The Fox

Karen Engstrom

While this is a work of fiction, many names, places, and events are real, some are real but have had their names changed, and some are the product of the author's imagination.

No part of this book may be reproduced, scanned, or distributed in any printed or electronic form without permission.

ACKNOWLEDGMENTS

Unexpected circumstances often create amazing opportunities. This book is the result of a set of such circumstances, and it is also proof that negatives can turn into positives.

That said, let me thank my writer friends who gave me support and many words of wisdom; my publisher, Michael MacBride of Salty Books Publishing, LLC, without whose unfettered enthusiasm I would never have completed this creative process; my three children, Tania Meixner, Britta Anderson, and Bert Anderson for their words of encouragement; and most of all, my thanks and love go to my partner, Bill Allan, for his endless patience and support. Writing this book was so satisfying I think I'll write another one. Meanwhile, I sincerely hope you enjoy The Fox.

Räven raskar över isen, räven raskar över isen.
Får jag lov och får jag lov at sjunga flickornas visa?
Så här gör flickorna var de gå och var de sitta och var de stå.
Får jag lov, och får jag lov at sjunga flickornas visa?

Räven raskar över isen, räven raskar över isen.
Får jag lov och får jag lov at sjunga gossarnas visa?
Så här gör gossarna var de gå och var de sitta och var de stå.
Får jag lov, och får jag lov at sjunga gossarnas visa?

- Swedish Children's Folk Dance

1948

CHAPTER 1

The fatal wound was kind. There was no pain. Only an immediate awareness of what he had known all along. All the things he'd missed. All the things he knew.

His wife, young and beautiful, ever hopeful he would be whole again, that he would be able to love her again as he had before. How he wished he could have. Their children would have been beautiful to him beyond his comprehension. Missing those beautiful children never born instantly flooded him with sadness.

Perhaps he should have gone home. He missed his mother, and she would have cared for him. But he couldn't bear sharing his pain with her, and she would have felt it no matter how hard he tried to hide it from her. His father would have appeared proud but would never have understood his burden.

No, he knew he had done the right thing hiding his pain from those he loved and everyone who had cared about him. Now there would be no more. No more pain. No more anything.

Without opening his eyes, he knew he was being hauled somewhere by his arms, his feet dragging in the dirt. He knew this is what some of those soldiers had felt as he had pulled them to the edge of a shallow grave in the French countryside pockmarked and barren from bombs. He knew some of the fallen hadn't died yet, but he buried them anyway. He knew they wouldn't have lived and there was no way he could have saved them. So, he had done his duty with the silent screams of war in his head.

But there were no screams or bombs now. The only sounds he heard were the wind in the trees and the lap of the waves on the shoreline. He felt someone rolling, shoving, pushing his body. He felt no remorse or fear, only calm. But he knew life demanded a final effort, so, despite his desire to be done with it, he opened his eyes one last time just before he dropped into the boat. He saw his home there on the shore of Lake Vermilion where he had finally been happy. In a flash of sweet memory, he saw the kit just as she had been that first spring when she appeared by the clump of birches in the yard, a fluff of red fur with a burst of white at the end of her tail, black on her snout and tips of her ears making tiny high-pitched wow-wow-wow sounds. As his eyes closed, his last awareness was of the fox silently watching from the corner of the cabin.

Lake Vermilion, Minnesota, is located one hundred miles north of Duluth and twenty-five miles south of Ontario, Canada. Its northern border lies within the Boundary Waters Canoe Area and the Superior National Forest. It is twenty-five miles wide from the Tower end in the east to the Cook end in the west. North of Lake Vermilion lies nothing but wilderness all the way to Hudson Bay and the North Pole beyond.

Lake Vermilion was first discovered in the mid-1600s by French explorers who traded furs with the Native Americans; first the Sioux, then the Ojibwe, who still reside in the area today. Its name is the French translation of the Ojibwe name "Lake of the Sunset Glow." The signing of the Treaty of Paris in 1763 made Lake Vermilion part of Canada. But in 1842, Britain and the US agreed on a border further to the north, as it is now. This minor concession gave the mineral-rich Arrowhead Region of Minnesota to the United States, which probably changed history, considering the importance of iron over the next one hundred years.

With 365 islands and 1,200 miles of shoreline, Lake Vermilion remains one of the most picturesque lakes in the Northwoods. There are a few sandy beaches and a few shallow reedy bays, but most of the shoreline is rocky, and the depth of Vermilion's waters reaches seventy-six feet at some points – all making for some of the best freshwater fishing in the country. Trout Lake, a spring-fed lake, feeds its cold, crystal clear water into Lake Vermilion from the north, while the Pike River meanders through iron-rich country to feed its clear tannin-brown water into Vermilion from the south.

CHAPTER 2

Elsa Swanson stepped out the door and reached up and to the left, the wind blowing her almost blond hair across her face. The thin chain was elusive as she stood on tiptoe to reach for it. Finally grabbing it, she yanked down quickly a few times. The clang of the dinner bell hanging from the eaves rang out over the rustling of the birch trees in the wind. Despite knowing he could hear the bell, Elsa called out to her husband anyway, "Carl, lunch is ready!" She heard a muffled answer shouted from the boathouse. Her corduroy pants and long sleeve cotton blouse were no match for the early June chill; shivering, she went back indoors.

At the far end of the cabin's main room, Elsa opened the door of the small cast iron stove door and put in another piece of wood from the stack sitting on a square of linoleum. Lake Vermilion was bright blue under a cloudless sky and a noon-day sun. Elsa wished she could shake the shadowed feeling she had.

Maybe it was because she had shared things she shouldn't have. She should have held it all in, but last week at her doctor's appointment, after he informed her, again, that she wasn't pregnant, she had gushed out all her concerns, along with a lot of tears. She was thirty. Was she too old? Despite having the shapely hips her aunts said were good for childbearing, maybe there was something wrong with her physically. Or with Carl. He often seemed unhappy and on edge, but he was kind and loving most of the time. Was it her fault? The doctor assured her there was nothing wrong with her or their lovemaking. He seemed more concerned with Carl's experiences in the war and the nightmares Elsa said he had.

"Most likely Carl is suffering from battle shock," the kindly old man had said. "If he is going to get better, your summer cabin should be the place to do it. The quiet up there should be good for him. But both of you need to relax. I've seen many couples who weren't able to conceive, and when they returned from a trip abroad or a prolonged vacation, sure enough, I'm next on their list of people to see," Dr. Smithson had said with a big smile and a pat on her shoulder.

Looking out on the sun-sparkled lake, Elsa took a deep breath, lifted her shoulders, and tried to restore her naturally optimistic outlook. "I can do this," she said to herself out loud.

In the boathouse, Carl, a trim forty-year-old of medium height, was almost done varnishing the last part of the bow of the open fishing boat. He was wearing hip waders over his stained white tee shirt and old khaki combat pants, standing in the water underneath the boat. A limp painter's cap kept his wavy red hair safe from drips.

When he first bought the eighteen-foot mahogany

Sportsman, Carl had built an over-the-water boathouse. It took most of that summer to dig out the shoreline to accommodate a boat and line the underwater walls with rocks to keep them from washing away. He had installed a set of winches inside the boathouse, one at each end, and rigged belly straps to go under the boat. One person could now easily lift it out of the water using the hand cranks. He hoisted it up to the rafters every fall, where it spent the winter safely above the jaws of the crushing ice. The winches were also handy for doing maintenance on the heavy wooden boat. It needed a new clear coat of varnish on the hull every year or so.

Carl put the brush, bristles down, into the open coffee can filled with turpentine sitting on the edge of the dock that extended two feet into the boathouse that gave him a walkway down the length of the boat. He grabbed the lid of the varnish can, set it in place, and tapped it on lightly with his palm.

"All done, for now, Bruno," he said as he pushed up to sit on the overhang, then stood up. The dog, occupying the doorway with his front paws hanging over the edge of the dock, responded by standing up too, albeit with a grunt. Carl hung the waders and cap on a hook outside the boathouse door, put on his shoes, and followed Bruno up the hill to the house.

Elsa was sliding grilled cheese sandwiches onto the plates when Carl came in shivering, followed by Bruno wagging exuberantly. The black lab greeted her as if he'd been gone for days. Elsa scratched the back of his neck after she put the pan down on a hot pad. Steam was coming off the bowls of soup and smelled warm and soothing. They started to eat without a word, comfortable in their silence. Bruno laid down near the table with a loud uff, ever hopeful.

"I sure wish I'd varnished the boat before we left for Chicago last September," said Carl taking a bite of sandwich. "But I guess it was just as cold then as it is now. Oh, well, it's almost done."

"That's good, honey. When can we put it in the water? I can't wait to get out on the lake," Elsa said with a smile and a mouthful of wild rice soup.

"Day after tomorrow. It should be dry by then."

"Let's go into town tomorrow. I have to pick up a few things we forgot to bring from home. Hey, we could have lunch at the Tower Hotel. That would be fun, wouldn't it?" said Elsa.

"If you want," said Carl without enthusiasm.

* * *

After lunch, Carl and Bruno returned to the boathouse to finish the job. The paintbrush felt good in his grip. His muscled arm and wrist made the most of each pass, spreading the thick clear varnish evenly. He was quick to catch the inevitable drips. The brush was one of his favorites, one he had acquired early on. It was light wood but strong with a six-inch-wide swath of thick boar bristle. He valued the tools of his trade and loved the feel of a good brush in his hand.

He had done a lot of painting in his life. When he arrived in 1927 Chicago, the first job he landed was working on a crew painting a water tower. Coming from a small village in rural Sweden, he had never even seen such a thing before and had stopped across the street from it in awe; his neck craned back, gazing at the enormous bulb-like structure on gigantic stilts. He watched, fascinated, as a team of men mounted scaffolding and were hoisted a hundred feet in the air to the line of fresh paint.

He was hungry and desperate for work, so he looked around for the job boss. He saw a man clearly directing the activities behind the chain-link fence. Carl crossed the street, walked through the gate marked 'Do Not Enter,' and approached the man. In very broken English, Carl asked if there was a job available.

After looking the strong young man up and down, the foreman said he had enough painters, but the scaffolding mover had just quit so Carl could have the job if he wanted it. Carl hadn't really understood what the man had said, but he nodded vigorously. Lindy was the boss's name. Lindy, Carl found out later, was a Swede, too, and his nickname was short for Lindholm. With a big grin on his face, Carl shook Lindy's hand.

When Carl showed up for work the next morning, Lindy took him up to the top of the tower on the scaffolding to show him how it worked. His job would be to move the scaffolding ropes around the perimeter of the curved metal tower so the crew far below him could paint a new section. As they ascended around the curve of the giant structure, he thought his heart would stop. He couldn't breathe and felt instantly covered in sweat. Carl hadn't mentioned he was afraid of heights because he hadn't even known he would be scared until he climbed the rigging that first day. But he hid his fear and showed up on time for weeks until Lindy gave him a job as a painter and he had been doing it ever since. First, he painted water towers for a year or so, then commercial properties. Later, as a crew boss, he painted residential exteriors. After a few more years, with Lindy's blessing, Carl and his friend Eric started their own company specializing in interior painting and decorating. Carl's good looks and willingness to do an odd job here and there made him very popular with wealthy Northside Chicago ladies who wanted their parlors to be the latest fashionable colors and their furniture rearranged. He was always in demand.

Standing in the cold water of Daisy Bay, Carl suddenly felt a flash of fear, as real and paralyzing as he had felt on his first ascent to the top of the tower. He felt it again. Panic. Heart-stopping panic. He wanted to run, but his feet wouldn't move. He couldn't breathe, and his pulse was pounding in the veins in his neck. Finally, the panic subsided. He worked to get his breathing and heart rate under control. The varnish brush still held in midair. His face had a sheen of sweat.

He hadn't thought about that first job in a long time. Every morning back then, he had had to overcome his fear before he could climb the ladders up the tank side to sit high above the city and wait, afraid to move until he had to manipulate the guy wires and winches. He often thought maybe that experience had helped him deal with other fears he had to face later. Usually, when his mood became dark with thoughts of the war, he would feel an overwhelming sadness that weighed down his very body – a weight so heavy he could only move or talk with great effort. But today's unwarranted panic was new and unexpected and disturbed him more than he wanted to admit.

"Geez, I'm glad Elsa didn't see that," he thought and wiped the sweat off his forehead with his shirtsleeve.

When he finished varnishing and was satisfied, he hadn't missed any spots on the hull, Carl took the cans up to the shed behind the house. He cleaned the brush in the turpentine and hung it on a nail, took off the waders and cap and hung them on another nail inside the small slant-roofed building. He stood in the doorway for a moment considering his next chore, then picked up the ax from where it was leaning in the corner.

The woodpile, a neatly stacked arrangement of split wood some four feet tall, was off to the side of the house. As he split the short logs lengthwise into at least four pieces, he thought about what his father used to say. Wood warms you twice - once when you cut it and once when you burn it. His thoughts went back to his childhood in central Sweden, where he had grown up with his parents and two brothers. The sawmill was the center of the local economy, and practically everyone he knew worked there, including his father. He remembered cutting wood after school with his brother, two years older. They used a small two-man crosscut saw, and together they earned twenty-five cents for each half cord of stacked wood.

One day when they were deep in the forest, they stumbled on a tiny furry animal hiding in a hole under some leaves. It was mewing like a kitten, but they saw it was a fox kit when they picked it up. The boys were sure it would die out there alone in the woods, so Carl took off his jacket and wrapped it around the baby grey fox. Eric carried the saw, and Carl carried the little animal. When they got home, they ran upstairs to their apartment in the company barracks to show their mother what they had found.

They kept the kit in a box in the kitchen for a few days, feeding it drops of milk from a spoon. The neighbors all came in to see it. One day, the supervisor came to see the fox and declared they couldn't keep it in the barracks, and took it away. He put it in a fenced enclosure near the sawmill entrance as entertainment for the laborers. Some would feed it tidbits of their lunch. Others would poke at it or tease it through the fence.

Carl was twelve when he had to work full time in the sawmill. He saw the fox every day, running back and forth along the fence, looking for a way out. One morning when Carl was seventeen, the fox wasn't there. It had died. The ideas that had been swirling around in his head like cottonwood fluff in the spring settled on the fertile ground of despair. He could not stay, only to die in a cage like the fox. Even though he loved his home, America was calling. Promising fortunes and free land in the west, the handbill pinned to the bulletin board at the train station had already lured several of his friends to leave. He had to follow his heart and soon after he broke his mother's when he left to find his fortune. The smell of fresh-cut wood always reminded him of home and the captive fox.

The swing of the ax was second nature, and it didn't take long to split the stack of logs left from last year. They were dry, and the work went quickly. Bruno disappeared off into the bush for a while to chase a squirrel.

* * *

Elsa spent time cleaning and organizing the things they had brought from Chicago. Feeling restless, she put on her jacket and went outside for a walk, stopping to talk with Carl for a minute at the woodpile. He seemed distant and she worried she was losing a battle that she had never known she would fight, a battle for his love. She felt she was fighting things that clawed at his memory, brutal things that clouded his eyes and made him distant, as though he didn't even see her sometimes.

"I'm going for a walk, honey," she said. She went to him and gave him a kiss and a smile.

"Ok, then. Take Bruno with you." Carl whistled for the dog.

Bruno came out of the woods and they took off together down the long gravel driveway lined with fragrant balsam and spruce whose needles crunched underfoot. In a quarter mile, they came to the paved county road and headed east toward Moccasin Point until it started to drizzle.

"Turn around, Bruno," Elsa said. Instantly, he whirled around and headed home like an old trail horse, twice as fast as he had left the barn. She laughed and hurried her step to keep up.

When they got back to the cabin, Bruno got comfortable on the braided rag rug that covered most of the unfinished pine floor. After she stoked the fire, Elsa sat askew on the sofa, chin on her forearm, under the front windows to look out at the lake. Birches dotted the rocky yard sloping to the water, their new yellow-green leaves barely hiding the goldfinches flitting from branch to branch. She thought about how different it was up here. More relaxed and peaceful. She wanted a child so badly, but they had had no luck starting a family so far. Perhaps that was just another awful consequence of the horrible war. But she was still hopeful. Each year he got a little better. Life in Chicago was more stressful, but he jumped at unexpected noises and fell into dark moods even here. Still, he was so much better than when he first got back from serving in Italy. He no longer cried out in the night, though he still had nightmares and often woke in a sweat. Although she knew it wasn't funny, she chuckled, remembering one night recently when they were sleeping, and he had suddenly sat up in bed, punched her, and yelled at her as if she were a Nazi soldier. It had scared her, but she reached out, pulled him close with soothing words, and he calmed without ever waking.

Elsa stared out across Daisy Bay, darkened now by the gray sky, thinking about the terrible things he must have seen, knowing she couldn't even imagine them if she had wanted to. Eventually, she stretched, got up, and started dinner.

* * *

They enjoyed a simple meal of macaroni and cheese from a box, canned beans, and canned sliced peaches for dessert. They talked about last summer, reminiscing about the fish they had caught and the people they had met.

Carl spent the evening cleaning and oiling the fishing reels. He removed the old, waxed cotton lines in preparation for winding on the new nylon fishing line he had bought at a sporting goods store in Chicago. Elsa held the spool of monofilament suspended on a pencil cradled by her thumbs so the line would easily flow as Carl wound it onto the spindle of the reel. They enjoyed each other's company in silence, and after a while, they talked about plans for the next day, agreeing on the errands and shopping they would do.

"We'll have to stop and see Harvey Pittella, too, so he knows we're back," said Carl.

"Sure. I wonder how many more years he'll be a Sheriff's deputy. He's no spring chicken, you know," Elsa replied.

"He's such a fixture up here. I can't imagine how they'll get along without him when he retires."

"Well, in some ways, it's a great job for an older guy like him. He could stay on for quite a while."

"What do you mean?"

"There's no crime up here. All he does is drive a few drunks home now and then. What's the worst thing that's ever happened up here anyway?"

"Well, the first year we were up here, remember, three or

four cabins over by Del Lago's Resort were broken into. Turned out it was kids from the Vermilion Boys Camp looking for cigarettes."

"See what I mean! Of course, he does play an important part in keeping the crowd in line at the 4th of July parade," she chuckled.

"Oh, don't be so hard on him. He really is an important fixture up here," said Carl. "Come on, Bruno. Let's go outside."

Carl looked up at the stars as Bruno lumbered off to finish his day. A few minutes later, Elsa joined him, and they sat on the top step, arms around each other. A barred owl hooted nearby. Bats, visible only against the indigo sky, dived-bombed delectable flying insects. Fireflies sprinkled the grass like confetti. The air was still, as if holding its breath in anticipation. After a while, Bruno appeared at the bottom of the stairs, and they all headed inside to bed.

Carl and Elsa undressed in the tiny bedroom. The floor space was limited, even with the bed pushed against the wall. Bruno curled up on the floor at the foot. They crawled under the covers one at a time, Elsa first, Carl holding the covers up for her. Their lovemaking started slowly but had an urgency to it. No longer newlyweds, they knew what pleased one another and enjoyed the unspoken give and take that came with loving intimacy. Satisfied, they spooned together and slept.

CHAPTER 3

Early in the morning, a few miles to the east on Pine Island, Bill Thompson, the foreman, stood off to the side, observing how work was progressing on the new house. He was a rather tall, thick man with an expressionless face and large veined hands held awkwardly at his sides, as if they themselves were tools he was holding. He wore a plaid lumberjack shirt, dark green Carhartt overalls, steel-toed boots, and a battered bucket cloth hat pulled down over graying, shaggy hair.

Despite the drizzle, several carpenters were making the forms needed to pour the concrete foundation. Big timbers were stacked near the site waiting to be hoisted into place as ceiling beams when the support walls were ready. The house would be nestled into the rock hillside, maximizing the yard between the house and the lake. A crew was working at clearing away brush. A man running a backhoe was leveling the ground in front of the house into tiers, each of which would become massive stone patios. There was a lot of work to be done, and Thompson was pondering if he could possibly meet the short summer season's schedule – or not.

Only a few weeks into construction, progress had been delayed multiple times by damaged supplies or sabotaged work. Day after day, there were setbacks. The men would show up in the morning to find buckets of nails dumped into the lake, gas cans emptied, or temporary supports torn down. A few days prior, Sanford had been injured when a stack of logs rolled, knocking him down and breaking both his legs. The crew had begun complaining they should get hazard pay. Thompson successfully negotiated with the owner, Stephen Stark, to pay the men who agreed to stay double their daily rate.

Thompson wasn't looking forward to informing Mr. Stark about the latest setback. There was no way around it; he'd have to tell him the cement had been tampered with. The boss had a temper that matched his huge ego, and Thompson knew he would get the brunt of it again. He reconciled himself to it, though, knowing he was being paid exceptionally well. He smiled at that thought and went to find Stark.

Minnesota Point is a flat sandbar that extends seven miles into Lake Superior, separating the great lake from the Duluth-Superior Harbor. In 1852, George Stuntz moved from Superior, Wisconsin, to that spit of land to become unofficially the first non-native resident of Minnesota Point. With its strategic location, others quickly followed. In 1870, over three thousand people lived there, and by 1890, there were thirty-three thousand. A contest of sorts resulted was held to rename Minnesota Point. Rev. J. G. Wilson was given two plots of land when he came up with the name Duluth which the populace agreed was a name they could live with.

The West End district became more of a melting pot than other areas of the city. During the 1880s, waves of immigrants began to pour into Duluth and would continue doing so for the next thirty years. Some were recruited for specific skilled jobs, such as Norwegian and Swedish fishermen. Some were well-educated western Europeans filling the need for professionals of all types. But most were families of unskilled laborers who left their homelands because of economic or political hardship. They came from practically every European country.

While the original Minnesota Point is flat, the adjacent land is some of the hilliest in Minnesota. Duluth has been called 'the San Francisco of the

Midwest' because of the steep, curvy streets and magnificent views of big water. Before WWII, Duluth even had a network of streetcars and an "Incline Railway" similar to San Francisco's cable cars. Duluth is Minnesota's second-largest city in terms of land area, surpassed only by Hibbing.

CHAPTER 4

Rainy days were especially hard for Ike. The light coming through the front windows wasn't bright enough to paint. He could sketch out a new painting but at his age, he needed natural sunshine to do the fine details. He had never worn glasses and never would. If his eyes couldn't see it, he wouldn't paint it. He had decided that a long time ago. But he was still frustrated when it was too dreary to paint. He had tried painting by the light of the kerosene lantern, but the colors weren't true. So, he waited for sunny days.

When he first saw the shack, he had had this room in mind and knew he wanted to live here. The shack became his bedroom. He had a well dug right outside and then built the main room over it. He had large windows installed across the length of the south side facing the lake. Not even a door broke up the expanse of light. He didn't care that the windows had many small panes. They were cheap, and he wasn't interested in the view. He just wanted the light.

Winter days were the best, and there were so many frigid but bright sunny days up here. The sun reflecting off the white snow, which never got ugly and dirty as it had in Duluth and Chicago, was brighter than any day in June. He'd always loved the winter days for the light but also because no one was around to bother him. Yes, the days were very short, but he could only paint for a few hours a day anyway.

These drizzly June days, he spent his time whittling, sitting on the narrow back porch that ran the length of the main room. Mostly, he carved small plaques with bas relief flowers or animals, then painted them just as he had done when he was young. The gift shop in Tower displayed them in the front window and sold them to the tourists. The shop owner supplied him with soft pinewood oval blanks and bought as many as he could make. The best seller depicted a black bear next to a birch tree with 'Lake Vermilion, Minn.' painted in a semi-circle across the top. But his favorite was of a fox standing on a rocky point overlooking the lake.

On an impulse, he decided he would make another paddle. He went to the shed and wrestled with the stack of cedar boards leaning in the corner until he found a long thick one that felt just right. He took it back to the porch, set it against the wall near the door, and then got his knife.

The red wood-handled Mora knife made of Swedish steel in its leather sheath had been a high school graduation gift from his father. He was the only one of his siblings to finish school, and his father had been very proud. Ike left home shortly after that, and the knife was one of the few possessions he took with him. It reminded him of happier times. He never used it much until he came to Lake Vermilion many years later. Now it showed the signs of being an oft-used tool. A wide band of scratches the length of the six-inch blade from being sharpened by hand. A slight concave profile to the edge. A few nicks along the spine. The leather sheath supple and darkened, repaired with deer sinew in a few places. The handle worn and variegated from the natural oils of his hands.

Ike sat down on the straight-back chair on the porch with the long piece of cedar across his knees. He sighed and ran his hands through his thick white hair. Then he laid them on the wood. He caressed its length, finding the place to start, feeling for its core strength. This chunk of dead wood would become alive again as an extension of a human arm. Together the arm and the paddle would gracefully push the water behind while almost effortlessly creating forward propulsion. Neither the human nor the paddle would be able to move through the water as smoothly without the other.

Across the narrow strip of yard which buffered the tiny cabin from the depths of the forest, he saw the fox trot by with a small rodent in her mouth. It was strange, he suddenly thought, that he had never given this fox or her mother or any of the others a name, except the first. This fox wasn't quite as friendly as her mother had been. He had worked at earning her trust, spending hours sitting quietly on the grass when she was nearby. She was still wary of him, and only now and again would she come close enough to take food from his hand. Her mother, in contrast, was like the first one and had actively sought his presence. She had spent a lot of time near Ike, watching him from the shadows. She would follow him when he went into the woods to cut firewood, sometimes running ahead, only to wait for him at the side of the path. He felt honored when one year she brought her young kit to his yard. Now she was gone, and this kit would be gone in a few years, too. Perhaps she'd surprise him next spring, he thought, and bring a new kit to his yard, a harbinger of the next phase in nature's endless cycle. It pained him that the life of the red fox was so short.

He pulled the Mora knife out of its sheath and began to pare away the wood. It came easy for him, and his mind wandered to his childhood. Born in Duluth in 1886, Ike was the oldest of five children born to Norwegian immigrants. His father, Anders Iverson, had arrived as a small child with his parents, siblings, and several other families from the same village near Bergen on the west coast of Norway. They ended up in Duluth because they had been fishermen back home. Unlike most immigrants who came for the free land, this group had heard about the big lake called Superior and came to fish. Those first hearty men worked on the commercial fishing boats, but many of the next generation, like Ike's father, ended up working the docks, earning less but having bigger families.

His mother, Sonja, the youngest child of a Swede and a Norwegian mixed marriage, was only 15 when Anders Iverson saw her for the first time at the Lutheran Church near the ore docks where he worked. She had been hired out by her father as a nanny to tend the children of a wealthy family on London Road, on the north side of Duluth, where she stayed during the week. She came home every Sunday and would attend services with her family at the church where many Norwegian immigrants, especially the dock workers, went to worship in their native language. Anders, a handsome young man, who worked with her father loading the ore ships, was smitten. One thing led to another, and after two years of servitude as a nanny, her father agreed for her to marry Anders.

Ike was her favorite child, her last. Sonja was a happy person, doting on her children and singing while she scrubbed floors in the office buildings in downtown Duluth at night. She kept a tidy house and never complained. Even with both her and Anders working, it was difficult to make ends meet. The children all had menial jobs starting at age eight. Ike was a small child but clever with his hands. His father wanted him to go out to work, but Sonja convinced her husband to allow the boy to contribute to the family finances by making things to sell to others in the immigrant community. The West End of Duluth where they lived was a hodge-podge of ethnic groups coexisting together on the steep streets, crowded and noisy, overlooking the industrial harbor. Ike learned a smattering of the different languages, although he never lost the heavy Norwegian accent his family spoke at home. He liked to whittle and became proficient at it. He carved small wall plaques and adorned them with sentimental sayings in Swedish, Danish, German, Austrian, Czech, Italian, Polish, Hungarian, Romanian, or Russian, to name a few. Later he painted nostalgic scenes of Europe or Scandinavia on the plaques, copied from magazines or picture postcards borrowed from neighbors who had received them from relatives back home.

His parents fought over his schooling, but again Sonja prevailed, and so he was able to continue in school as long as he brought in his share. He would go to school during the day and create sentimental trinkets at night. A quiet, serious boy devoted to his mother, he did well in school and graduated from high school, but with little fanfare. By that time, all his siblings had left home, and Ike had been contributing to the household more and more as his mother's health started to fail. It was a big disappointment to his parents when Ike told them he wanted to leave home, too, but in the end, they gave their blessing. With a small satchel and a few dollars, he rode the train, hobo style, to Milwaukee, where he stayed for a year, working on a loading dock and living in a boarding house. He heard about the large ethnic neighborhoods in Chicago, big as cities in themselves, and decided that was the next place to go. He had saved a little money, so he bought a ticket this time and rode the train to Chicago as a paying passenger.

He had thought Milwaukee was a big city, but he realized his mistake when he came to Union Station in Chicago. This really was 'the big city.' He decided to explore the different neighborhoods until he found one where he could fit in and find a job. He was easy-going, so he thought it wouldn't be hard. He learned the streetcar lines and rode from one ethnic neighborhood to another, looking for work. Weeks went by, and Ike could only find odd jobs, most of which lasted just a short time, menial, heavy labor, and not at all to his liking. But he had to eat and pay for his room at the boarding house on Ashland Avenue in West Town.

One day, he walked past an Italian bakery on Halsted Street on the Southside of Chicago. The front door was propped open, and as he was passing by, the smell of freshly baked cakes literally turned his head like a dog who has just spotted a squirrel. He stopped and after a moment of hesitation, backed up a step and went in. He looked in awe at the beautiful pastries and decorated cakes displayed in the large glass cases. The splendid array of tiered spun sugar in all manner of colors enthralled him.

Never before had he seen art that you could eat.

"May I help you, sir?" said the girl behind the counter. She was the most beautiful girl he had ever seen. She was dressed in a white uniform buttoned to her neck, pale slim arms extended from short capped sleeves. Her long black hair was braided and pinned like a crown around her head. Short ringlets adorned her temples. Her cheeks and lips were brushed with the palest pink that contrasted with her dark eyes. Truth be told, her nose was too large and her mouth too small, but that only accentuated the exotic beauty that took away Ike's breath. When he didn't answer, she asked again, "What would you like, sir?"

"I'd like a job painting cakes," Ike blurted out.

The girl laughed and told him to wait while she went to get the owner, Mr. Ferrara, who put him to work in short order filling cannoli. Mr. Ferrara found Ike had a steady hand with the pastry bag, and the young man caught on quickly. Soon, he was decorating the wedding cakes and other bakery delights Ferrara's was famous for. He experimented with icing colors, blending them in swirls and patterns, and applying the sweet fluff in new and different ways. At first, Ferrara was adamant his shop wouldn't have such nonsense. But when the girl behind the counter, who happened to be Mr. Ferrara's daughter, Angela, asked her father to put one of Ike's creations in the window, he couldn't refuse. Everyone was surprised at how many orders it generated, most of all Ike.

The other thing which surprised him was the strange feelings he started having when he was around Angela. He couldn't stop thinking about her either. He came to realize it was what everyone called 'love .' He was shy, but he could tell by her side glances at him that Angela had feelings for him too. It surprised him that he had always made her laugh, even when he wasn't trying to be funny. After a year, Ike got up the nerve to ask her out for a date. A year later, he asked Mr. Ferrara for her hand. When they were married in December 1913, the wedding cake was so spectacular the Chicago Examiner included a photo of it with a small article on page seven near the society column. Mr. Ferrara was thrilled with the publicity.

They moved into the apartment above the shop, where Mr. and Mrs. Ferrara had lived when they first started the business. The young couple were happy and busy. Ike had written home to tell his parents the news; the answer from his father wished him well and informed him his mother had died of the flu the previous winter. Time passed, but unfortunately, there were no grandchildren for Mr. and Mrs. Ferrara. Mr. Ferrara secretly congratulated himself on not signing over a part of the business to his son-in-law right away and decided he wouldn't, at least not until there were grandchildren.

When the envelope from the War Department came in June of 1917, Ike, Angela and the Ferraras gathered at the kitchen table to open it. Once it had been passed around, they were silent, each contemplating how their lives would change. All able-bodied men between the ages of twenty-one and thirty-one were being called up to serve, so they had all been expecting it, but still it was a somber moment. Ike had been feeling stifled in the close quarters of the bakery and small apartment with the cloying family demanding the young couple produce children He needed a break from the life he hadn't bargained for when he fell in love with the baker's daughter, so he sat quietly as his wife sobbed.

Ike thought going to war would be just a sabbatical from his new family that he needed. He would return a hero, take over the bakery, and have lots of children with his pretty wife. He and Angela talked it over, and she finally agreed not to worry.

When he came home a year and a half later, everyone was happy, especially Ike. At least he told himself he was. But scenes from the battlefields of France filled his thoughts; he cried for no reason; sleep was almost impossible. He was sure things would get better, back to normal, but he no longer knew what normal was.

It had all happened so quickly. One day he was home with his wife, secure and safe in a routine of work and family. Then he was whisked away from his life, no longer in control of any part of it; he followed as best he could, dazed and scared. After just weeks of training, poorly fed and poorly equipped, he and tens of thousands of other foot soldiers were sent to Newport News, Virginia, and loaded on huge transport ships for the trip to France. Onboard, Ike happened to meet some men who were assigned to the Pioneer Troops as food specialists. They took a liking to Ike, and when they learned he had experience as a baker, the Sergeant arranged for him to join their ranks as support troops.

However, once they landed in France, he was assigned to a different platoon, which had yet to receive its orders. There was a lot of confusion for some time, and finally, after weeks of temporary camps and marching here and there, his platoon was assigned to battlefield sanitation. The platoon's duty was to clean up after the fighting and medical troops had left the area where a battle had taken place. The fifty-three men in Ike's platoon buried thousands of men and horses. They also filled in latrines and covered mess garbage pits. Their chaplain did his best to keep track of the dead, their numbers and dog tags and personal belongings, but it was an impossible job. During his spare moments, the chaplain would try to comfort the living. Only two of Ike's company died from combat wounds, but thirty-three others died from accidents, dysentery, and other diseases. He could barely remember the details of his first months in the Army, but his days on the battlefields with the dead never left his thoughts.

One Sunday, shortly after he arrived back in Chicago, the Ferraras had a dinner to celebrate his homecoming. His father-in-law stood at the head of the long table filled with family and friends and clinked his glass with a silver knife.

"I have something I'd like to say," Mr. Ferrara said. "I'd like to welcome home my dear son-in-law, Ike. And to tell him how proud we are of him."

Everyone clapped, and Angela grabbed his arm and smiled at him. He numbly smiled back.

"I've got a gift for the man who has made my daughter so happy." And with that, he walked over and handed Ike the keys to a brand new 1919 Paige Roadster. "It's parked out back, and it's all yours. Go," the old man shooed them. "Go take your sweetheart for a ride."

After he thanked his generous father-in-law, that's precisely what Ike did. He took Angela for a long ride that late Sunday afternoon, and while he was driving, he pledged he would do his best for her. He loved her with all his heart, and she still loved him, but he knew things just weren't the same. Still, he would do his best. That's all he could do.

For over a year, he tried. He was thankful he had lived when so many soldiers had died or come home in horrible condition.

His thoughts often wandered as he decorated cakes. He would stand, pastry bag in hand, staring into a freshly dug grave filled with bodies and pieces of bodies he had laid gently on one another. When he sprinkled powdered sugar on top of pastries, he saw corpses in their freshly dug graves covered in the white lye powder he sprinkled on them. Angela would have to call his name, sometimes more than once, to get him to come back to the present.

He went through the motions, but even those were stilted and uncomfortable. He jumped at noises. He flinched when she touched him. He hardly spoke. Angela never laughed anymore.

Late one evening in June of 1920, after Angela was in bed, he sat at the kitchen table and wrote her a note.

'I loved you with all my heart, but now it's too full of holes to be good for anything. I'm so sorry.'

The First World War began in July 1914, but the United States did not join its allies until April 1917, when 14,000 US soldiers were sent to France. One year later, in April 1918, there were 1,000,000 US troops overseas. By November 1918, when peace was declared, there were 2,800,000 US Armed Forces in Europe. During the 19 months of US involvement, 116,000 US military personnel died, of which only 53,000 died in combat.

All war-related supplies were shipped from Newport News, Virginia. The SOS, as the Service of Supply Division of the Army was called, was in charge of shipping troops, supplies, and equipment needed at the battlefront in Europe. All medical and Red Cross supplies were shipped from there, including four hundred complete hospitals and one thousand infirmaries. Hundreds of thousands of horses and mules and all the supplies needed to maintain them were part of the massive support sent overseas. Four thousand soldiers were kept stateside to man the SOS in Newport News, Virginia.

CHAPTER 5

Gregory Morgan was having his morning coffee in the Florida-room of his sprawling Mediterranean-style house overlooking Biscayne Bay. He was dressed in a light, silk guayabera shirt and gray pleated slacks. He adjusted his glasses and reread the letter.

Dear Uncle Greg,

I know we both have had some bad memories because of my father, but I want to make the case that we should be well past that point in our lives. I know I am. I mentioned in my Christmas letter that I am building a fine house on the lake property I reacquired. Construction is in full swing, and I would like you to join me as the project is very exciting to watch unfold. You are my only relative, and we really should get together more often. And, while I know you prefer your home in Florida, I also know it can be very hot there during the summer – as you have complained in the past.

I have enclosed a rail ticket for you to come to Lake Vermilion to spend some time with me. I will be there to meet the train in Tower. Or I will have someone else meet you if the project demands my attention at that particular time. I have very comfortable accommodations right on the construction site, but if you prefer, there is an entirely adequate resort not far away where you could have your own cabin, boat, etc., and if the construction gets too hectic or noisy for you. I have reserved a nice cabin for you there in case that would be your preference.

I look forward to your company.
All my best, your godson,
Stephen

Cup in hand, the gaunt, gray-haired man stood and looked out at countless boats lazing on the sparkling turquoise water. He had sacrificed to get here, maybe too much. But here he was, nonetheless, and he liked where he was. His thoughts went to the past, which seemed to fly before his eyes.

He and Stephen's father, Nathan Stark, had been friends literally their whole lives. They had been born within a month of each other in the East Hillside neighborhood of Duluth. Their families lived next door to each other in rowhouses, each only twenty feet wide. Their mothers were best friends, so they became best friends. Neither one had siblings, so they grew up as if they were brothers. There was no fence between their tiny backyards and they played together every day. It wasn't much of a stretch to stay friends as they got older. They were as close to being family as they could get.

As kids, they were an odd pair. Nathan, stocky and muscular, was the typical Minnesota boy who, as they say, played hockey in the winter and baseball the other three months of the year. Gregory, too, liked hockey and baseball. He went to all his friend's games. He cheered and watched but never once felt the need to participate. He gleaned a sense of accomplishment from his friend. Nathan shared his successes with Gregory, naively thinking Gregory wasn't envious.

Gregory was always one of the kids to be picked on in grade school. Since they walked to and from school together, Nathan would usually be around to intervene and often got into fights to protect Gregory. As far as Gregory was concerned, what others said about him didn't matter, and he didn't much care if he got bullied or punched now and then as long as they didn't damage his glasses. He had his books, his imagination, and his friend, Nathan. His secret sense of superiority offset his envy because Gregory knew that, although Nathan was better in so many things, he was the smarter of the two.

In high school, Nathan was bigger, faster, and stronger than Gregory and most of his classmates as well. He played all the sports, had girlfriends, and got passing grades. Gregory was, as everyone pointed out, a brainy wimp. He survived high school by staying under the radar. When he went to watch Nathan play in some game or another, he would sit near the home team bench where he was known and grudgingly accepted as somewhat of a silent mascot. As much as he told himself he didn't care what others thought, he felt humiliated when he was bullied or belittled. Gregory's jealousy festered, especially when girls crowded around Nathan, ignoring Gregory, but Nathan's good-natured friendship never faltered, even when Gregory sometimes railed against it.

When they entered UMD, they both had scholarships, Nathan to play baseball and Gregory to study pre-law. They stayed friends even though the rigors of their two very different academic paths kept them from socializing or even studying together very much. They both graduated in 1912. Stark got a job in a sporting goods store in downtown Duluth. He enjoyed his job and eventually became a department manager. Gregory went on to law school and then worked in a small law practice downtown Duluth doing business contracts, wills, and divorces. The firm's partners agreed, behind Morgan's back, that he would never make it up the ladder - Gregory didn't have the ego to go with the job. Everyone saw him as weak.

Then the war came. For three long years, the US watched the drama unfold in Europe. Patriotism ran high, and young men were anxious for the US to join the fight. Most welcomed the draft and the chance to serve. Gregory, by that time, had become proficient at manipulating the legal system and, oblivious to the stigma of being unpatriotic, managed to avoid the draft by calling in a favor from a politician whose particularly nasty divorce he had handled.

Nathan, on the other hand, had been anxiously awaiting his draft notice for months. He was active in the "Preparedness Movement" and met regularly with similar-minded young men to practice maneuvers and exercise, so they would be ready when called. He never got the privilege or honor, as he saw it, to go overseas, but he made the best of his assignment when it came, ever hopeful he would get to serve in a more meaningful way. He spent his time in the Army as an SOS Lieutenant in the shipyards of Newport News, Virginia. Nathan helped send the 'doughboys' and the supplies they needed off to fight the good fight. And later he helped unload those few unlucky soldiers who made it back in pine boxes. Most were buried on the battlefield without the dignity of a coffin.

When it was over, Nathan returned to Duluth and got his manager job back, sending the lady who had stepped in for two years back to her secretary desk without so much as a thank you. Gregory watched, again from the sidelines, as Nathan resumed his happy-go-lucky lifestyle. Within a short time, Nathan married Sophie Knotek, a young woman Gregory saw as a gold-digging tramp, and they had a son. Being named Stephen's godfather was an ongoing dilemma for Gregory: he was genuinely fond of the boy but couldn't stand his mother. But, Gregory thought, life has a way of fixing things. Sophie proved herself as shallow as he had foreseen. Nathan, who enjoyed the out-of-doors, took off for fishing and hunting in the Northwoods as often as he could. Sophie liked the comforts of home and wouldn't even think of bringing a small child up to the wilderness where, as she put it, 'anything' could happen. It suited them both. Gregory felt smug, no longer jealous of Nathan's marriage.

After one particular camping trip to Lake Vermilion, Nathan went to see Gregory at his apartment. He talked to his old friend about the potential for developing a nature lover's vacation paradise – camping and cabin sites, resorts – nirvana for fishermen from all across the Midwest. Travel to the lake was not complicated as the railroad ran every day from Duluth to Tower where, across from the train station, there was direct access to the lake via the small river. Steamer ferries ran several times a day from one end of the lake to the other. The logging industry was booming, and Tower was a bustling town. Gregory said no but Nathan kept on, and after many meetings, Gregory eventually gave in. The two formed a business partnership and things were looking great. Then came the storm.

That was years ago, twenty, twenty-five, maybe. Now, Gregory thought, Stephen wants to ignore the old wounds and get together for a vacation – at the same place in that God-forsaken wilderness. What was he thinking?

Tower, Minnesota, "Gateway to Lake Vermilion," is situated at the lake's southeastern corner on the East Two River. Its population has fluctuated between several hundred and several thousand since its incorporation in the early 1880s. The most influential factor in Tower's history was the Gold Rush which started in 1865. The search for gold lured a few thousand fortune seekers to the area. No gold was ever found, and by 1867 the population of Tower decreased back down to a few hundred as the prospectors abandoned their futile search. With the discovery of iron ore came another cycle of boom and bust.

Open-pit mining and later underground mining each caused significant fluctuations in population. For instance, in 1882, when the first open-pit mine was started, Tower's population was three thousand, and it had doubled to six thousand in 1884 when the mine opened. After the mine's peak production in 1886, the population steadily declined despite an overlapping timeline with the timber industry boom and bust. At the turn of the century, the population was only thirteen hundred. The desirability of the lake for fishing and tourism has provided the only constant, albeit small, source of revenue throughout the years. In 1948, Tower had been in decline for almost thirty years, and the population was only seven hundred.

CHAPTER 6

Coming through the tight cloak of trees, around the curve, and then down the incline into Tower, the road suddenly became a broad street as wide as a big city grand boulevard. Built during one of the boom times, Main Street was empty except for a few cars parked in front of the half dozen businesses that managed to stay open. The five streets that crossed Main were named creatively Cedar, Pine, Spruce, Birch, and Poplar and were lined with two-story wooden houses painted in bland colors. A handful of businesses kept the people living in the tiny remnant of a once bustling town happy and their needs met - for the most part.

Carl drove the new Frazer four-door sedan down Main Street to Zup's Grocery, and with no traffic around at all, he made a leisurely U-turn in the broad street and parked in front of the Tower Hotel. Carl and Elsa had agreed to run a few errands separately and meet back there for lunch, then shop for groceries together just before heading home. Carl turned to look in the backseat and said to Bruno, "Who are you going to go with, Bruno? One for me, two for your mom." Bruno looked from Carl to Elsa and back. He woofed once. Carl and Elsa laughed and got out of the car. Elsa headed in one direction while Carl put on Bruno's leash, and off they went in the other.

At the far end of Main Street, they stepped into the small storefront of the lumberyard. A weathered man in his fifties stood behind the counter. His deeply tanned and wrinkled face suggested he had spent many years fishing without a hat. His name tag said "Eric," and he was talking with an irate customer. At first, Carl thought the man was mad at Eric or the lumberyard, but he listened more carefully as he walked around looking at the various hardware items on the sparse shelves. The man was frustrated about someone stealing nails. That's an odd thing to steal, thought Carl. When the man finished his tirade, Eric took a minute to write in a ledger book.

"Okay. I've got all of it on your account, then," Eric said to the man as he handed him his receipt. "Go 'round back to the loading dock. Melvin is back there to help you load up."

When the man had left, Eric smiled at Carl and said, "Nice to see you again, Mr. Carl. And Bruno! How ya doing?" Eric came around the counter and, using both hands, enthusiastically scratched the big, black dog behind both ears. Bruno thumped his tail in appreciation.

Carl glanced back at the door, released Bruno from his leash, and said, "What's with that guy?"

Eric shook his head and said, "That poor bastard's gonna bust a gut. He's having a log cabin built out on Pine Island. Hrumph. More like a mansion, I'd say, but he's calling it a cabin anyway."

"What was he so upset about?" Carl asked.

"I dunno," Eric replied with a flip of his hand. "He says somebody's been stealing supplies and messing up stuff out there. It's happened several times now. Must be some kids."

"Yeah, well, that would be a bother," said Carl. "Anyway, I need to get a couple of one-by-eights for some shelves I'm adding to the kitchen cupboards."

As they discussed the length of the boards and the prices, Bruno sniffed around where the angry man had been and followed his steps to the door. He sat and waited there until Carl was ready to leave. Eric rounded the counter and gave Bruno another vigorous scratch before they went out the door. "See ya, big guy," he said.

Carl, carrying the lease, and Bruno went around back to the lumberyard. The irate customer was already gone, so Carl chatted with Mel as they picked out the best of the clear pine boards. Bruno sniffed around and strategically marked the yard while Mel cut the two straightest into four six-foot lengths. When Carl had the boards snug under his arm, he and Bruno walked across the street side by side, Bruno's leash folded up in Carl's back pocket. It was a funny thing, Carl thought, if Bruno had the leash on, he'd walk as far ahead as the leash allowed, but if he didn't have a leash on, he walked right next to Carl. "Va' snäll hund, Bruno," said Carl in Swedish.

There were two gas stations in Tower, one at either end of Main Street. The Arrowhead Garage was a Standard Oil station at the east end and was the last building before the road entered the forest again. Carl and Bruno went inside, and Carl leaned the boards he was carrying upright against the wall behind the door.

A jingle-jangle from the door closing brought Arno Peyla in from the repair bay through a side door. Carl could see a 1942 Dodge Deluxe up on the lift, a mess of tools on a red cart underneath it. The big man wiped his hands on the rag hanging from his back pocket and grinned.

"Well, hello, stranger. Nice to see you." He knelt down to look Bruno in the eye as he rubbed behind the dog's ears. "How ya doin', big guy? You're sure not getting any smaller, are ya then?" Bruno thumped his tail in silent enjoyment of the attention. This was his kind of trip to town.

At least a foot shorter than Arno, Carl reached out and shook the Finn's hand. Peyla's grandfather had been an immigrant at the turn of the century, forsaking the hard life of a timberman in the forests of Finland for what he hoped would be a better life in the north woods of Minnesota. His two sons and four grandsons all had remnants of the old man's speech with a Finnish lilt and broken English phrases.

"Yah, we sure had a great time last year at the Old Settler's Day cookout. Thanks for coming out for it."

"It was fun. Thanks for inviting us. Maybe we can do it again this year. I know Elsa enjoyed visiting with your wife, too. Well, you sure look busy enough," said Carl looking out the window at the small but full parking lot. "But I have to say you are one smart businessman, running two businesses out of one place. You are still delivering gravel, too, aren't you?"

"Yep. We're busy enough, but in a small place like this, and what with the history of layoffs at the mine, I gotta make hay, if ya know what I mean. So whatddya need up at your place, then?"

They chatted about what would be the best type of gravel for the Swanson's driveway and picked a delivery date in the middle of next month. It couldn't be sooner, said Peyla, because his nephew was running the backhoe out at a building site on Pine Island until then.

"Well, whenever you get to us is okay. We're in no hurry."

"Yah, I say the middle of the month, ya know. I hope it's not going to be longer than that. They seem to be running a week or two behind out there. I could always have Aronson's barge bring the Cat over to your place for a day, ya know, such as when they don't need it out there, yah."

"No, don't bother with that. Like I say, we're in no hurry. Well, I'd better be getting along. I'll stop in again after the 4th of July," said Carl.

He shook Peyla's hand again. Bruno waited by the door as Carl picked up his boards and held the door for the dog to go first, which, of course, he always had to do.

* * *

The US Post Office was located near the other end of town, just four blocks away on the same side of the street as the lumber yard. It was housed in a little red brick building typical of small-town post offices. A window and a door faced the street with a flagpole directly outside. The floor was black and white linoleum in a checkboard pattern, the walls a minty green.

The matron behind the counter had driven the rural routes for many years and now had earned the dubious privilege of serving the community face-to-face. Her face, however, made it crystal clear she would rather be back in her car, leaning far across the bench seat to open mailboxes and silently insert whatever was next in the giant mailbag resting on the passenger seat of her reliable four-door sedan. Customer service was not her forte. Her name tag said, "Midge." She was talking to a man dressed in catalog clothes. At least, that's how Elsa thought of them. The kind that city guys buy from a catalog to try to look like sportsmen on the rare occasion they actually do get outdoors. Too much plaid. Too much flannel. Midge was frustrating the man no end and vice versa.

Elsa reminded herself, as she waited, that although midges were ubiquitous pests, they didn't bite. Finally, the man in plaid finished. He had requested that his mail be delivered to his new cabin out on Pine Island. He had told Midge the mail boat should look for a mailbox on the new dock on the eastern shore of the entrance to Canfield Bay. "Stark" would be painted on the side, he said. Midge had laboriously written it all down, taking her sweet time. In a condescending voice, she told the man his mail delivery service would start the day after tomorrow – if there was any mail for him. The man rolled his eyes and left.

She was next, so Elsa stepped up to talk to Midge with a smile, hoping she could get one in return. No such luck.

"Hi," she said. "My husband and I are here for the summer and would like our mail delivery to start. Carl and Elsa Swanson. We're over on Rural Route 2, about a half mile before you get to Gruben's."

"Sure. I remember you," Midge said with a smirk, "You're the folks from Chicago with the oversized mailbox and ya never get any mail except the week-old Chicago Sunday newspaper."

As Elsa left the Post Office, she stopped at the glass-fronted bulletin board by the door. Half of it was taken up with Federal Postal notices. The other half was devoted to the six men from Tower who had lost their lives in WWII. Their deaths happened a few years before, but the people of Tower didn't want to forget them. Elsa looked at each of their faces and silently thanked her lucky stars Carl had made it home.

She went next door to the Tower News newspaper office. This building could have been made from the same set of blueprints as the Post Office, Elsa thought as she pulled open the door, except that the back area in this one hummed with the noise of printing machines. The lady behind the counter had the opposite demeanor from Midge. She was smiling and seemed genuinely happy to see Elsa.

"What can I help you with?" said Edith. She and her husband had owned and operated the Tower News for years.

"I'd like to start receiving the Tower News," said Elsa. "We're here for the summer. We got the paper last year and we enjoyed it immensely."

"Well, that's nice to hear. What is the name?"

"Elsa and Carl Swanson. We're on Rural Route 2 before you get to Gruben's."

"Sure. I'll add you to the route. Would you mind if we put an announcement in next week's edition that you and your husband are here for the summer?"

"No. Not at all. It'd be kind of fun to see our names in the paper."

The two women chatted about the announcement Edith would write about the Swansons. Then the topic changed to the weather, last year's and hopes for this year's, and things coming up over the summer. Edith told her the Fourth of July celebration was still in limbo because the city fathers couldn't agree. Finally, after chatting for a bit, Elsa paid for their summer subscription, said her goodbyes and left.

Across the street in front of Martilla's Drug Store, she paused briefly to check out the displays in the windows on either side of the heavy beveled glass door. She also saw her reflection there - a slim, pretty woman with bobbed hair and a confident demeanor. A tiny bell jingled pleasantly as she opened it and entered Tower's only Pharmacy and Emporium. It had started as a soda fountain back in the early 1900s, selling tobacco, sundries, ice cream sundaes, malts, and other goodies. There had been two soda fountains back when the population was much larger during the lumber boom. Martilla's had survived by adding the pharmacy some years back.

Once inside, Elsa stopped for a minute taking in the familiar sights and smells. It reminded her of the small store just like this one in Thorsby, Alberta, where she was born and raised. She thought about going there with her parents as a child. She was jarred out of her reverie by a couple of boys laughing at the soda counter.

To her right, a long glass counter cabinet ran the length of the store. Behind the counter, the wall was covered with closed cupboards. This was Mrs. Martilla's realm. If a customer asked Mr. Martilla for something outside of his purview of pharmacopeia, he would stiffen up and call for his wife with a bark. She was the only person who knew what was behind each cupboard door. When someone asked for cotton balls or bunion compresses, she would fling open the correct cupboard door and produce the item with a magician's flourish.

The cash register was stationed midway on the glass counter, and behind it was Mrs. Martilla's stool, where she sat most of the time. Through the glass counter to the left of the cash register, Elsa could see all sorts of hair ornaments, boxes of permanent wave kits, shampoos, brushes and combs, bobby pins, hairpins, and curlers. To the right of the cash register were all the tobacco products and men's shaving things.

Across from Mrs. Martilla's domain and taking much of the floor space was a soda fountain, complete with a double-curved counter like a big "S" and about twelve stools attached to the floor on chrome pedestals. A mirror with etched advertising lined the wall above the chest-type refrigerator unit and the countertop where the malts and sundaes were made. While they tasted ever so good, the quantity was often lacking. The Martillas were known to be stingy. Everyone in town knew a single scoop had about enough ice cream for a toddler, and if you liked ice cream, you needed to ask for a triple scoop. Steam leaked out around the cover of the hot fudge pot. The smell of melted chocolate made Elsa smile as she inhaled a long deep breathe.

Down the center of the tin-ceiling room were a few racks with items customers could peruse themselves - a selection of paperbacks, the latest magazines, newspapers from the big cities, gum, candy, and postcards. Running across the entire width of the store at the back was the pharmacy counter, and behind it, Mr. Martilla's domain. His pitch-black comb-over belied his age and Mrs. Martilla's skill with the liquid shoe polish applicator.

Elsa loved Martilla's because it reminded her of home, but she hesitated to get any actual medication there. Today, her list included double-edged razor blades for Carl, some Pepto Bismol, Band-Aids, a tin of licorice to have in the boat, and a magazine or two. As Mrs. Martilla gathered the items from different cupboards, Elsa leaned an elbow on the counter, turned, and took it all in – including the two boys at the soda counter having root beer floats. She moved to the magazine racks to pick out a couple, and from there, she could hear what the boys were saying.

"…in that house. My mother wouldn't be able to find me for days it's so big. And I hear it's just that one guy from Wisconsin who's building it. Bet he's gonna throw some big parties, eh?" said the taller boy.

"Yeah, and I bet he's got more money than old Mr. Iron Mine. And, hey, ya know what? I hear something funny is going on out there. My brother Dennis has been working out there, running my uncle's backhoe, and he says somebody has been doing some bibbidy stuff out there," the shorter one said.

"Whaddya mean?" his friend said, leaning in close.

"He says things keep disappearing, like nails and wood and stuff. And someone keeps breaking stuff too. Oh, and he said someone put some gunk in the cement mixer and it ruined everything they made that day. Stuff never hardened up like it's supposed to."

"No kiddin'! That's a hoot! What do ya do with soft cement, eh?" laughed the short kid.

"Guess they had to shovel it out and start over. My cousin didn't mind. Got paid again for the same work. But the owner wasn't happy. Irvin says he's really a weird guy. Got himself a tent he's living in up there that's fancier than your house or mine, neither. He drinks fancy whisky and is always fussin' about and shoutin' at people."

Mrs. Martilla gave Elsa a start with a slap on the counter. "Here's your items, Missus," she said. Elsa went over to the counter and handed the magazines she had chosen to Mrs. Martilla, who rang everything into the cash register with a grand flourish. After paying, Elsa took her bag and headed out of the store with a wistful glance at the boys' root beer floats.

* * *

Carl and Elsa saw each other down the block and waved, walking toward one another on the wide sidewalk. They reached the car at the same time. Elsa dropped her purchases off in the front seat while Carl rolled down the back windows a foot on both sides. A cool breeze made it a pleasant place for a canine nap. Carl said, "Hop in, Bruno. You have to stay for now." The big dog jumped into the cavernous back section of the Frazer and plopped down, head on paws, eyes going from Elsa to Carl and back again like the eyes on a Kit Kat Klock.

The Tower Hotel and Café was the third in a string of three clapboard buildings pressed close together on the north side of the street, empty lots at either end. The bar along the wall in the café also served as the front desk for the hotel rooms. It wasn't a hotel anymore in the strict sense of the word. It was more of a rooming house for a few old men down on their luck who rented the rooms upstairs. But the bar and café on the first floor were still popular with the locals.

Elsa and Carl took the table by the front window so they could keep an eye on the car while they ate. She ordered the chef's salad, and he chose the cabbage rolls, a favorite because his mother had made kåldolmar, the Swedish version of cabbage rolls smothered in a cream sauce. They talked about their errands and what they had left to do, including a quick rundown of the groceries they needed.

"I got two nice boards to make those extra shelves under the sink you wanted last year, and I never got around to," said Carl, "Nice and straight with no knots. Shouldn't take long at all to put them in."

"Thanks, honey. It'll be nice to have a little extra storage for canned goods."

"You know, there was a guy in the lumberyard office who's building a new cabin over by Canfield Portage. The guy was complaining to Eric. You know Eric, right? The counter guy at Tower Lumber?" Elsa mm-hmmed while she chewed without looking up. "Well, this guy was complaining things were going missing from the job site. Somebody had stolen sacks of nails and some other stuff. The guy was there getting replacements. How aggravating would it be to have your building project delayed by stupid kids stealing things like that?" continued Carl.

Elsa looked up at Carl and put her fork down. "When I was in Martilla's I overheard a couple of boys talking. One of them was saying how his brother was working on a new cabin and it was going to be really big and fancy. But the interesting thing was his brother told him somebody had tampered with the concrete mixer, put something in it or something like that. And the concrete didn't harden up, so they had to do whatever they were doing all over again," she said. "The boys thought that was a hoot."

"Whoa, that is kinda funny," said Carl. "Oh, and I stopped to see Peyla down at the Arrowhead Garage. He said to say hello, by the way. And he said we can't get delivery of the gravel for our driveway until the end of the month because his backhoe is being used out on Pine Island. His nephew, Dennis, is running it for him out there. He said they're way behind because of some trouble. It's going to be a big house, evidently."

"And somebody doesn't like it. Maybe they're jealous or something."

"Sure looks that way," Carl said.

"Say, that must have been the owner I saw at the Post Office.

He was telling Midge he wanted mail boat postal delivery to a new box out on a pier over there by Canfield Bay. He said his name was Stark," said Elsa as she took another bite and kept talking. "Seemed like an OK guy considering he was dealing with dear sweet Midge. He kind of matched her grump for grump though, now that I think about it. Kind of down in the mouth, too, like he was frustrated at something else besides Midge. He walked out like the world owed him big time."

"Well, we'll have to take a boat ride out that way and check it out. Some good fishing spots near there," Carl said as he wiped his mouth with his napkin. "Let's get a move on. Bruno's been in the car a while and we've still got to grocery shop."

They left a tip on the table, went to the end of the bar to pay their bill.

1920

CHAPTER 7

The smell of stuffed cabbage rolls greeted him when he opened the door. The Tower Hotel dining room wasn't crowded, so Ike chose the table by the window. The barkeep waved him over and said he would take his order, that the waitress would be right back. Ike set his things down, went up to the bar, and ordered a patty melt and a beer.

"Sorry, Bud. It's soft drinks only now, thanks to that scumbag Volstead. Our local brewery used to make a great lager, but now it makes root beer, ginger beer, and sarsaparilla. Which one would you like?"

"I'll take a ginger beer," said Ike.

The bartender filled a mug from a wood-handled tap and set it in front of Ike who took it back to the table by the window.

Just a few days earlier, he had been in Chicago – lost and suffocating. The people who cared about him had no idea who he was, but then, neither did he. He had written the note, left it on the table, took the small bag he had hidden in the front hall closet, and went downstairs to the garage in back. He got in the Paige and drove around the block to the front of the bakery. He looked up at the windows where he knew Angela was sleeping. No tears came. He knew he should feel something more, but nothing happened.

He headed north without thinking and then made a choice. He would go to Duluth to see his family. It was late in the afternoon a day and a half later when he parked across the street from the apartment where he had grown up on Wadena St. He had received letters from his father when he was in the Army. He knew his family loved him and wanted to see him, but he couldn't make himself get out of the car. Finally, he stopped trying to feel anything and drove away.

Again, he headed north. For a few summers when he was a boy, his family had rented a small cabin on Nichols Lake. It was just one room with a fireplace, lots of well-used stuffed furniture, a long table with benches on each side, a kitchen along the back wall, and a loft where his parents slept. There was a large screened-in porch where all the children slept on the cushioned benches which lined the walls below the screen. If it rained, they took the cushions, moved inside, and slept on the floor. Here it was that he learned to swim and fish and that a person could do without a lot, and that simple pleasures were fundamental to happiness. He knew his parents loved each other, and they loved their children. Scraps between the boys and snits between the girls meant nothing. They were a family, and they were happy to just be themselves with each other. Those summer days at the lake were his best memories.

Ike loved the noise of the wilderness. For him, there was a

quiet in it unlike any other. The wind, the waves, the animals, the insects, the birds, all made a ruckus that melded to make the most peaceful sound in the world. His soul had longed for nature's quiet noise when he was in the battlefields where there we no birds, no animals except the dead, and no leaves on the few remaining trees to rustle in the wind. Only the smells and sights of death, tearing at his sanity.

He had heard about Lake Vermilion many times when he lived in Duluth. It was famous for being wild and beautiful. It was far away from any city, 100 miles north of Duluth, and that sounded great to Ike. From his childhood memories, his uncle's description of the lake and Pine Island were intriguing, too, so he headed that way. He kept driving north until he got to Tower, a small mining town between Virginia and Ely, Minnesota. There wasn't another town north of Tower, just 30 miles of wilderness to the Ontario border, then more wilderness beyond that. Nothing but wilderness, then ice, all the way to the top of the world.

He stopped at the first store in town, Martilla's Emporium, and bought a local map even though he had an old map of his own in his bag. Somehow the new map made his plans seem more plausible. It was possible, he realized. There was a real place here, not just the rambling memories of a dying old man or the myths of bragging fishermen.

He decided to take a chance on this distant place and went into the Tower Bank to open an account. All the money left each week from his earnings at the bakery had gone into a joint account that he had left for Angela. But he had brought with him what he had saved from his Army pay and a little cash he had saved over the years. He deposited most of it into his new account, kept a little cash in his pocket, and left the bank to find a place to stay.

It was a glorious early June day, and many people walked up and down Main Street. Even here, there might be too many people, he thought. He asked around town about the Lake Vermilion and was directed to Aronson's boat livery office on Pine Street. They ran a ferry service from Tower out to various resorts on the lake. There were no roads to the far reaches of the lake, and the ferry was the only transport. He was told the next one would depart in two hours, so he bought a ticket and then went to find a bite to eat while he waited. He left the Paige parked in the lot behind the livery office where the clerk had told him to. He walked down Main Street to the Tower Hotel and went in to eat.

Ike looked at the map on the table as he ate, folded carefully down to a small square as he had done with the burial maps on the silent battlefields. He folded and refolded it to see the different sections of the area but still kept it neatly next to his plate. When he finished eating, and the waitress took his plate and silverware away, he ordered another ginger beer and spread the map open in front of him on the polished pine surface. He ran his finger from one end of the lake to the other. It was a complicated lake with many bays and narrows. Forty miles long, they said. More than three hundred and fifty islands, they said. The shape reminded him of an ant with a segmented body and many foreshortened legs. He started to count the islands, then realized a map couldn't possibly show all three hundred and fifty, if there really were that many.

Ike sat back and pondered how it would be to live on an island. He decided it would suit him just fine. Pine Island looked like it took up about a quarter of the length of the lake. An island that big would always have enough firewood, he thought. As he leaned forward again to take another look, the shapes on the map began to seem familiar to him. After thinking about it for a minute, he reached down into his satchel on the floor by his feet and pulled out the old map he hadn't looked at since he was a boy. What he saw made him nod. Even if it wasn't the Pine Island his uncle talked about, it was close enough. Pine Island, it would be. It was meant to be.

He called the waitress over and paid his tab. He was anxious to get on the ferry and see the lake. When the ferry finally departed, Ike made his way to the bow and stood looking forward. The forty-foot steamboat held fifty people or so. An enclosed cabin with windows all around and rows of seats took up most of the main level with an outside walkway all around it. It was early in the summer, and there were only about twenty people on board, most of whom were inside the cabin sheltered from the wind, looking out at the lake and chatting with their fellow travelers.

Ike was struck by the beauty of what he saw. The deep water was clear, yet all blues and browns, like the finest Murano glass. The expanse of water was fringed by endless boulders, veins of quartz threading through the rock masses like pieces of thick white yarn. Ike could plainly see that the area had been logged. Young trees, most barely a man's height, made the rocky landscape beneath their branches appear to be sprouting a green stubbly beard. At various places in the distance, there were tall stands of old-growth pine trees, their dark, rich green in sharp contrast to the paler yellow-green of the young birch and poplar trees.

The ferry motored past Hoodoo Point and Puncher Point, weaving between the many islands at the north end of Pike Bay. Then turning northwest and passing between Echo Point and Ely Island, the expanse of Big Bay lay before them. Ike was used to big water, having grown up on the shores of Lake Superior, then living in Milwaukee and Chicago by Lake Michigan. But the Great Lakes, as grand and spectacular as they are, aren't welcoming or approachable. As they crossed Big Bay, he thought this was the most beautiful lake he had ever seen. It beckoned to him. He would have a boat. He would get to know this water.

The ferry took him to the Idlewilde Hotel on a small island on the northwest end of Big Bay. The main lodge, perched high on a bedrock outcropping, had an expansive lake view. He rented a housekeeping cabin which came with a rowboat. The resort owner told Ike that Pine Island was ten miles long, and the view from his cabin looked at the southwestern corner of it across a large channel. Every day, he used the little rowboat to cross the channel and explore the shoreline of the big island, venturing farther each day as he became more familiar with the lake and his body got used to rowing. One day, Ike spotted a shack near the shore on the south side of Pine Island facing Big Bay. It was clearly abandoned, so he went ashore and walked around. The loggers had clear-cut the entire island some fifty years before. Here and there were a few big pine trees, which had probably been tiny saplings when the big trees were cut. These stood tall above the light forest which had grown up around them. I'll cut back the woods a little to have a bit of a yard and let some light into the cabin, he thought. He paced out the size of the room he would add to make the shack livable, with a new roof across the whole structure. He stood on the shore and looked south across the wide expanse of Big Bay. This is where I want to be, he thought.

He made all the arrangements with the authorities and after a few weeks, became the owner of the shack and a few acres around it. He never cared about the borders of his property. It was all forest, and which trees were his didn't matter to him. He sold his car and bought a small wooden boat and a 1919 Johnson Waterbug two-horsepower motor. He went to the Tower Lumberyard and contracted to have some work done. First, he had a short dock built and added extra pilings to withstand the ice, as someone had suggested. He had a well dug and the main room built onto the shack, then an outhouse. He added a long narrow porch across the back as an afterthought. Within a few weeks, the work was done.

While the work was going on, he went back into Tower several times. He visited the Herman T. Olson Mercantile on Main Street and purchased an icebox, a big cast iron stove, some furniture, and other things he needed, like a broom and some tools. On one trip, he purchased winter boots and a heavy coat, mittens, hat, some work clothes, underwear, and handkerchiefs at the Chas. Roland Department Store. On another trip, he bought kitchen basics, some linens, a shotgun and shells, and more groceries. His savings account was sorely depleted, but he reckoned he still had enough to buy needed supplies and a few necessities to get through the next year. He felt prepared.

Tower was alluring to most people, with its movie theatre, saloons, and cafes, but Ike couldn't wait to get back to the island. He could get an ice chunk from Morcom Inn or Gruben's Marina when he needed it for the icebox. He could get eggs, milk, and bread at any resort on the lake. He figured he would only have to go into Tower every couple of months. He was finally settled.

1948

CHAPTER 8

Zup's was short for Zupanicich. It was currently the only grocery store in Tower. It had grown out of a small meat market named after the owner and butcher, a short cheery Slavic man with a stiff accent. He had immigrated to Tower as a young boy with his family, most of whom became miners. Now his son ran the store, and the old man came in twice a week to do what he loved most – cut meat and make sausage. The piroshkis were terrific, the pot roasts generous, the pasties superb, and the porketta to die for. But Elsa had learned not to buy steaks from Mr. Zup. His opinion was if you had that much money to spend on meat, why not buy twice as much sausage which "had some flavor."

The other thing she found out the hard way not to buy was the Swedish sausage, which she frequently bought from a meat market on Clark Street back home in Chicago. While Zup made eight different varieties of Polish, Ukrainian, and Latvian sausages, which were all delicious, the Swedish sausage was horrible – dry and bland like mushy, uncooked oatmeal stuffed into sausage casing.

Thursdays had been hot bologna day at Zup's for over thirty years. The tradition had started back when the miners were paid on Thursdays. Zup's cooked up big juicy chunks of bologna ready for the miners to eat on the spot before they went to their favorite bar. The fat sausages floated in a big pot on an electric hot plate on a folding table in front of the meat counter. Elsa stopped to lift the lid but decided the grey color and garlic smell was unappetizing.

Elsa had realized the store was laid out like a maze with short aisles and dead ends, forcing a customer to walk down every row. The only way to avoid that was to weave through the first three aisles, cut across the back by the meat counter, skip the center two aisles, and then weave to the front through the last three aisles. The meat counter ran the width of the store all along the back wall.

Meats were one thing, vegetables another. Deliveries came up once a week by train from a supplier in Duluth. Potatoes, onions, parsnips, turnips, and rutabagas were always plentiful. Everything else, not so much. Zup hated to throw anything out. Spoilage was not in his budget, so any unpurchased oranges or apples stayed in the cooler until they became unrecognizable except by unpleasant odors. However, when local berries and vegetables were in season, people from around the area would bring in flats or containers of whatever they grew or picked. Zup would pay them fairly, but he still made a good profit because both the tourists and the locals would pay top price for the precious fresh produce.

Elsa had planned to buy the various items they would need for the coming weeks. They would go to Gruben's for milk and eggs and a few other perishables and try not to come back into Tower for at least two to three weeks. Elsa piled flour, sugar, canned goods, a few spices, and other things from her list into the shopping cart, while Carl chatted with other customers and the stock boy as he pushed the cart up and down the tight aisles on the winding journey to the cash registers.

When they got to the front, they saw both registers were being used. A mother with four disheveled young children and a cart full of groceries to match was being helped at one, so they chose the other register where the single customer was just about to pay. Elsa recognized the man from the Post Office, Mr. Stark.

"Hello," Elsa said, "Are you the gentleman who's building the new cabin out on Pine Island? I'm Elsa and this is my husband, Carl. We've got a place over on Daisy Bay."

"Yes, I'm Stephen Stark," the man said. "But I guess you already knew that. You were standing right behind me at the Post Office, weren't you?" He turned back to the cashier, who was holding down a piece of paper with the tips of her fingers. He signed it, then turned back to Elsa, "Stop out sometime, and I'll show you around. It's going to be grand!" and with that, he left. The grocery boy followed close behind, pushing the cart filled with groceries.

Elsa stood in shock for a moment, realizing the man who she had found so rude earlier had just invited them to visit him. Trying to flush out her feeling of reticence, she turned to Carl, "What do you make of that?" but he just shrugged leaving her even more frustrated.

As the cashier rang up the Swanson's items, the bag boy returned with the empty cart and started bagging their items. He finished just as Carl was putting his wallet back in his pocket. Elsa led the way, and Carl held the door for the skinny kid pushing the cart. They walked out of the parking lot and down the sidewalk to where the big Frazer automobile was parked. Bruno greeted them with a woof. Carl opened the back-hatch doors, the window section going up, the lower section going down flat. Elsa went around to the side door and leaned in to lower the back seats. Bruno hopped out and sat on the sidewalk as the grocery boy began to load the bags into the back.

"Hey, Dirk," Carl said after glancing at the boy's name tag, "What do you know about the guy you helped just before us? We hear he's building quite a fancy place out on the lake."

Dirk stopped loading bags and haphazardly leaned on the cart with his elbow as if he were standing at a bar, one ankle crossed over the other. Fortunately for him, the cart was up against the curb. "Seems he owns a bunch of property out there on Pine Island. This guy, now he came to the store couple of weeks ago and asked for Mr. Zup. So, I went back to meats and got him. Mr. Zup came up front and talked to him right out there by the registers so as even though I was doing my job I could hear what they was saying, yah know what I mean? So, the guy told Mr. Zup he was Nathan Stark's son and that he used ta' come here as a kid when his dad was trying to build a bunch of cabins out there to sell. Gonna make a whole city out there, he was.

"The guy says he's building out there on the big island now. Not the whole whizz-bang like his dad wanted, but just a cabin for himself. Mr. Zup started out by saying how sorry he was 'bout his dad and all. Seems he knew the guy's dad back when. Said he remembered the guy as a kid. Seems his dad told Mr. Zup he was gonna have to expand the meat market on account of all the people who'd be coming up here from the big cities if all went according to his plan. He must a' went and died or something is what I thought. But when I told my grandpa about the guy when I got home that night, my grandpa said the guy was a crook and that he up and took everybody's money and never came back so nothing ever came of the place out there on Pine Island.

"Bottom line, though, Mr. Stark wanted Mr. Zup to open him up an account like his dad used ta' have. That's so the guys working out there, or whoever, can come into town, get some groceries and put it on Mr. Stark's tab. Sounds like some of them are camping out there 'til they be done with getting' his cabin built."

Carl thanked Dirk with an extra two-bits and shut the hatch doors. Dirk took off back to the store as the Swansons headed for City Hall.

Down a block from the Post Office and kitty corner from Martilla's was City Hall, a sparse-looking two-story cube of white stucco. The section which faced Main Street had been partitioned off for commercial use and housed the municipal liquor store. The minimalist Art Deco ornamentation was painted matte gold which had faded and from a distance looked more like a couple of stripes of missing paint. That is not to say the building was in disrepair. It was, in fact, well taken care of and a source of pride for the residents. Not every town with such a small population had a city hall this grand. Back in its heyday, Tower had a population more than five times what it was now in 1948. The Saint Louis County Sheriff's Department had a branch that served this remote northern section of the county up to the Canadian border, and the Deputy Sheriff had his office in Tower's City Hall.

The government portion of the building faced Birch Street. Four wide steps led up to the double glass doors, which opened into a central foyer, a hallway straight ahead and stairs going up on the right. The main floor was taken up with the city hall offices, which had a service window opening onto the foyer, and the rear of the building at the end of the hallway was given over to the Sheriff. There was an exit door out the back, too, with a parking lot for employees and official vehicles. Upstairs in City Hall was a large meeting room, the library, and two smaller rooms now used for storage.

Outside, at the top of the wide marble stairs, Carl held the door for Elsa and Bruno. They paused once inside to adapt to the dim light, absorbing the dusty smell of old marble floors. They waved at the lady behind the sliding-glass service window next to the entrance to the city offices as the three of them passed her and walked on down the hall. She smiled and looked back down at her work.

The Deputy Sheriff's office door was open, and the lights were on, but no one was inside. There were two desks in the room. The large one toward the back held a sign which read "Deputy Sheriff Harvey Pittella." The sign on the smaller desk by the door said, "Patrolman Peter Korchenko." Carl and Elsa were about to leave when they heard the back door in the hall open. Pittella came into his office, running his hand through thinning grey hair. When he saw his visitors, a big grin spread across his face.

"Hey, now, look who's here," he said as he offered his hand to Carl. "You guys back for the summer, eh?"

"Yep, we sure are," said Carl, taking his hand. "How are things going?"

"Good, good. Same as always. Hey, Bruno, want a treat?"

Bruno, wagging his tail a mile a minute, went around the desk to get the Milk Bone the tall, pale man was taking out of a box in his bottom drawer. Yep, this was definitely Bruno's kind of trip to town.

Carl and Elsa sat on the two chairs positioned in front of the big wooden desk. Bruno lay down near the desk drawer just in case it would open again.

"So, when did you two get up here?" asked Pittella.

"Just a few days ago. We've had a fire going since we got here. When's it going to warm up?" replied Elsa with a smile.

"Soon. Soon. You know how Minnesota weather is. If you don't like it, just wait a few hours and it will change. How was the winter in Chicago? And your business is doing good, Carl?"

"The winter wasn't too bad. Not much snow and only about a week of below zero temperatures. Business is great. We managed to hire on a couple of experienced painters. My partner, Eric Lindberg, is healthy again after his surgery last fall. So, I get to come up here for the summer while he runs the business. Then the lucky bastard will take off for Florida while we deal with Chicago winter."

"Yah, I remember meeting him one time when he came up with you to go camping a while back. Nice guy."

"How's Minnie and the family?" asked Elsa.

"She's fine. Thanks for asking. She's out at the reservation several times a week taking care of her parents and a few other older people there, her real aunts and uncles, I think. But I can't tell 'cause they all call everyone in their tribe some relative name."

"Ya, just like at home," said Carl. "Anyone old is called aunt or uncle and anyone even older is called grandpa or grandma. But we don't call people our own age 'brother' or 'sister'."

"It's good Minnie has her extended family out there. Keeps her busy. We still miss the boys a lot. We get a letter from John every now and then. I think, you know, I mean, we might have told you that when he got back from Germany, he came home but he didn't stay but a few days. We were hurt, but now I think we've finally come to realize he just isn't the same happy-go-lucky kid he was when he signed up to be a hero. We hope he'll come back to us but, honestly, I don't think he will ever be the same. But at least he can provide for himself, unlike some poor fellows who came back wounded or worse. Last winter, he moved from Gary, Indiana to Detroit. Still working as a smelter. My understanding is they can make good money working the steel mills there."

"As for Jim, there's no describing the loss. It's like it happened yesterday, even though it's been four years now. We thought he'd be safe on a ship as a merchant marine. It's ironic John was infantry and saw action constantly, but Jim is the one who got killed. It was an unbelievable tragedy, his ship going down. So many young men died. I was hoping the pain would get less for Minnie, but sometimes I still find her crying when she thinks I can't hear her."

"Oh, I'm so sorry. For you both. I can't imagine how hard it is to lose a child," said Carl.

"But we still have our Winnie. Her new baby is the light of

our lives, and her husband is a good man. Fortunately, they decided to stay in Tower, and he didn't have to serve on account of his one leg being shorter than the other. He's a good son-in-law to us," Pittella said, nodding.

"How's Ike? Have you seen him lately?" Elsa asked.

"Oh, he's the same. Getting up in age though. Hah, about the same as me, I guess. He was in town a few weeks ago for supplies. Stopped in to say hello. He asked if you were up yet."

"We'll go over to see him as soon as we can. I can't imagine how long the winter must be for him," said Elsa.

"Say, we heard from several people in town there's a big house going up on Pine Island," said Carl. "Just curious, what's the scoop with the owner? He seems like quite the jerk. We just bumped into him at Zup's and he was quite full of himself."

Pittella paused and folded his hands on his desk.

"Well, I'm not one for gossip, so I'll just tell you the facts as I know them. His name is Stephen Stark and he is the son of the man who disappeared, oh, must be twenty years ago now. I was just new on the job, and it was my first missing persons case and, unfortunately, it remains unsolved. Still keeps me awake at night, now and then," Pittella shook his head.

"Now, the young Mr. Stark is building a substantial home on the very site where his father had been planning a real estate development. He has been to visit me several times to file complaints about malicious activities on the property. Things have gone missing or been destroyed. I've been out there but can't find any hard evidence of who is doing the damage," said Pittella.

"That's too bad," said Carl.

"Yep, and Ike's property is near his and he's stopped in to

see me too, complaining about the noise and disruptive activity at the construction site. Aaronson's barge comes and goes bringing supplies and equipment, and that barge's big diesel motor stinks, I know. And there's machinery going all day and hammering, of course. Poor Ike doesn't like to be disturbed, let alone having a neighbor. Come to think about it, he lucked out, I guess, when the elder Stark's planned community didn't come to be way back when. Let's see, that would have been close to when Ike arrived up here – that's a long time ago, you know. And he loves his peace and quiet. If I remember correctly, Ike was approached by Stark and his partner, can't remember his name, to sell to them back then, but he refused. Far as I know, they just planned around his property. Guess it wasn't really a concern to Stark anyway on account of him planning on walking away with the money and never really building anything there in the first place."

"It sounds like Ike could really use a visit. I think I'll bake him some bars, too. Maybe cheer him up a little," said Elsa.

"He'll love that. Say, Carl, the Game Warden told me there's lots of northerns this year. I know you like to fish for them, just like me. You and I are about the only people I know who actually keep 'em and eat 'em. Me, I don't mind the bones, the taste is so good. Should be a good year for walleye too, from what he tells me."

As the conversation about fishing picked up steam, Elsa interrupted to say she was going to run upstairs to the library. She backtracked to the foyer, stopping along the way to look at several of the framed photos of historical events from Tower's past which were hanging in the long hallway. It was so quiet in the cold building, her shoes made a loud shsssh noise on each step on the way up the granite staircase. The door to the public library had the word "LIBRARY" stenciled on the frosted glass. It probably had been the mayor's office back when Tower had a much bigger population and the mayor needed a big office. Nowadays, a part-time mayor had a partitioned-off area for his desk in the main city office downstairs.

The library had been started by a generous donation of hundreds of books from the Reverend Dr. Preston Bradley, an immensely popular radio preacher from Illinois. For over twenty-five years, his inspirational words, broadcast worldwide, had compelled young and old alike to do good things, work for equality and justice, and send their donations to him. He had been coming up to Lake Vermilion for many years. Back in the 1920s, he bought Black Duck Island in Frazer Bay, where he built a log cabin as a summer retreat for himself and celebrity guests.

The one-room library was filled floor to ceiling with books. An overwhelming majority of those books were of a serious nature and had been used as fodder for his sermons at the People's Church in Chicago. In order not to repeat himself too many times, he would periodically purge his bookshelves and have them brought to the Tower Library. Over the years, hundreds of books had been donated by Bradley's wife and other people as well. These were predominantly summer reading, mysteries, romance novels, and the like. Since the library volunteers had no better method of keeping track of the books, they were alphabetized on the shelves by author's last name. Browsing for a good read was like being on a moral seesaw from one book to the next - *The Many Mansions of Christ*; *One Night to Love*; *The Definitive Lutheran*; *The Mystery of the Torn*

Bodice; *Finding Peace Through Poetry*; *Hot was Her Favorite Color* and so on.

Very little light came through the glass of the door, and the library looked closed. Elsa tried the handle anyway and found it unlocked. The familiar smell of musty books met her when she walked in. She knew from previous visits there was no librarian, and the few volunteers came in whenever they felt like it, so she was not surprised no one was in the room. She stood for a moment trying to decide, then chose the nearest row of shelves on her left and proceeded to walk slowly along the rows of shelves, moving her lips as she read the book titles, skipping over the preachy ones. The light from the double-hung windows overlooking the street seemed sufficient to read the titles, so she didn't bother turning on the overhead light.

She chose four mystery novels with exciting titles and a fifth book about the history of Tower. It had a drawing of a gold miner and a lumberjack standing together on the cover. She carried them to the table closest to the door that held a small box and a few pencils. She took the 3x5 cards from the little paper pockets glued to the inside front cover of the books and filled out her name and the date on each of them. When she was done, she put the cards in the little box on the table, picked up her newly found literary treasures, and went back downstairs.

Carl stood when Elsa came in and said, "I'm all done. Got a few good ones! Ready to go?"

Bruno stood and stretched, then began loudly sniffing the bottom drawer to see if more treats would appear, and everyone laughed. His antics panned out, though, and Bruno was still licking crumbs off his lips as they left.

"Be sure to drop by any time you're on Daisy Bay," Elsa said.

"I will, I will," Pittella said, smiling. The two men leaned across the desk to shake hands again. They said their goodbyes, and Carl and Elsa made their way outside and down the front steps.

They made a quick stop in the liquor store for a bottle of rye and one of sweet vermouth to make Manhattans. It was a small store, and any liquor other than beer was kept behind the counter. The walk-in refrigerated beer cooler was filled with long neck bottles of Fitgers, Schmidt, Hamm's, Blatz, Pabst, and Grain Belt. Six-packs filled the cooler shelves, and cases of the same brands were piled high down the center of the room.

Carl said, "I think I'll get a case of beer, too. It's gonna get warm one of these days."

They were helped by a pleasant, matronly woman who tended the cash register from behind the counter. On the way home, Bruno stood with his head thrust over the front bench seat between Carl and Elsa, making conversation difficult for them. They rode in silence, all three staring ahead at the road, thinking their thoughts.

Carl and Elsa headed back on 169 and at the "Y" turned right on Hwy 77. They kept going past Birch Point Road toward Moccasin Point, where the road ended. They pulled in on the long gravel driveway which led to their cabin and stopped. Elsa got out and checked the mailbox - just in case Midge was wrong. Nothing there. They drove the quarter mile into their cabin, unloaded the groceries, and carried them inside. Bruno supervised the process, accompanying Carl up and down the steps to the car each time he went for another load of groceries. When they finished, Carl parked the car farther up the driveway in a graveled area off to the side.

"Tomorrow we'll get the boat down and go for a ride," Carl said after dinner as he helped carry the dishes into the tiny kitchen.

"I hope it'll be a little warmer tomorrow. But unless it's raining, I'm up for it, no matter how chilly it is," replied Elsa.

She did the dishes while Carl fussed with the Stromberg Carlson. It was a model 1121, table-top radio with AM/FM/shortwave bands, a large rectangular case covered in tan leather with gold-tone trim. The half of the front flipped up to reveal a wide display with a channel selector behind a glass face showing all the numbers of the radio stations for the different bands. Tiny letters listed the names of far-away cities and countries above golden numerals. Carl loved to fine tune the black Bakelite knobs to find an interesting program or music channel. He would pull up a chair next to the tall table it sat on and lean toward it as he carefully moved the knobs, practically willing it to find a station with clear reception. After dark, if the weather and atmosphere were just right, he could tune into stations thousands of miles away. It was a pleasant way to spend an evening -- listening to a radio drama or a concert from Carnegie Hall or a program in a foreign language from the other side of the world. Sometimes they'd get the Jack Benny Program or the Fred Allen Show clear as day, and they'd laugh along with the studio audience, as if they were there.

CHAPTER 9

The next morning, Elsa fixed fresh pork sausage and eggs and perked coffee on the stove burner for breakfast. No trendy new Nescafé instant coffee for us, she thought. A jar of jam sat on the table by the butter, waiting for the toast to be done. Carl reached over and opened the pull-down door on one side of the old Redi-Heat flip-flop toaster, and the piece of bread, toasted on one side, slid down and flipped over as he closed the door. Then he did the same for the door on the other side for the second piece of bread.

"Toast will be done in a minute," he announced.

The lake looked beautiful in the morning sunshine, thousands of shimmering ripples beckoning them to come outside. So early in the summer, the leaves of the poplar and birch trees were such a bright green and fluttered so vigorously in the breeze that it was almost as if the trees were covered with green butterflies. Elsa poured more coffee for them from the stainless-steel percolator. She liked the coffee pot because it had a glass insert in the top which allowed her to see how dark the coffee was getting, so she could take it off the stove at just the right time. Carl liked his coffee nice and dark. When they finished the meal, they cleared the table together.

"That was excellent, my dear," Carl said in a funny, deep voice, tipping an imaginary hat.

Elsa laughed and thought his stiff Swedish accent made the W.C. Fields imitation a real hoot. Carl kissed her cheek as he headed for the door. He picked up the fishing poles and tackle box and gave Bruno a nod of his head and a look that said, "Coming?" Bruno stood up, stretched full out from head to toe, and wagged all the way to and out the door.

"You coming, too?" Carl said to Elsa, still holding the door open.

"I'll be down shortly," Elsa said, "soon as I finish tidying up."

Carl and Bruno walked down the slope to the boathouse. Carl set his armload of gear by the door and continued to the end of the dock.

Their property ran for 100 feet to the east of the boathouse and 200 feet to the west along a slightly convex portion of shoreline, so there were no neighbors or other indications of civilization to be seen from where he and Bruno stood.

Carl loved Lake Vermilion because it reminded him of his home in Sweden. The landscape was the same as the area around the small village where he was born. He had fished the waters of Stor Sjön in Hälsingland as a boy, and, truth be told, the shoreline of Vermilion looked so similar, sometimes when he was casting from the shore, he forgot he was in Minnesota.

There were no weeds or bulrushes, or any sand either, to be found in their part of Daisy Bay. The shoreline and lake bottom were all rocks, rocks, and more rocks. Cedars and birch grew along the water's edge, adding to the picturesque view.

He had started coming up from Chicago to camp years ago, long before he married Elsa. The lake was located 600 miles north of Chicago, so only serious vacationers or people trying to get away made it this far north. But the trip was worth it. Lake Vermilion's 365 islands and 1,200 miles of shoreline made it a sportsman's dream. And Carl loved to fish.

An old friend from Chicago had bought a large section of land sight unseen in the early 1930s. The friend, Werner, loved to tell how he came to own the property. He and his wife had emigrated from Sweden after World War I and lived in Evanston, Illinois, just north of Chicago. One day he was in a grocery store there when he heard the elderly lady in front of him telling the clerk her husband had died. She went on to say she didn't know what to do with the property he had purchased sight unseen on a lake in northern Minnesota some years before. It was just wilderness, she had said. Her husband had wasted their money buying a place he never even went to see, she said. Now she was stuck with it. What was she to do?

Werner and his wife had been dreaming about starting a resort somewhere in the lakes region of northern Wisconsin and he knew Minnesota was full of lakes too. So, he politely told the lady without so much as a breath's hesitation, "I'll buy it from you." When he related the story to friends and acquaintances, he always ended it by saying how lucky he was because he gets to go the piece of heaven the guy he bought it from didn't even get to visit it.

Carl had been invited to come along on the Werner's first trip to see his new property, and they both fell in love with the place. Werner told Carl he could camp on the land whenever he wanted, which Carl had done until he married Elsa. It was then he had asked Werner if he could buy a piece of the property. The land Carl now owned was a small piece of what Werner had purchased from the old lady in the grocery store six hundred miles away sight-unseen twenty-some years ago.

So much had happened since then, he thought. It couldn't have been easy for Elsa while he was gone for four years. Not just gone, but in harm's way - at war. We're lucky, so lucky, he thought. She waited. I lived.

Now here he was, with his own piece of heaven, ready to spend the summer with his beautiful wife, fishing and relaxing. What more could a man want? Well, maybe a couple of kids to pass it down to, Carl thought. He stood at the end of the dock gazing into the water and contemplating the perfect family. A boy for me. A girl for Elsa. No. It really didn't matter, he admitted to himself. Any children would be welcome. Was there still time for us? Even though they barely spoke about having children, he could tell Elsa was longing for a child. Maybe yet this summer. His thoughts wandered to the war, the friends he'd lost and the children they'd never have, the way they'd died. The dark thoughts were consuming him, and he struggled to come back to the moment. None of that, he said to himself and raised his head to look out over the water.

This day had one of those perfect mornings with only a slight breeze, few clouds, and thin cold sunshine. The lake was cold and clear but had a dark brown color like root beer after the ice melted in an untouched glass. When the sun was at the right angle early in the morning and there was no wind, the rocky bottom was visible for a long way down and a long way out from the shore until it got too deep to see. The light rays shone through the water all the way to the bottom where they played on a field of gray-brown rocks. A sunken log here or there would break up the bumpy pattern of the stones. Sometimes, what looked like a submerged log wasn't really a log but a giant muskie lounging midway between the surface and the bottom.

Bruno lay at the end of the dock, also gazing into the water. He liked to stay perfectly still and watch for a 'big one' to pass by. Carl could always tell when that happened because Bruno's tail would whack against the dock until the giant fish had drifted out of sight. No amount of fancy bait or expensive lures could entice one of the huge ones to bite. They were so old and wise that nothing fooled them. Carl and Elsa had seen one, or perhaps the same one, several times last year floating under the dock. Carl leaned over to pat Bruno's head. Watching the big dog watching for the big fish made him smile. What's he thinking, I wonder, Carl thought.

"Well, got to get to work, Bruno," Carl said, "Let me know if you see our friend down there."

He opened the boathouse door and began to untie the safety ropes that made sure the belts didn't slip out from under the boat during the winter. Then he took down the crank handles that hung on nails along the wall. He put each one on the correct winch crankshaft and put a cotter pin through it.

He walked back up the path to the cabin and continued around back to the shed. He got out a couple of flat cushions for the seats and the two-gallon gas can. He closed the shed door and started back down to the boathouse.

He stopped at the cabin and shouted up at the door, "Ready when you are!" and kept going down the path to the dock.

A few minutes later, Elsa came down the path. Bruno got up to greet her, and they both stuck their heads into the boathouse where Carl was cleaning the oars with a rag. He had thrown the seat cushions and fishing gear into the boat still suspended in the low ceiling. He set the oars on the seats. The gas can he left sitting on the lip of the dock.

"OK, we're ready to go," he said from where he had moved to near the back of the boat, "You take the front winch. I think the action is a little easier than on that one."

"OK, I'm ready. I'm going to start slow." Elsa started cranking. Ropes and wood creaked, and the front end of the boat began to rise. "Oops! Wrong way," she said.

Carl worked his way around the boat to her and flipped the lever which made the ratchet work in the other direction. "There you go. Let's try it again," he said and kissed the top of her head as he made his way along the narrow ledge past her.

This time, with both of them cranking, they produced the desired result, and the boat lowered slowly to the water. Carl disconnected the wide belts from the clips at the ends of the winch lines. The lines hung over the boat's centerline, two feet in from each end. They served a dual purpose, holding the boat out of the water during the winter and keeping the boat centered and away from the boathouse walls during the summer when it floated in the water tethered by hooks on large springs hanging from the ceiling. Carl attached the boat's short mooring lines to the hanging hooks with snap clips.

He stepped in with the gas can, set it in the boat between the back seat and the stern, and lowered the outboard motor so the propeller was in the water. Then he filled the gas tank located on the top of the motor and set the can back behind the seat.

Elsa got in. Then with a bit of coaxing, Bruno got in. They unhooked the mooring lines and pushed the boat forward. Elsa ducked under the truncated front wall as they slid the boat out of the boathouse. Carl did the same in turn. Bruno was lying down between the seats, so he didn't have to duck.

Elsa held on to the dock while Carl pulled the starter rope. Two tries and the Evinrude purred. The four-cylinder 9.7 horsepower Evinrude outboard motor did a great job moving the heavy eighteen-foot mahogany open boat through the water. No, not fast, but smooth and steady.

"Hurray! Summer is officially here," Elsa called over her shoulder to Carl at the back of the boat, and they took off toward Daisy Island directly across the bay from their place. When they got there, they turned west and rode the entire length of Birch Point along the southern shore of Daisy Bay, then came back along the northern shore. They waved at the fishermen sitting with their anchors dropped near the reef markers by Rainbow Island and at anyone they saw onshore or sitting on a dock. It was a beautiful morning for a boat ride.

When they arrived back at their place, they turned the boat around, propped the motor up out of the water, and slid under the front wall into the dark of the boathouse. They went to opposite ends of the boat and grabbed the large tightly-coiled springs hanging from the ceiling. They each attached a spring to a short rope which allowed the boat to float freely between the sides of the boathouse. When they stepped out of the boat, Bruno jumped out, too, and rushed on past them, sprinting up the hill to the cabin.

CHAPTER 10

They enjoyed a few clear days when they boated and fished close to home. After that, it was cold and grey for the next two weeks, drizzling off and on every day. It turned out to be a rainy June. Elsa kept a slow fire going all the time, so the cabin was warm. She was glad she had checked out more than one book from the library because she was already through two of the mystery novels. She did some baking, darned a few socks with holes in the heels, and patched up two pairs of work pants Carl had managed to tear while cutting firewood. Carl spent his time doing small projects around the house, in the shed, or in the boathouse – anywhere but outside. Before dinner each day, they would relax with a cocktail, a nice sweet Manhattan with extra cherry juice for her, a stiffer one for him. After dinner, they would have tea and play cribbage at the table or read on the sofa. The Stromberg Carlson was on whenever the reception was decent, which wasn't often in bad weather.

On one particularly dreary day, they went into Tower just to see a movie. They had seen the ad for it in the Tower News. The Rex Theater on Main Street was playing a John Garfield flick, "Body and Soul" with Lilli Palmer. Elsa was a big fan of the handsome leading man, so they went. Carl actually liked the movie, and they stopped at the new bar at the end of Main Street for a burger and a beer before they headed home.

After yet another dreary week and feeling a bit of cabin fever, they went back into Tower for groceries and a few errands, dodging from shop to shop in the rain. Elsa returned the books to the library and checked out some more. They stopped at the Deputy's office, but he wasn't in. In the shop windows all over town, they saw posters for the upcoming Fourth of July festivities. The highlight of the day was to be the parade down Main Street.

Carl and Elsa looked forward to this bit of small-town Americana, mainly because it was the anniversary of their meeting. While he was still working with Lindy, he had saved enough to buy property on the Fox River northwest of Chicago. He built a small house and a garage utility building and started a marine gas station the following summer. The old man next door took care of it during the week, running out to pump gas when a customer rang the bell by the pump. On the weekends, Carl manned the dock and repaired outboard motors in the garage when it was quiet. As fate would have it, he had been working the gas pump on the Fourth of July nine years ago.

The boat Elsa had been riding in had docked at the marine gas station to refuel: that's when he first saw her. Carl knew the couple who owned the sleek Chris Craft cabin cruiser. They kept the boat at a marina just up the river a half-mile but often gassed up at Swanson's Sales and Service. As they waited for service, they introduced him to their guests in the boat, people they knew from their work and had invited out for an excursion on the river.

The dishwater blonde in the back of the boat was a knockoff of Ingrid Bergman and Carl could hardly take his eyes of her. She smiled when he was introduced and said hello to her. That was it, right there, right then - he was smitten. They all chatted and laughed for a bit as the boat was refueled. Then the boating party left, and another boat took its place at the gas dock. It was a busy day for Carl and served his customers with a faraway look. A big holiday on the river generated a lot of income for his business - but he had a hard time concentrating.

As the days went by, Carl couldn't forget the pretty young woman with the yellow scarf tied around her hair sitting at the back of the boat. A perfect smile that made her eyes wrinkle at the corners. He kept talking himself out of thinking about her. He wasn't interested in having his heartbroken again. He had been married briefly, but it ended badly when his wife ran off with a man while he was at war.

Still, he kept thinking of the girl in the boat, so the next time the couple with the Chris Craft stopped for gas a week or so later, Carl asked them how he could reach her. He was pleasantly surprised when he called the boarding house where she was living, and she came to the phone. I've been hoping you'd call, she'd told him.

They had dated for a year and were married eight years ago in a civil ceremony at his house on the Fox River. It was a beautiful day in September, and the wedding took place on the broad front lawn. They didn't live there for long, though. They sold the house and the marine gas station for a good profit and moved into Evanston. Carl had recently partnered with another Swede painter named Eric Lindberg, and the two of them concentrated on interior painting and decorating – a lucrative business in the wealthy north shore suburbs of Chicago. Elsa quit her job as a secretary and became the primary bookkeeper and scheduler for the new endeavor.

It was fortunate for the business that Eric had flat feet. He had been turned down at the Army recruiting station in August of 1940 when he and Carl went to sign up together. They had been willing to shut their business down while they served, but since Eric couldn't serve, he and Elsa kept the company going while Carl went to war. When he returned unharmed and the business became more successful after the war, they agreed to cover for each other for long periods. Eric would spend winters in Florida, and Carl would spend summers on Lake Vermilion, and they worked together during the busy seasons of fall and spring, hiring crews to expand the business.

Now another Fourth of July was coming up, an anniversary of sorts for Carl and Elsa. They finished their shopping at Zup's and happened to get the same grocery boy.

"So, Dirk, what have you heard lately about Mr. Stark's new cabin out on Pine Island?" asked Elsa.

"Oh, the workers come in now and then to get supplies. They don't hesitate to load up when it's going on Mr. Stark's account, that's for sure. I heard them talking the other day about how they're way behind schedule. Guess there's still weird happenings going on and then, 'course, there's all the bad weather, too," he said as he set their bags in the back of the car.

"Oh, that's too bad. I'll bet Mr. Stark isn't very happy about it," said Elsa.

"The guys working out there don't even bother to go when the weather's too bad. The house ain't far enough along to be able to work inside. Leastwise, that's what I heard. I even heard Mr. Stark came into town and has been staying at the hotel, keeps his boat on the river, and goes out to the site every couple days. Who knows, maybe he'll give up and just go home."

"I don't blame him. Must be terrible camping in this weather. This drizzle is awful," said Carl as he closed the back of the car.

"Yah, but ya know, seems like he's the kinda guy who'd be miserable even in nice weather. Take care, then, eh," Dirk said as he turned back to the store.

They took their leave and headed home.

There were at least two resorts on Lake Vermilion at the turn of the twentieth century. By 1915, there were eight, almost all serviced by steamboat launches. The Duluth Mesabi and Iron Range Railroad ran two trains a day to Tower. In 1921, the railroad promoted the area with a pamphlet listing fifteen resorts. Most had three to ten cottages and a lodge building. As Lake Vermilion's reputation as a great fishing destination grew, so did tourism. In 1925, with even more resorts being built, the area could accommodate over six hundred visitors.

The Ole Gruben family had immigrated from Norway in 1886 and had a farm near the west end of Big Bay. Ole and Elsie had two daughters and five sons, two of whom became known as 'the Gruben Brothers'. They bought the Idlewilde Hotel on an island eight miles from Tower in the late 1920s. It was immensely popular, had accommodations for seventy-five people, over fifty rowboats for guests, and a dance hall with in-house entertainment.

The Gruben brothers changed the name to Isle of Pines Resort in 1932. The brothers also bought the property on the mainland closest to the island and opened Arrowhead Point, a lodge with a few log cottages. They added a marina and a grocery store and built a bridge linking Isle of Pines with *the mainland. When the old Tower school building was going to be torn down, the Gruben Brothers bought it. Once the lake froze solid the next winter they had the square two-story structure lifted onto skids and pulled across the ice by a team of horses some six or seven miles to its current location where locals and visitors still buy supplies and stop for an ice cream.*

CHAPTER 11

Finally, one morning in late June, the sun came out with the promise of a fine day. At breakfast, Carl said, mouth full of scrambled eggs, "How about we head over to Big Bay to fish today?"

He watched as Elsa put another piece of cinnamon bread in the flip-flop toaster and said, "Okay. I'll pack a picnic, and we can stop at one of our favorite spots."

"That'll be great. We can troll whichever shoreline is the calmest and maybe even go by Canfield Bay and check out the new cabin."

"Let's stop at Ike's and say hello. I think I'll wrap up a cardamom braid to take to him," Elsa said.

"Hmm. I thought you baked all of that for me," Carl said with an exaggerated pout.

Elsa laughed and said, "There's more where that came from. I'll bake again next week. I promise. I'm awfully glad we put in a decent stove. At least, when I do make something, it usually turns out pretty good. The heat seems to be nice and even, even though it's an electric oven."

They each busied themselves with getting ready for a day's outing on the water. Elsa made lunch, wrapping the ham and cheese sandwiches in wax paper, along with some chunks of Zup's summer sausage and pieces of hardtack for a snack on the way home. A few almond cookies in a small, lidded tin, and the lunch was complete. She wrapped cold bottles of beer in newspaper and filled a thermos of coffee. She packed it all in a two-handled Longaberger picnic basket made of woven strips of maple wood. She added a small screw-top metal tin filled with strike-anywhere matches, a bottle opener, a small plaid tablecloth, and a few mismatched cloth napkins. She set the basket by the door.

In the closet off the main room, she dug out one of her hats which she knew would stay on even in the wind. Her favorite boating jacket made of oilcloth with a plaid flannel lining, a smooth woven scarf, and a pair of low leather boots she had waterproofed with lanolin last year, and she had everything she needed. She put the boots on and piled the jacket, hat, and scarf on the picnic basket, and waited for Carl to finish getting ready.

When they finally got in the boat, Carl announced they should stop at Gruben's to top off the tank in the outboard motor and fill the gas can, too. Bruno perked up when he heard the name Gruben's because they always had a homemade dog treat for him and any other dog which came into the store. When Mr. Gruben smoked venison in the fall, he always included any gristle or small tidbits he couldn't sell. He did the same when he smoked whitefish. A crispy fish tail or a piece of smoked deer gristle, Bruno didn't care which - either would make him happy.

As they pulled up to Gruben's gas dock, Bruno bounded out of the boat and started to run up the hill to the store. He stopped abruptly as a boy came out of the icehouse, a chunk of ice the size of a case of beer dangling from the metal ice tongs he held in his right hand. Bud waved at the Swansons and said, "Be right with you, let me just run this up to Mr. Okerwall's car." Bruno went along trying to get a lick of the ice, but Bud laughed and kept it out of the dog's reach.

The icehouse was a large wooden, windowless shed that held sawdust and ice in a huge pile on the floor. Each winter when the lake was frozen several feet thick, a group of men would get together to cut big blocks of ice and haul them to Gruben's icehouse. The ice chunks were piled in and covered with sawdust which acted as insulation. The ice would last all summer in the cool dark shed buried in the thick pile of sawdust. By the end of August, Bud would have to poke around for a bit to find the shrinking chunks, but most years, there was ice until the following winter. Some people still had iceboxes, non-electric refrigerators which held a large chunk of ice in the upper chamber made of tin with thick insulation. The floor of the upper chamber was not insulated, and the cold from the ice kept the food in the lower chamber refrigerated.

Bud was Bill Gruben's son. He worked in the store, manned the marine gas pump, and helped his dad with the minnows and bait. He knew just about everything there was to know about outboard motors because he'd been working on them since he was old enough to hold a screwdriver. Now he was a big, strapping young man, all angles and elbows, but with a lot of baby fat yet to be shed. He was a pleasant guy, quick to smile and always blushed if a female of any age smiled back. Nice kid, Carl thought.

"How ya doin'?" Bud asked when he came down to the gas dock. "Ya up for the summer, eh?"

He pumped the handle on the side of the tall glass-topped gas pump until it was filled with the golden liquid giving off a strong smell of gasoline. Carl had unscrewed the gas cap on top of the Evinrude, poured in what little gas remained in his can, and set the empty can on the dock. The boy brought over a quart of outboard motor oil and opened it with a beaked can opener. He poured some of the oil into the gas can. He gently shook the oil can to hear how much was left and poured in a little more. Finally, he took the gas nozzle down from the side of the pump and filled Carl's gas can to the top.

"There. That should do ya," Bud said as he judged how much gas had drained from the glass container atop the pump by checking the lines painted on the glass, "Ya comin' up to the store for an ice cream or something?"

"No, we're on our way up to Bass Lake portage for some fishing. We'll be on our way. Say hello to your mother for us," said Carl.

"Okay, then. I'll put the gas on your book." As Carl was starting up the motor, Bud reached in his pocket, then leaned down to give Bruno a treat. "Take care now," Bud said pushing the boat away from the dock.

As they left Gruben's, the lake was calm, but as soon as they passed Moose Island at the tip of Birch Point, the lake became much rougher. The wind was coming from the east and had the entire length of Big Bay to whip up some big waves. The water was a cold, gray-blue, and flecked with dabs of white at the cap of each wave. Carl had to slow down so the waves breaking over the bow of the boat didn't completely drench Elsa. Even with her oilcloth coat and waterproof shoes she looked cold and wet after a few waves.

They cut a course straight down the middle of Big Bay. Carl's plan was to ride all the way to Indian Point, which was a distance of about four miles, tie up on the south side of the high rocky point of land and have lunch on the big rock ledge which faced west and had a fabulous view of Big Bay and Pine Island. Then they would fish the mainland shore in Bass Bay which would be much calmer water. That was the plan, anyway.

Because of the rough water, the trip across Big Bay had taken over an hour and a half by the time they pulled up to the shore on the south side of Indian Point. The wooden boat, a Sportland eighteen-footer, was prone to scratches and damage if it was pulled up onto rocks, so they took care not to let that happen. Carl had a routine to land the boat whenever there was no dock. He dropped anchor when they came up close to shore, yanking on the rope to make sure it had hooked securely on the lake's rock bottom. He motored close to the shore, feeding rope to the anchor as they went. With the nose of the boat as close to land as possible, Elsa held onto the front rope and jumped out onto the shore. Carl shifted the motor between reverse and neutral to keep the boat in place. She wrapped the rope around a tree by the water's edge, and holding the rope taut with one hand, she took the picnic basket out of the boat from the front seat where had been stowed. Bruno hopped out after the seat was clear. Then Carl backed away from the shore a little way, Elsa feeding him rope slack as he went - the rope still around the tree. Carl turned off the motor and secured the anchor rope so the boat would stay out from the shore just far enough to keep the bottom off the rocks. Elsa pulled on the front rope, bringing the boat as close to shore as possible so Carl could jump out onto dry land.

They were starving by the time they finally unpacked the picnic basket onto the little tablecloth Elsa had spread on the solid rock ledge, high above the lake. The sunshine felt warm and the rock smelled of lichen and pine needles. The lake below receded into the distance, looking soft like a wrinkled steel grey blanket dotted with fluffs of white cotton lint.

"Food always tastes better outside, I think," Elsa said, "What a gorgeous day and what a view. It really doesn't get any better than this."

They chatted about this and that and then sat silently, eating and taking in nature's visual arts masterpiece. Between gusts of wind, they heard a whining sound that piqued their curiosity. It was a distraction from the breathtaking view.

Looking over at Elsa, Carl said, "What IS that?"

"You've been hearing it too?"

"It sounds so far away, but it's still annoying." Carl looked over toward Pine Island, squinting as he visually concentrated on the portion of Pine Island where he thought Canfield Bay should be. "I'll bet it's noise from the construction at Mr. Stark's new cabin. Oh, well, I guess they're up and running again," he said. "Isn't the view from here so beautiful? I wish I had brought the camera."

They finished their picnic lunch in silence, enjoying the moment and the simple food. After shaking out the napkins and little tablecloth, Elsa folded and packed them back in the picnic basket. She stowed away the bottles and the used wax paper and stood up, looking around.

"Did I miss anything, Carl?" she asked.

He had been standing at the edge of the enormous rock, looking out over the water toward where the noise was coming from. He turned, looked around where they had been sitting.

"Nope. Looks just like when we got here. That was such a good lunch, honey. You know, we lost a lot of time coming across the rough water. How about we skip Bass Bay and cut across the channel right there and start trolling along the Pine Island shore toward home," he said, pointing to the end of Windy Island in the channel on the south side of Pine Island, the shortest stretch of water to cross to the lee side of the big island.

"We can stop at Ike's and say hi. Then we can troll around Canfield Bay and along Pine Island up to Isle of Pine and head home from there. We just can't stay too long at Ike's, or it'll be getting dark," he said.

"That shouldn't be a problem," said Elsa, "You know what a hermit he is. You can tell he likes the company, but it's not like there's a lot to say. I can't imagine what he does all winter. There's no one up here most of the time, and he can't even go into town for groceries during the freeze or thaw - both of which take a month at least."

"I know what you mean. The man has such talent and he used to have a family. I wonder what made him run from all of it," Carl said. "You've seen his paintings. I think he could have been famous, don't you?"

"Yes, I do, too. I'm glad we bought one of his paintings last year. I really love it. But, you know, I'm kind of torn because the money we paid him enabled him to hide out by himself for yet another winter. Maybe he'd move into town to the senior housing if he didn't have a choice. I really think that might be better for him in the long run."

Carl shook his head, "Nope. That'll never happen. He's way beyond that. He is destined to live and die out there at his hidey-hole. But don't feel bad about it. It's as happy as he's going to get. He loves the woods. He's happy when he paints. And he has a few friends, which is all he want- at this point at least."

Carl smiled as Elsa put her arms around him. He returned her hug and they stood like that for a minute, looking out over the broad expanse of Big Bay, each thinking about the solitary existence their friend had chosen. Finally, they gathered their things and returned to the boat. Bruno stayed behind to check for any missed goodies. When Carl start the motor, he ambled down to the boat and jumped in, and they headed out into Big Bay.

1920

CHAPTER 12

The first months on the island passed quickly. Each day had a routine. He was always busy until nightfall when he would fix a meal and go to bed. There was so much to do before winter came. He completed the cabin, winterized the door and windows with felt window trim, built the bookshelf, hung the curtains, and completed several other small projects. He built a shed and cut firewood. As the leaves started to change color, he spent more time cutting wood, splitting, and piling it in an orderly fashion, with enough airflow between the rows of split logs to allow for them to dry out quickly. He was hoping it would be dry enough to fuel the big Glenwood cast iron stove by the time he needed it to survive.

He knew there would be a period of time when the lake would be impassable, but he had no idea when that would be. He took several trips to Tower, each time thinking that trip would be his last until the lake was frozen solid, and he could walk to Tower if he needed to. Ike had always lived in the city and really had no idea how things would go for him during the winter. But he was resourceful and most of all, he was careful. He knew there would be no one to rescue him if he had an accident with the ax or fell through the ice.

It was a bright sunny morning when he decided to make one last trip before the freezing water would make using his boat impossible until spring. For the last two weeks, ice had been growing along the shoreline, but the water of Big Bay was open. He kept the boat pulled up on the shore, and it was easy to push it out into open water over the border of ice. Keeping hold of the front rope, he led it to the dock and got in. The trip to Tower took over an hour, but it was uneventful, and the lake was calm. The cold air was exhilarating, the lake beautiful under the crisp, blue sky. Ike had no cause to be concerned and enjoyed the trip. He had bought top-of-the-line Red Wing boots but he could still feel the cold water through the boards on the bottom of the boat.

When he got to the river to go into Tower, he found it was full of slush and had some large chunks of ice floating in it. He was afraid it might be jammed with ice further in, so he decided to backtrack to Hoodoo Point. When he got there, he looked up at the pale sun barely visible against the even paler sky. He never suspected what the strange glowing halo around the sun meant. He tied up his boat and began the mile and a half walk into town. After a few minutes, a car approached from behind. As it came alongside him, it slowed and stopped. The St. Louis County Sheriff's Department logo was painted on the door. The man behind the wheel leaned over, grabbed the window crank and rolled down the passenger side window. Ike stopped and walked over. It was the friendly thing to do. The driver was a big man with pale hair and eyebrows. The reach across the big Packard patrol car was hardly a stretch for him.

"Hop in. I'll give you a lift into Tower," Pittella said as he pushed open the door.

Much as Ike preferred to walk alone, he accepted the ride from the law officer without hesitation just as a matter of respect.

"I was just visiting with some old folks out on Puncher Point. They live alone out there and need checking on now and then. It's a pleasant drive but not a pleasant walk, I'd say, eh? I don't think we've met," said the officer as he drove. "I'm Deputy Sheriff Harvey Pittella. First year on the job and I don't know everybody yet," he said as he reached to shake hands and keep driving at the same time.

Ike took off his mitten and shook his hand. "T'ank you for the lift, Deputy."

They rode in silence for a minute, then Pittella said, "And your name is?"

"Ike Iverson. I have a cabin out on Pine Island."

"You tie up at Hoodoo Point, then?"

"Yah. Need a few things before the lake freezes over and I can't make the crossing no more. River looked too icy."

"This your first winter here, Ike?"

"Yah."

"Not many folk live on the lake year-round. Nobody lives on an island year-round."

Ike didn't respond, and they rode in silence until they got to town. The going was slow because it had begun to snow big, fluffy flakes, and the deputy was a cautious driver on the dirt road.

Ike could sense that the officer glancing at him, trying to be subtle about it. Ike remained stoic, looking straight ahead through the big windshield of the cruiser. Pittella wondered why he would even venture out on a day like this. Everyone knew when there was a sundog, that pale ephemeral ring around the sun, the weather would turn bad and, more than likely, it would turn bad quickly.

As they approached town, Pittella said, "Hey, why don't I pick you up in front of the grocery store in, say, twenty minutes. I've got to run some medicine back up to the Korpola's on Puncher Point anyway, so I can give you a lift back to your boat."

When Ike came out of the grocery store carrying three paper bags of groceries in his arms, light snowflakes dotted the air suspended like the dandelion fluff of summers past. Pittella was waiting there in the patrol car, parked by the curb. The Deputy again leaned across and pushed the door open. Ike got in without a word and pulled the door shut. Holding the bags on his lap, he swiped a hand across the little bit of snow that had accumulated on them and his coat front, brushing it onto the floor. It melted quickly in the warm car, leaving dark spots of moisture on his wool pants.

"I think it would be best if you stayed in town tonight. There's no telling how much snow we're going to get. You could head home when the weather clears tomorrow," said Pittella.

"I'll be fine. Got to go home."

"Even if it wasn't snowing, it's iffy crossing this time of year. It gets dark so early."

"T'anks, but I'll be fine. 'Preciate the ride."

"You get all the supplies you need? It might be six weeks or more before you can cross again, if we don't get hard freezing weather. Snowy weather can be deceiving. Puts a layer on the lake but insulates it from making thick ice. If you decide to walk out on the ice, I'd suggest you carry a knife in case you break through. It can really make a difference. I've been here two winters now and have already seen a few accidents where people have fallen through the ice. Believe me, having a sharp object to help you crawl up onto the ice can mean the difference between life and death.'

"T'anks for the advice. I'll keep it in mind."

They rode the rest of the way in silence, watching the windshield wipers bat away the big, flat snowflakes until they came to the boat landing. Pittella stopped the car and got out when Ike did. Although it wasn't that cold, it was snowing heavier, and the young officer was concerned.

"You sure you won't change your mind and stay the night? If the cost of the hotel is an issue, I've got a cot in city hall for the occasional late-nighter. You can sleep there if you like."

"Nope. T'anks for the ride, Sheriff."

Pittella laughed good-naturedly, "Just Deputy. I'm not Sheriff yet."

Ike loaded his groceries into the little boat, covered them with a piece of canvas he kept under the seat to keep them dry, untied the back rope, and started the motor. Pittella hesitated before going to the front of the boat to untie the rope there. He reached in his pocket for something and gave it to Ike. "You might need this," said the Deputy.

Ike looked at it, put it in his pocket, and gave the Deputy a nod of thanks.

Pittella untied the front rope, tossed it into the boat, and shoved the boat away from the dock. He gave a wave as Ike drove off through the whiteness. Ike disappeared from sight sooner than Pittella expected. The snow quickly covered Ike's coat and hat and made him seem to disappear like a rose under the swirl of a magician's white silk scarf.

"Good luck," Pittella said to the silence.

CHAPTER 13

There was no wind, and the little motor ran smoothly, leaving a small wake behind the boat. Ike steered toward the end of Pike Bay and decided to give a broad berth to the reefs near Puncher Point. He could see Echo Point to his left and felt confident about where he was. The snow was falling heavier now. When he realized Echo Point was becoming hard to see through the flakes, he drew closer to it so he would be ready to turn north into Big Bay.

He saw the tiny island that marked the end of the point and aimed the boat's bow toward Ely Island. The snow began to fall faster, the flakes were smaller, and the visibility got worse. Fifteen minutes later, Ike could see he was close to Ely Island on his right. At least that is what he thought it was. He continued on the same course, and immediately ahead was a much smaller island. His confidence came back then because he knew this was Birch Island and felt now he could make it home easily if he just aimed directly across the big expanse of water. He couldn't see the shore on the other side. He couldn't see the row of small islands that ran up the middle of Big Bay, but he wasn't worried. He was headed in the right direction, and he wasn't going very fast, so if he kept his eyes open, he would surely see any hazards ahead. He held his hand steady on the motor's throttle handle and stayed the course.

The snow came down even heavier, and Ike could barely see the front of his boat. He had no idea how long he had been going. Time seems to stand still when it's snowing, he thought. Fortunately, there was no wind. He had to keep blinking as the snow clouded his eyelashes and made it difficult to see. The snow in the bottom of the boat was several inches deep, covering the ribs of the hull and the tops of his boots.

The mounds of snow which covered the grocery bags, the gas can, and the seats brought Ike to another place. A battlefield in France where the dead were not recognizable as bodies, just odd shapes under a white blanket. The snow cover hid the blood and empty eyes of the dead soldiers. Ike stared at the mounds until his tears stopped. He wiped his cheeks with the back of a glove, not sure how long he had been staring at nothing. He focused on the white-gray around him, trying to gauge where he was; but the lake, sky, snow were all the same color with no trace of the sun.

Doubt started to creep into his thoughts. Then dread took its place. He began to realize how serious his situation was. He no longer could tell if he was going straight or how long he had been traveling. He realized that no matter how steady he kept his steering arm, if he was aimed just a few degrees off, he could end up far from his cabin, or even worse - he could be going in a huge circle.

Suddenly he remembered Pittella's gift. He took the compass out of his pocket and immediately had to wipe the snow off it. He put it on his knee and cupped his right hand around it to keep the snow off, glancing at it frequently to find north and keep on course.

He gasped as he passed close to a rocky shore he hadn't anticipated, his heart racing as the bottom scraped on the rocks, thankful he had been going parallel to the shore. He realized he had no idea what land it was. He slowed the motor to a crawl hoping not to crash onto a reef. A few scratches wouldn't hurt the boat, but a hole in it would be the end of him. As he drove on heading ever north, he could no longer see the middle of the boat because the snow was falling so heavy. The light was starting to fade, but there was still enough to see the compass. North. He pulled his cap down tight over his ears and drove on, hoping by the time he found Pine Island, which must surely be directly ahead, the snow would have ended, and he could follow the shore home.

Then without his becoming aware of it, darkness had fallen. Now instead of straining his eyes and ears against the complete whiteout, he was surrounded by the opposite. He was struck by the fact that both made him equally blind. Time seemed to drag. Minutes. How many, he had no idea. Surely it couldn't be hours. It was only a mile and a half north to south across Big Bay. Perhaps earlier he had veered far enough that heading north was now causing him to pass the end of Pine Island. The wind had begun to pick up, and he was worried he was being blown completely off course since he could no longer see the compass. Perhaps he was now running parallel with Pine Island. The snow, which had been falling straight down earlier when he could see it, was hitting him now at a sharp angle. He wished he could tell which direction it was coming from.

When the hull hit the rocks, he was thrown forward onto the floor of the boat. Even at the slow rate of speed, it crashed with a horrible cracking noise. He immediately righted himself and made his way to the front, where he stepped over the prow onto the rocks, grabbing the rope as he did. Whatever land it was, he desperately wanted to be on it. The rocks were slippery and covered with ice. He fell, bruising his shins, so he put his hands out in front of himself and crawled. His hands and feet broke through the icy layer between the rocks, and his mittens, pants and boots became utterly soaked. When he thought he was past the ice, he stood up hoping it was a rocky shore, not a reef. He swore out loud but was glad, nonetheless, for the contact with land.

The waves were splashing violently against the shore, drenching him where he stood. The sound of the wooden boat grating loudly on the rocks shocked Ike into action. With a great effort, he struggled to pull the boat off the jagged rock it had snagged on and kept pulling until its tip was on the shore.

"Now what?" he said aloud to the darkness, leaning on the gunwale to catch his breath.

The snow was still coming down heavily, and the wind was whipping it around, stinging his face and eyes. Holding onto the rope with frozen fingers, he walked back and forth the short distance of its tether, arm extended, falling every few steps, unable to see a thing. There were trees nearby - he could tell from the sound of the wind in their branches. That was a good thing, he thought, at least I'm not on some reef. He was cold.

He leaned on the boat for a moment with both hands as the soaked mittens started to harden. I could freeze to death if I don't act quickly. He thought about what to do, then got started.

He pulled the boat up further onshore and made his way by feel to the back of the boat, his feet sloshing in the icy water. He untied the back rope and added it to the front one, then tied it to his wrist so he wouldn't get lost. He walked cautiously, stumbling often with one arm extended, as far as the ropes would go in all directions. When he came to some trees not far away, he followed the rope back to the boat. He took the motor off the back and carried it up next to the nearest tree. He went back for the grocery bags under the canvas, took them to the tree, and set them against the motor. He scouted the area close by the front of the boat using outstretched hands and found what he was looking for – a large boulder that he had literally bumped into shortly before. He dragged the boat as close as he could, wriggled it into place, tipped it on its side, and then pulled it up onto the boulder upside down so the bow was well off the ground. Supported by the big rock, it created a shelter of sorts.

The wind was howling now, and the drifting snow made walking even more difficult. It was pitch black. He groped around until he found the groceries and brought them to the boat, leaving the motor by the tree. As he was shoving the bags wrapped in the canvas toward the back, the boat tipped off the rock and crashed against him, landing flat on the earth with his legs trapped beneath. He struggled and managed to pull himself out from under the weight of the boat. His right leg was hurt badly; he could tell without seeing it. It was extremely painful to bend his knee, but he was reasonably sure nothing was broken. He sat there for a moment in the black, taking in the situation.

I've got to get shelter, but I don't see another option. So, crying out in pain as he stood, he again pulled the front end of the boat up onto the boulder. This time testing its purchase before crawling into the space under it. Inside the tiny shelter, on his hands and knees he painfully used his shoulders to hoist the boat farther up on the boulder until it felt stable. Turning around there was just enough room for him to sit upright with his back against the rock. He used the snow under the boat to fill the gaps where it didn't meet the boulder, compressing it to create walls down from the gunwales as protection from the biting wind and snow.

Now that he was on dry land, he wasn't as concerned about drowning in the ice water. As he leaned his head back against the rock, he was tempted to rest. I'm so tired... I can't feel my hands...No! Don't fall asleep! He had shelter but he was soaked, and the temperature was dropping. Luckily, he had purchased a couple dozen utility candles to have in case something happened to his kerosene lantern during the winter. He felt around to find the grocery bags and dug for the candles and wooden matches he had bought. He lit one and, with one hand, scraped away more snow until he uncovered a flat rock, dribbled wax on it, and set the candle in the pool of hot wax to hold it in place.

Almost immediately, he began feeling better, the tiny source of heat warming the small space. He took off his mittens and wrung them out. He rubbed and blew on his icy fingers. He removed his boots and socks and put the boots back on, afraid if they froze in the wrong shape, he wouldn't be able to put them on again. He hung the fish stringer between the upside-down seats over the candle and draped the socks and the gloves over it to dry. Thankful for the Army surplus wool pants that provided warmth even when wet, he probed his legs to find out how seriously he was hurt. He cried out when he touched his knee which felt swollen now. He thought he should put some snow or ice on it to take the swelling down but decided it was better to be warm with a sore knee than wet and freezing. In a short while, he stopped shivering.

There wasn't much to eat in the grocery bags. Mainly they contained staples - flour, sugar, and canned goods. And he didn't have a can opener. But there was a loaf of bread. He always bought a loaf of freshly baked bread when he went to town. He baked his own the rest of the time. The caraway rye from Zup's was his favorite. He was thankful he had splurged on a big smoked bone-in ham. He planned to make many meals from it, and it looked like this would be the first one. He unwrapped it from the butcher paper and cut several slices with his pocketknife. He put them between two pieces of the fragrant bread, leaned back against the supporting boulder, and ate slowly. He scooped a little snow and let it melt in his mouth to drink.

When he awoke, the candle was still burning. The wind was howling. He moved his body lower into the tight space, avoiding the rock where the candle was burning, pulled his hands up inside his coat sleeves and lay back to sleep some more. The next light he saw was daylight reflected through the snow filling the small spaces where the boat met the rock. The candle had burned down and gone out. Inside his boat cocoon covered with snow, he felt warm. He reached up for his socks and mittens. They were dry enough, and he put them on. His thigh muscles throbbed, and his knee was excruciating when he moved, but he had no choice but to get going.

Ike tried pushing the snow aside to get out through the way he had come in. But the storm that had started with fluffy snow had turned to heavy wetter snow during the night and then the temperature dropped. He scratched at the icy snow without much result. Finally, he again went on all fours and used his back to push against the boat seat, flipping it over and away from the rock.

As he was getting to his feet, Ike saw he was not alone. A fox, standing not more than thirty feet away, met his eye, then sat down to watch as Ike hobbled through the deep snow to a tree and relieved himself. The fox was gone when he turned back.

The snow was over a foot deep with a crust of ice. The wind blew fiercely from the northwest and drifted what little snow wasn't frozen. The sun was shining, and the temperature was at least fifteen degrees colder than the previous day. Ike pulled his hat down and tied the flaps under his chin. He walked to the shore and tried to get his bearings, looking back and forth across the lake, now covered in frothy white waves. From where he stood, he could see several islands. It took a few minutes to orient himself, and then he knew. He was on Pine Island directly north of Comet Island, looking out on Big Bay. Off to his right he could see the end of Birch Point, with Moose Island on one side of it and Isle of Pines on the other. To his left, he could see Spider Island, which was just out from where his cabin was.

He went back to a tree and broke off a dry branch, then returned to the shore. The snow-covered water that he poked at close to shore was solid ice. But when he threw the heavy stick farther out, it lay on top of the water for a while, then slowly disappeared into the slushy lake. He was feeling confident he could make it home in the boat, but when he went to turn it over, he saw that one of the boards on the bottom of the boat had cracked enough to let light in through its jagged edges. Guess I'll have to walk. At least I know my way now.

He took the two ropes off the boat and used one of them to tie the canvas around the grocery bags. He threw the make-shift canvas sack over his shoulder and started the long walk home, looking like an overworked Santa's helper.

The pain in his knee was only half the problem. The deep snow hid rocks and fallen logs, and the contours of the earth reached out to trip him, like a hungry cat scratching at your legs to be fed. He fell repeatedly, and his shoulders ached from the heavy bag. He was in Canfield Bay by the time the sun was high in the sky. He stopped to brush the snow off a fallen log and sat down to rest. He cut more ham and ate it with the bread, looking around at the breathtaking winter scene. There on his left, ahead of him on the route to his cabin, was the fox. It was sitting, looking at Ike as if waiting for him to continue his journey.

When he finished eating and the ham and bread were stowed away, Ike used the second rope to tie the sack around his waist so it would drag along behind him as he walked. This let him use his hands for balance and to break his frequent falls. His legs felt like they weighed a hundred pounds each. Every step took a huge effort to lift his foot out of the deep icy snow and set the heavy wet boot down ahead just a few inches. He looked around as he went and saw the fox was always ahead of him, sometimes off to the left, sometimes to the right, hidden most of the time by the trees. The fox seemed to dance across the top of the snow like a dragonfly flying over calm water.

He thought about cutting through the woods to save some

time but decided against it and stuck to the shore. As evening fell, he was glad for his decision as there was only a sliver of a moon visible over the open water. If I were in the woods now, I'd have no way to know which way to go, he thought. He stopped to rest often, feeling he was pushing himself far beyond his limit. At times, he wanted just to sit down and sleep, but he resisted the urge. Finally, he came to the clearing where his cabin stood, but he kept walking along the shoreline, too exhausted to realize he was home. Only when he stumbled on his dock did he look up.

His cabin stood cold and empty, but he hurried, despite the pain, to get inside. He had made it back, exhausted, hungry, and thirsty. Relief overcame him. When he came in the door, the first thing he did was light the fire in the woodstove. He left his boots by the door and padded around in his socks. He left his coat on as he opened a can of beans, dumped it in a pan, added a few chunks of ham, and put the pan on the stove. When the ice in the kettle had melted, he primed the pump at the kitchen sink, filled the kettle to the top, and set it back on the stove.

After a few minutes, he poured warm water into a shallow, blue-speckled enamel wash pan, returning the kettle to the stove to boil more water for tea. Under his coat, he was soaked with sweat, and he shivered uncontrollably as he undressed by the kitchen table. He washed and dried himself and went to the bedroom to put on some clean clothes. He pulled a chair close to the stove and ate the ham and beans as the tea steeped in a brownstone teapot. He drank a cup, feeling the warmth permeate through his bones, thinking about the lake, the snow, and the big man who saved his life with a small gift.

When he went outside to relieve himself before bed, he

wondered if he would see the fox again. He thought how strange it was it had followed him so far during the day. Actually, I was following him, I guess, he thought. He hadn't seen it since it had gotten dark hours ago and wondered where it had gone.

In his bed, as his eyes closed and he fell into the elongated moment of time between wake and sleep, he heard a ky-yipp, ky-yipp, ky-yipp repeated in rhythmic sets of three until he heard it no more. The fox.

CHAPTER 14

Spring came slowly with a force as strong and primal as the need to push during birthing. The wind and cold kept trying to keep spring at bay, but nature's desire to bring forth new life always prevails. Ike watched the lake devour a little more of the ice each day. Finally, when it was gone completely, Ike gathered the things he needed and trekked back over to where his boat was. He patched the crack in the hull with a square of canvas held on with pitch he had harvested from balsam trees and some sawdust to give it more to bond with. He had been experimenting with the patch solution all winter and felt it would hold even though it wouldn't be totally cured for many months, possibly years. It would be like waiting for honey to dry.

He flipped the boat over and slid it down to the water's edge and put the little motor on it. He grabbed an oar in one hand, stepped in and used it to push away from shore. He pulled the starter rope a few times and fiddled with the choke. After a few tries, the motor came alive and, running just a little rough, brought Ike back to his cabin. He knew he had come very close to dying that day last fall but felt no responsibility for having saved himself. It just wasn't his time. He had done what he could, and, at that particular time, it had been enough. He would be smarter and more cautious in the future, only because that is what he was supposed to do, not because he had any illusion his actions would save him in the future. He was home on Lake Vermilion, for better or worse, until the end.

Pittella came to see him a week after the ice went out. He stopped his boat at the dock and tied up. He stood there looking around. He noticed the patch on Ike's boat, pulled up on the logs. It was obvious Ike had had a close call. Pittella waited for Ike to come out, but when he didn't, he went around back to the door and knocked. Ike opened it and asked him to come in. They stood there by the stove for a few minutes conversing about the weather. Then Ike went over to the kitchen shelf and brought the compass back to Pittella.

"Here you go, Deputy. T'anks for the loan. It did come in handy dat day."

"Call me Harvey," Pittella said. "You keep it. Glad it was helpful."

"Yah, I've got a few things yet to learn about the Northwoods, I guess," said Ike.

"I noticed you're limping a little, Ike. Anything serious?"

"No, just my knee. A small mishap earlier in the winter. It'll heal eventually."

They shook hands, and Pittella left feeling he had made friends with a man who could use one.

After the first year in the woods, Ike felt he could finally bear the pain, that he had found a place to heal. Well, not exactly heal. He knew he would never be whole again. But the nightmares were not consuming him as they had when he first returned from the war. He hadn't expected to be happy, but he was at least comfortable in his own skin for periods of time during each day, almost as if he was a normal person. He found small pleasures in the day-to-day activities of feeding himself, fishing, carving, and painting. He went into town infrequently, avoiding casual conversation, spending only what money he had to for necessities.

He started to paint again. A few hours a day by the front window would produce a calm for him, which he needed so desperately. He would occasionally take a painting to town and barter it for more canvas, paints, or other supplies. He got a reputation and soon could sell a painting whenever he wanted. But still, he only painted what struck his fancy, usually copying some travel postcard or an outdoorsman magazine photo. His routine suited him, and time passed.

CHAPTER 15

Carl loved Evinrudes in general and this motor in particular. The 9.7 horsepower motor hummed at full speed, but when he throttled back to slow for trolling, it purred. It was like the propeller was an extension of his hand when he torqued the throttle handle back to go slower. Trolling, he firmly believed, was how a fish would fish. Moving evenly and slowly through cold, clear water in a boat powered by a smooth-running motor, seeking the most tentative nibble of a walleye on a lure trailing twenty feet behind tied to a thin line. The incomparable panorama of the wilderness sliding past, both above and below the waterline, was the kind of nirvana Carl thought was worth all the work and sacrifice he had to make the rest of the year. This was heaven. Trolling on Lake Vermilion.

Catching a fish wasn't all that important to Carl. It was more about being in the moment, knowing if needed he could set the hook with just the right amount of jerk and land the prized walleye. Yes, he loved when Elsa fried the fish he caught, and, yes, the taste of the fresh cold-water catch was indescribable, but ultimately, that wasn't what mattered to Carl. He loved to fish. Period. Whether he ever caught another one in his life, he would fish until his dying day.

And he knew Elsa understood. It was part of why he loved her so much.

They set off from their picnic spot on Indian Point heading north and cut across to Pine Island, close to the little Windy Island. It didn't take long to get over to the shore of the big island. Pine Island stretched to the west for seven miles. Carl slowed to trolling speed, and they let out their lures with their rods pointed to the back of the boat. Carl kept the boat an even distance from shore, just the right amount where the lure wouldn't snag on the bottom. He intrinsically knew what was going on with the mechanics of the interactions of the lure, water, and the boat's propulsion, although he didn't know that's what it was called or even how to describe it. For Carl the physics of fishing came naturally. He had an instinct about the ratio of how deep the water was, how much the lure weighed, and how fast the boat was going. All this came naturally as he steered the boat.

Trolling was an active sport for Carl. He was totally engaged, constantly monitoring the surface of the water for hazards, watching for variations in movement. Occasionally, he saw a 'deadhead,' which is what the locals called the long timbers that somehow got one end stuck in the bottom of the lake. Deadheads floated at odd angles so only the uppermost tip showed above the water's surface, regardless of how long the log was. Hitting a deadhead usually meant shearing a cotter pin or breaking the propeller. There were also outcroppings of rock right under the surface which only an experienced eye could discern by the variations of the surface patterns of the water. Carl would veer away from whatever the danger was in such a way the trailing lure would also not be affected by it. That was the sign of a good trolling fisherman - they seldom got stuck and almost never lost a plug.

As Carl and Elsa trolled their way westward along the southern shore of Pine Island, the noise of the construction they had heard earlier became louder. It was an annoying buzz when they got to the slight indentation of lakeshore where Ike's cabin stood in a rocky clearing up against the woods. They slowed even further as they approached the short dock. To the right of it, Ike's small wooden boat was pulled up on the shore, resting on a few horizontal logs. A canvas tarp was tied over the top of it. And to the left of the dock, a canoe was resting upside down, also on a couple of logs.

They tied up the boat and stepped onto the dock. Bruno was the first ashore and made his way up to the small green cabin, disappearing around the back. Facing the lake, Ike Iverson's cabin had four wide windows but no door. He had built the small house over twenty-five years before and had lived there alone ever since with no electricity or running water. One time, Carl had asked him why there was no door on the lake side. Ike had said he didn't need two, the back door being necessary to get to the woodpile and the outhouse.

* * *

Elsa, carrying the package they had brought, followed Carl and Bruno around to the back. Ike came out to meet them, standing on the back porch under the narrow overhanging roof. "Hey, dere. I see I got comb-panee," he said in the lilting accent picked up from his immigrant parents, "Come on in." Which sounded like 'comb-o-nin' with emphasis on the last syllable. Elsa smiled at Ike, and as they approached, she thought, "It's strange. Carl's Swedish accent was still noticeable, but he's worked hard to lose it because he wanted to be American; but Ike never felt the need to change I guess because he was born here."

Elsa entered first and set the bag on the bare wooden table. The cabin smelled of wood smoke and slightly of turpentine, the familiar smells making the small place feel cozy to her. Carl often smelled of paint thinner when he came home after a long day painting wealthy people's homes. She appreciated that he worked hard for them, even though once in a while she felt a little jealous of the rich ladies who got to watch him change the color of their huge dining room from Sherwin Williams 'Belvedere Cream' to 'Copen Blue' on a whim. They would offer him a cold beer midday and ask for favors when he finished the job. She knew it wasn't only his precise brush work that made the company he owned with Eric so popular among the homeowners of Wilmette and Winnetka. Both Carl and Eric were good looking, engaging, and generous with their time - rearranging furniture, hanging a new painting for the lady of the house or sitting at the kitchen table to share a tale with the lonely rich. She wondered sometimes if there was more to it, but she trusted Carl and dismissed those thoughts on the rare occasion they came to mind. More often, she was amazed at the 'throw-aways' that they would offer Carl and Eric for doing simple handyman tasks. The small house she and Carl shared had amazing, original oil paintings on the walls, oriental rugs on the floor, and a crystal chandelier in the eating area because wealthy ladies were bored with the beautiful things they had thought they loved a mere few years before.

As she entered Ike's small home, about the same size as their summer cabin over on Daisy Bay, she was thought about what it is about a home that makes a person happy. Those beautiful Northshore Chicago mansions were the ultimate of what money could buy but they were no guarantee of a happy home. The irony struck her as she realized this two-room shack was equally not a guarantee of happiness; a wave of thankfulness flowed over her.

Ike's cabin was similar to Carl and Elsa's, but the floor plan was even simpler. The door opened into the main room and to the right was a small bedroom with a curtain covering the doorway. That was it. What passed for a kitchen was up against the wall which separated the main room from the bedroom. There was a stretch of counter for the sink, a cupboard below it. The old-fashioned icebox was against the wall next to the window overlooking the lake. It was an old-fashioned icebox with the upper chamber holding a block of ice. A large cast-iron wood-burning stove which did double duty for cooking and heating stood near the door. A stack of firewood waited on the porch just outside. The six-quart wood-handled kettle which sat atop the stove was used to heat water for dishes, shaving, bathing, and laundry – all done in the kitchen sink.

A hand pump perched at the edge of the sink was the water source. The well had been dug before the structure was built over it. The sink drained out a pipe that ended in a small rock-filled pit buried below the frostline; some distance from the cabin. No curtain covered the space under the countertop. There wasn't much there anyway, just one shelf that held a cast iron frying pan and one large aluminum pot, a few odd household things, a few canned goods, and a wire basket half full of potatoes and onions. A flour sack dish towel hung from a nail. An open wooden toolbox containing a few hand tools was on the floor against the far wall. Two open shelves hung on the wall to the left above the sink. One held a few plates and bowls stacked together, three cups, and two glasses, and an empty coffee can held a few eating utensils. The other shelf held a set of metal canisters, painted white with red wooden knobs on the lids and decals declaring the contents -- Flour, Sugar, Coffee. They sat on the shelf like siblings posed in size order for a family photo. Beside 'Coffee' was a round blue Morton's Salt box and a tin-lidded glass shaker of ground black pepper. A blue enamelware metal mug holding a double-edged razor and a toothbrush also sat on the shelf, a bar of soap rested on a little tin plate. Above the sink was a small mirror. To the right of it by the doorway to the bedroom hung a calendar – a gift from the Standard Oil Station in Tower.

"We brought you something," Elsa said.

"T'ank you. Sit. Sit," he said. A saggy brown sofa took up the end of the room. There were two pressed back wooden chairs pulled up to the unpainted table. A third was situated in front of an easel near the front window where Ike did his painting. When Carl and Elsa sat to the table, Ike brought the other chair over and joined them.

"Here's a little treat for you, Ike. I did some baking yesterday and I know you like cardamom coffee bread," Elsa said, taking the braided loaf wrapped in wax paper out of the bag. The smell of the familiar spice pervaded the small space. He thanked her and got up to put the bread on the counter.

"And I brought you something, too," said Carl with a grin. He reached into the paper sack and brought out a framed photograph.

"I hope you like it," he said as he handed it to Ike.

It was a black and white photograph blown up to an 8x10 and set in a plain black frame. Elsa remembered the day Carl had taken it the previous summer. Carl happened to have his camera along when they stopped to visit Ike. They had been sitting at Ike's table the same as they were now when Ike had looked out the back window and said they must excuse him because he had a visitor. He got up, grabbed something from a tin on the kitchen counter and went outside. They watched through the screen door as Ike lay down on his side in the grass. A fox was standing at the edge of the woods, ever so tentatively.

Elsa and Carl had looked at each other – just a glance that said so much. Carl silently made his way to where he had left his camera on the floor near the door. He slowly got the Argus out of its case, adjusted the aperture based on a guess, and quietly pushed open the screen door just enough to get a clear shot.

The photo showed Ike propped up on one elbow lying on the grass holding out a small piece of smoked fish to the fox. The fox was stretching its neck as far as possible to reach the food without getting too close, its body poised to flee, and its tail curled tightly around his body like the Cheshire Cat sitting on the tree branch. Ike was holding the food out but not far from his body. The fox was no more than a foot or so away, close but wary, reaching for the food. It was a beautiful animal, full of life, its shiny, lush fur evident even through the black and white grain of the photo. Ike's expression was stoic, patient, seeming to comprehend the fragile friendship between man and animal and the need for patience.

Elsa was struck by Ike's expressionless face as he picked up the photo and looked at it. She felt sad that this gentle man carried such a burden that he no longer could smile.

"Oh, yah, I remember. This fox looks so much like her mother, but she's not as friendly. Her mother would come much closer to me. Sometimes she even let me touch her, but not this one," he said as he set it on the windowsill. "T'ank you."

Elsa went over to the easel to admire Ike's latest work. It was a large painting and seemed to be almost completed. It depicted a young woman walking down a mountain trail in the Norwegian fjords with a waterfall in the background. The girl was looking down at her hands, knitting as she walked. The postcard he was copying the image from was propped against the canvas on the ledge of the easel.

"Oh, Ike. It's beautiful. I hope we aren't interrupting you."

"No. I wasn't painting today."

"We love the painting of the two wolves we got from you last summer. Did you sell many paintings last year?"

"Enough. Yah, enough to get by."

They chatted for a short while, talking about the winter weather and, of course, fishing. Finally, the topic turned to the new cabin being built not far away. Ike's face darkened, and he became silent. His lips quivered as they tightened into a taut line.

"I'll bet the noise bothers you. I'm sure it will get better in a few weeks when they have the main structure up. Have you met Mr. Stark, your new neighbor?" Elsa asked.

"He should go back where he came from. He doesn't belong

there," he said and stood up without another word and started for the door.

Elsa exchanged a glance with Carl, and they stood as well.

"Well, Carl, we should get going," she said. "Come on, Bruno, you big, lazy guy. Let's head out." Bruno stretched his length as he usually did when rising and still managed to get out the door first.

They were saying their goodbyes on the porch when Elsa stopped to admire Ike's handiwork.

"I see you're working on a new paddle." She went over to the piece of wood leaning against the wall near the only chair on the porch, the fourth pressed back chair which should have been inside at the kitchen table. Well over half of the long piece of wood was thin, whittled down to a long straight shaft, the end already shaped into a curved T-shaped handle. Elsa knew a properly made end grip, especially custom-made for the user, could alleviate knuckle pain or blisters. The other end was obviously going to be the paddle blade. Ike had started to thin and taper it, and although it was far from done, the finished product could be envisioned. It would be a fine piece of craftsmanship, functional and artful at the same time. A wood-handled knife in a leather sheaf lay on the floor next to the chair. As she set the paddle back against the wall, she asked Ike if he was making it for himself.

"Yah," he said. "I'll have it finished in a week or two."

Carl picked it up to admire its size and heft. "It's really nice work," he said, turning to Ike. "Maybe we can convince you to make one for each of us sometime." He set it back in place.

"But we'll have to get a canoe first," Elsa said with a laugh as she led the way to the front of the cabin. Ike stopped at the corner and watched as they got in their boat. He looked at them without moving as they waved goodbye and pulled away from the dock. Bruno wagged his tail and let out a solitary woof.

Finally, Ike broke his stare, turned, and disappeared behind the cabin.

The Colorado Gold Rush, which started in 1859, played out as the Civil War began. At the end of the war, Minnesota legislators decided another gold rush was just what the country and Minnesota needed. In 1865, Minnesota Governor Miller authorized the continuation of the state-sponsored geological survey which had been suspended because of the war. He appointed Henry Eames as the Minnesota State Geologist and his brother, Richard Eames, as Assistant State Geologist. They were charged with exploring the northern areas of the state and producing a report of the mineral-bearing rocks and their commercial value. The two brothers established headquarters in Duluth and spent the summer of 1865 north of there, taking and analyzing samples. Specimens were sent to the Federal Mint in Philadelphia, and the results confirmed they were high-value samples. When they reported finding veins of gold and silver-bearing quartz at Lake Vermilion, the news spread like wildfire across the country.

The Civil War was over, and the rough and tumble people who survived were ready to try new adventures. Fortunes were made by the lucky. And they were lucky. They had survived a civil war unlike any other. Now was their time to grab fate by the short hairs and take what they could.

The land between Duluth and Lake Vermilion was so marshy and full of peat bogs the journey could only be made during the frigid winter months when the swamps were frozen. Groups of enterprising people and investors formed major companies to exploit the new opportunity. In January 1866, the Mutual Protection Company crew began clearing a road, starting forty miles north of Duluth. At the rate of two miles per day of cutting timber and laying a trail wide enough for ox-driven wagons and despite heavy snow and forty below temperatures, they finally made it to Lake Vermilion on March 5th, 1866, after seventy days of labor. Other companies soon followed, using the hard-won trail, and the people who arrived on the shores of Lake Vermilion in those first months built a town they named Winton. The mining and exploration operations commenced and grew and grew. During the winter of 1866-67, eighty wagon teams a day left Duluth for Lake Vermilion, hauling equipment, supplies, and more people.

CHAPTER 16

When Ike was 12, his uncle came to live with his family. The man was his mother's oldest sibling, and his name was Rolf Petter Braar. Ike and his brother had given up their bedroom for the old man, the brother squeezing in with the younger children and Ike sleeping on a cot in the pantry. The man was in his late fifties but looked twenty years older. He had come back to Duluth to die from emphysema. Fate and years in the Tower-Soudan underground mine breathing iron-laden air had forced him to spend his last days living with his youngest sister and her family, struggling for his every breath.

Uncle Rolf Petter would stay at the kitchen table after the evening meal, wanting to talk about his days as a prospector, explorer, and miner. The rest of the family, bored with his repetitive chatter, would move to the tiny parlor or the bedrooms in the winter, and in the summer, they would head outside to the street to chat with neighbors or watch the children play on the steep streets. But Ike had patience for the old man when the others didn't. He listened attentively, asking questions, ignoring the repeated phrases and stories, always alert for new tidbits of fiction or fact. How the old man loved to talk and talk and talk about his glory years. What he talked about didn't sound very glorious to the rest of the family. To them, it sounded like lots of boring hard work for a whole lot of nothing. Ike was fascinated.

In 1865, like thousands of other men and women across the U.S., Braar had been smitten by the lure of gold. Braar was one of the first to make his way up to Lake Vermilion because he was already in Duluth. He had emigrated from Norway a few years earlier. He was working the docks when he first heard talk of gold and finally gave in to its call. He left Duluth in the winter of 1865-66 and made his way with hundreds of others along a frozen trail northward.

Braar had a small nest egg when he left Duluth, and he used it to set up a claim on Pine Island. He built a shack on the southern shore overlooking Big Bay and spent his days searching for gold. By 1869, his stake money had dried up, and it was obvious his claim on the small parcel of land was not the mother lode. In fact, none of the others who had succumbed to the lure of gold found any either. By the end of 1869, the gold rush was over, and Winton became a ghost town. However, all the digging and scratching at the land had revealed another mineral worth mining - iron.

Braar took a job in the open pit iron mine located just east of Tower, although it was many years before he stopped looking for the glint of gold even in the pits belonging to someone else. He married a young woman from Embarrass and had a family.

His two daughters died from influenza within days of each other as small children. His three sons all died as young men in an open pit mining accident in 1882. Shortly after that, they closed the mine. When it reopened as an underground mine, he signed up and worked there until his health gave out. His wife had died shortly after his sons were killed. It was a heart attack, but Braar was sure it was grief that killed her. When he got too old to work anymore and there was no one else to take care of the old man, he ended up at his younger sister's. He slept in his nephew Ike's bed, and the pain of his futile life endlessly ran through his head.

One muggy summer evening, Ike and his uncle were alone in the third-floor apartment. The old man was too weak to venture down the two flights of stairs to get some fresh air outside. Still, he spoke animatedly about the portages and canoeing and blasting rocks and bleeding hands searching for the sparkle in the quartz as if he were still a young man just taking a moment's respite at his sister's kitchen table. Ike looked up when his uncle stopped speaking.

"What's the matter?" Ike asked.

"Do you think we're really alone?" Braar said quietly, looking around.

"Yah. I'm sure of it," Ike said, placating the old man's obvious concern.

"Then I want to give you something, Ike. But it's for you only. You can't share it with your father or anyone else. I want you to keep it until you can use it yourself," he said cryptically. "Now go in your old room and under the bed is my satchel. Put it up on the bed and open it up wide. If you look closely at the zipper flap, you'll see there is another smaller zipper hidden under it. Open the zipper and bring me what's in the pocket."

Ike thought he was looking for a favorite pocketknife or a pouch of snuff that the old man was forbidden to use. When he reached in and pulled out a wrinkled piece of oilcloth, he was disappointed. He tucked the satchel back under the bed and brought the oilcloth out to the kitchen table. The old man's face lit up. He unfolded the oilcloth and laid it out flat on the table. It was a map of the Lake Vermilion region. "This, my young man, is a real live treasure map," he said as he patted it with a gnarled hand. Even after fifty years, the lust for gold still shone in the old man's eyes.

"Let me tell you how I came about having it." And so, Braar told Ike about his encounter with Henry Eames.

One evening in the fall of 1867, Eames was sitting in the Tower Hotel, drinking heavily. He was scheduled to join his brother back in St. Paul the following day and was despondent over the failure to find gold. Braar came in and sat at the bar after ordering supplies at the Mercantile. The two men got to talking as they drank, and Eames became more inebriated as the evening went on. Through thick lips and with a hand-smack to the bar, he told Braar that, despite what his boss at the Capital and the Governor thought, he had, indeed, kept a good record of where he had found the initial gold-bearing samples. It wasn't his fault, he said. His new fountain pen, just like President Lincoln's, was a gift from his brother. How could he know that the ink would blur beyond recognition when the rain saturated his satchel that day. The printed map was there, but nothing he had written of his findings remained. When he realized what had happened, he was sure could find the lode again when he returned the following year. But he hadn't, and it looked to Eames like he never would. His funding was being withdrawn, and he had to return to the capital to face a failure he didn't deserve. The man was in a drunken state of despair and ranted on, repeating various parts of his story.

Braar had just finished buying the most recent round of drinks when Eames suddenly folded the map up and tossed it in front of Braar, saying, "Take it. It's just a useless rag." Then he abruptly left. Braar never saw the man again.

For the next three years, he searched Pine Island using the map. Finally, when his money was gone, he gave up and got a job in the iron mine, but he never quit thinking about the gold.

"You got to promise me, Ikie, you'll keep this safe until you get older. Maybe someday you'll figure out where the gold really is. Remember, Eames was pointing at the big island, Pine Island, when he was drunk and showing it to me. Too bad about the guy. I wonder what ever happened to him," and with that, Braar ruffled Ike's towhead affectionately and went off to bed.

During the initial weeks of US involvement in WWI, the American dead were buried by their fellow soldiers. But that arrangement quickly became untenable for three reasons. First, the number of soldiers and civilians alike falling ill because of the unsanitary conditions was unacceptable. Second, the number of casualties was enormous, and all able-bodied soldiers were needed to fight. And third, the job of burying the dead, both men and horses, was so demoralizing the soldiers often would not fight again after burial duty.

The solution, it was decided by the Chief Surgeon of the First Army Corps, was to assign one platoon of Pioneer Troops, about fifty men, to each division (approximately 10,000 men) to handle the odious task of cleaning up a battlefield. This ratio was increased as the severity of the fighting increased, and the number of dead continued to rise.

The clean-up platoons assigned to battlefield sanitation were responsible for burying men and horses, disposing of refuse, and filling latrines. One chaplain was assigned to each platoon, and it was his job to keep the dog tags, personal belongings, and records of each dead soldier and mark the map where the temporary graves were located. After the war, Graves Registration personnel would use the maps to find the graves and disinter the bodies so they could be brought home. Since the Civil War, the US Armed Forces policy has been to return the remains of fallen combat troops to their loved ones for proper burial.

The Pioneer Troops, from which the clean-up platoons were reassigned, were non-combatant soldiers who supported the infantry in areas such as engineering, medical, food service, or supply chain logistics. Pioneer Troops were often highly trained professionals in specific fields of expertise before the war.

1922

CHAPTER 17

One day in 1922, Ike found the carpetbag he had brought with him from Chicago pushed far under the bed. Lying at the bottom was the map his uncle had given him. When he first settled on the island, he wasn't interested in gold. He just wanted to be away. Away from people and the chaos of their relationships, which brought memories of people he cared about who were no longer in his life. Then he found the map in the old bag, and his curiosity was piqued.

For six years, he combed the woods and rocks on Pine Island. He no longer really cared why he was doing it. He just knew he should do what his uncle asked. He should keep looking until he found it. He wasn't sure he would know if that ever happened. He had no idea what it looked like in nature or what to do if he found it. Many times he saw the fox watching him as he walked, always looking for the gold his uncle was sure existed.

One day, he was searching a section of the map to the northwest of his cabin. Carefully looking at the rock formations under the vegetation, he moved slowly along, with his head down, when he heard a noise. He stood upright and looked around. Off to the left, he saw two men through the trees. They were arguing, gesturing wildly, faces contorted. Their fighting brought back memories. Soldiers were watching now to see if the captain or the lieutenant would win the argument. Should they venture further onto the battlefield yet or wait until the fighting had moved farther away?

It was quiet. No bombs were going off in the distance. The silence told him the argument had been won. A man was down. He was dead now, and the chaplain kneeled next to the body. Blessing the dead soldier by placing his hands on the soldier's face. Holding his hands there, delivering his blessing. The chaplain straightened up and looked in Ike's direction. Their eyes met for a few long seconds, then the man left, leaving Ike to his duty – burying the dead as he had done so many times before.

Ike knew his job. He went back for his shovel where he had left it at his bivouac. When he returned, he dragged the body farther inland where the earth was soft, and the trees would shade the new grave. Doing his duty. What he was supposed to do. He dug the hole deep. There was no shelling now, so he had time to do the job right. He removed the soldier's jacket. He saw the head wound as he lowered the body into the grave. Ike covered the man's face with the jacket before he began to shovel the dark earth on top of him.

The fox was curious about the noise. The gentle sound of earth landing on earth grew louder as she approached where the man was working. The fox crept closer, stopping behind the trunk of a large spruce tree, watching.

When he finished covering the body, Ike realized the bombing hadn't started up again, so he felt he had some time. Time to really honor this fallen soldier with a marker for his grave. He went back home and, sitting on his porch, he carved the date and RIP into the paddle he had been working on. It seemed like a fitting tombstone, and, although he knew it was wood and might rot eventually, it was more than most of the soldiers he had buried had been given.

As he made his way back into the woods where the soldier was buried, the fox trotted ahead. He knelt at the end of the mound of dirt and dug the paddle handle down into the soft soil. *Now*, he thought, *this soldier can rest in peace. I've done my job. I can go home now. I need to sleep.*

When he got back to his cabin, he put the shovel in the shed and lay down on the earth outside the back door. It was early evening, and he was exhausted. He fell asleep almost immediately and dreamed he had found gold and his uncle was very proud of him. But just as his uncle was telling him what a good boy he was, his uncle turned into a fox, and when the fox touched his hand with her nose, he awoke. He sat up with a jerk. The fox, startled, jumped back and stared at Ike for a second, then trotted off into the woods.

He knew he had to remember something, but he didn't know what. He went inside and took the map he had been carrying out of his pocket and laid it open flat on the table. He pointed to a spot without really knowing why. Then he grabbed a pencil from the shelf and marked the spot with an x. This somehow made him feel relieved. He had done a good job. He was okay.

He folded the map and put it away on the low shelf under the window. He went to bed, determined not to look for gold again. Thunder woke him at some point in the night, he wasn't sure when. He lay awake listening to the rain pound on the roof, the trees beating each other furiously. Most of the time, when he awoke abruptly to thunder, it was fear he felt. Tonight, he felt calm. He knew he was a good soldier. He had done his duty today. And he knew there was nothing more to do. He fell back to sleep with the storm still raging and the fox ky-yipping in the distance.

1948

CHAPTER 18

Carl, Elsa, and Bruno loaded back into the boat and pushed off from Ike's small dock as he walked back behind his cabin.

"I'm so glad we have a boat house. At least we don't have to pull our boat out of the water and cover it every time we use it," said Elsa.

Carl shrugged. "I don't think Ike uses his boat except for going into town. I'll bet he thinks using gas is wasteful. I'm pretty sure he catches fish from the dock or once in a while he might use his canoe to fish for northern back in the weeds in Canfield Bay."

They dropped their lines and began to troll again as soon as they were away from the dock. Bruno found a comfy place to rest his head on top of the life jackets up at the front of the boat and closed his eyes. Elsa laughed and said, "I think Bruno's motto is 'Sleep when you can. Wag when you can't.'"

As they trolled along the shore further west, the noise of the saws and construction became even louder. The rocks along this part of the shoreline canted sharply into the water and indicated to Carl the drop-off was steep. He steered the boat closer, trying to find the perfect spot where a walleye might be, just be lying in wait for his crazy action Silver Creek Wobbler to pass by. Walleye weren't known for their fight and gamesmanship, but Carl didn't care because they sure were the tastiest. Elsa's lure was an iridescent Lippy Sue running straight behind the boat. Neither lure was doing the trick today.

With Spider Island just off to their left, the opening to Canfield Bay appeared as they rounded the gentle curve of Pine Island. They continued to follow the shoreline around to their right, where the new cabin was being built. They could see into Canfield Bay, where a dozen or so small cabins were crammed right next to each other close to the shore. Last year, after trolling the shoreline of the whole bay, they had wondered why those cabins were all bunched together like they were. Later, they had asked Peyla about it, and he told them the small lots had been part of a campsite development some years before.

It was a beautiful day, and the comfortable temperature had prompted Elsa to take off her jacket and fish in her sleeveless blouse. Carl had taken his jacket off, too, and rolled up his sleeves. They refrained from talking because they knew how voices carry across the water, content instead to continue their fishing until they were passing directly in front of the building site. The construction noise had stopped.

"Must be quitting time," said Carl quietly. "It is after five."

As they moved slowly past the new cabin, Elsa realized what the gossip they had heard in town meant. This was going to be a huge house. She could see why some people would call it a mansion. A lower level of concrete seemed to recede into the rocky background with the natural stone ledge wrapping around it on three sides. Sections of concrete were still unfinished, but work had already begun on the log construction of the upper level above the foundation sections which had been completed. The cabin stretched at least a hundred feet side to side, and because of its placement part way up the rocky incline, it seemed to loom over Big Bay like a challenge to the expanse of water.

* * *

A few hundred feet further, a craggy outcropping of rock stuck out into the lake and created a barrier between Big Bay and the small quiet waters of Canfield Bay. There were no trees on the huge boulder, and it looked like the top of a bald grey giant's head rising up out of the water except that someone had built a footing and poured a flat concrete slab on it, like some alien landing pad. A narrow wooden footbridge crossed the twenty feet or so of half-submerged rocks between it and the shore. Two rough-hewn wooden chairs and a short thick table sat out on the concrete pad, impervious to the wind and waves of the massive body of water it hovered beside. Stark was sitting on one of the chairs, looking not out at the big body of water but back towards the new cabin. He had a highball glass in his hand, and a whisky bottle sat on the table. His posture said he was relaxing there, admiring his new place, contemplating what it was to be.

As the young couple slowly motored by with trolling lines following along, Stark gave a cursory glance toward the noise of their motor. Then with a flash of recognition on his face, he abruptly stood and, raising his glass, called out to Carl and Elsa,

"Hello! Welcome!" He gestured back to the dock over by the tents and yelled, "Go on around to the dock. I'll meet you there." The dock was just beyond the natural breakwater.

He proceeded to work his way off the outcropping of rock and along the shoreline. Carl and Elsa shrugged at each other with a curious look. They reeled in their lines and stowed their rods. Bruno roused himself, stretched, and prepared to get off the boat as they pulled up to the dock, which had a couple of other boats tied up to it.

Several men in plaid flannel shirts and denim overalls were putting tools and supplies away into a shed. Off to the side were several good-sized tents. Army Surplus, Carl thought. He had slept in quite a few of those during boot camp and again in Italy during the war. A man could stand comfortably inside. They looked large enough to have multiple rooms. One of the tents was wide open with the canvas sides rolled up, and they could see someone inside tending a camp stove, preparing food.

Stark and another man in work clothes met them at the dock. He extended a hand to the lovely woman who accepted his help and came ashore with the rope from the bow in hand. The workman took the rope from her and tied it to a metal ring in the dock. Carl stepped onto the dock and did the same with a rope at the back.

"Welcome. Glad you came by," Stark said to his guests. "This is Bill Thompson, my crew boss. He's up from Duluth. Came highly recommended. If anyone can handle a big job like this, Bill, here, can. He and most of the rest of the crew stay on site." Stark clapped the man on the shoulder and said, "Thanks for the update, John."

The foreman nodded at Carl and Elsa and headed toward the

construction site.

"Come up and have a drink," said Stark. It was obvious the one in his hand was not his first or even his second, for that matter.

"Well, this is a nice surprise," Elsa said.

Stark led them up to the biggest tent and held the flap open. They entered a pleasant enough temporary abode. There was a front room with four folding chairs, the kind they called director's chairs when they are tall bar stool height. These were regular chair height and had black canvas seats and backs. There were a few random folding tables with kerosene lamps, an eating table with a bench on the long sides and two more canvas chairs, one at each end. A collapsible bookshelf complete with two dozen or so books and a metal ice cooler were near the door. A sleeping area walled off with canvas was visible beyond a half-open flap door. The drab tent canvas floor had been covered with well-worn oriental rugs. Architectural drawings spread across the table. A large portfolio and a briefcase lay on one of the benches.

"Wow, this is quite the place you've got here," said Carl looking around.

"Do you mean this tent or the cabin we're building?" Stark said with a smile. "Hmm, either way. No need to be uncomfortable in the wild, don't you agree?"

"Yes, of course. But it's a bit different from our place over on Daisy Bay."

"Can I get you a Scotch on the rocks? Manhattan? Gin and tonic?" Stark asked.

"Oh, a Manhattan would be lovely, thanks," said Elsa, and Carl agreed with a nod.

Stark set his glass on the end of the table away from the plans and proceeded to open the metal cooler, exposing a large block of ice. Atop the bookshelf was a silver tray with three crystal glasses matching the one he was drinking from and various bartending utensils - a shaker, strainer, ice pick, and silver coasters. He took the ivory handled ice pick and struck at the block, chipping off enough ice chips to fill three glasses. He made them each a drink from the liquor bottles housed on the bottom shelf of the bookcase. He gave them their glasses and motioned them to come closer to look at the building plans.

They chatted about the project, Stark pointing out the master suite, multiple guest suites, a massive central salon, a library/smoking room, a long deck stretching across the entire front of the house, and the kitchen wing with housing for the help canting off to the rear, away from the lake views all of the other rooms would enjoy. He told them about the large boathouse he planned to build over the water with a honeymoon suite above four boat slips. There would be an airplane hangar for a floatplane farther along the shoreline, he gestured, obviously proud of the magnificent place it was going to be.

"Now, if we could just get it built," Stark said, slamming his glass down. A few drops splashed on the large sheet of paper, and he brusquely wiped them off.

"What's the hold up?" Carl asked.

"We've been having a bit of sabotage going on. At first, I thought it was just punks from those shacks over there in Canfield Bay. But this has gone way beyond the point of mischief for mischief's sake. I think someone around here doesn't want this cabin built." His voice got louder, and he began to slur his words. The more he talked, the angrier he got.

"My supplies have been stolen. Water poured into my boat's gas tank. That cost me a pretty penny, let me tell you. Then they put something in the bottom of the concrete mixer the workers didn't notice and when they mixed up the concrete and poured it in the foundation forms, it never set up."

"Sugar in the generator. Holes in the shingles. So many malicious things have been happening I can't even tell you. I think I might know who it is but I'm not ready to take my suspicions to the Deputy Sheriff yet. Which I will do when I have some proof. But if I catch the bastard red handed, I'll just kill him on the spot myself."

"It's not even built yet," he practically shouted. "Think what will happen when it's finished, and we leave it unoccupied for any length of time. It will be vandalized and ruined. I can't let that happen. This has been my dream for a long time." His face nearing a shade of purple, he spit out, "It's mine and whoever is doing this can't stop me from having what's mine."

He realized he had come on too strong when the young woman sat down abruptly and averted her eyes as she sipped her drink. Trying to lighten the tension in the room, she said, "I've been reading a history of the Lake Vermilion area which I took out from the Tower library. It talks a lot about the gold rush and then the timber boom. One part talks about how Pine Island was going to be developed into a real city with roads and parks, and schools, and stores. The whole shebang. I found it fascinating. Where would all those people work anyway? And winters up here can be really harsh. Seems like it was a pipe dream to me." She paused and took another sip. Carl continued to look at the drawings, but Stark was staring at her now angry at her for doubting the glory of his endeavors.

"Have you had the land long? Did you buy it from some of those people who were going to live here?" she asked.

Stark calmed down somewhat and took a moment to pour himself another drink, then sat down in the chair next to Elsa, close enough to enjoy the smell of her skin lotion, rotating his glass around and around between his palms for a minute before speaking.

"Can I tell you a story?" he asked, raising his head slowly to looking her in the eye.

"Of course," she said. And so, he began.

"It pains me to this day. How my father abandoned me," Stark said softly, then stopped to sip his drink before continuing.

"But I should start at the beginning. My father's name was Nathan Stark. He was born in Duluth and grew up next door to his best friend and business partner, Gregory Morgan. They were best friends all their lives. My dad was a great athlete and served in the Army during WW1, working in some shipyard in Virginia, the state, not Virginia, MN. My mother told me she had worked in a government office in Duluth, and when my father came home, they met and fell in love. It's such a sweet love-at-first-sight story. She said she had been at a dancehall when my dad first saw her, and he fell in love right then and there. She was on a date with a merchant marine who was on leave from some ship docked in the harbor. When my dad approached her to ask her to dance, her date took offense, and my dad and the guy got into it. It was a no-contest. My dad was a real athlete, you know, and, anyway, he ended up taking her home. When he asked her to marry him three dates later, she said yes without so much as a moment's hesitation. They had a beautiful wedding. I've seen the pictures. The wedding even made the Duluth Tribune. Then I came along. My mom was so happy. We all were -- until my dad disappeared," he paused for a few sips before he continued.

"My father loved the outdoors and spent a lot of time up here. He brought me with him many times, although I was pretty young then. My mother wouldn't hear of roughing it, though. She liked the comforts of home. Uncle Gregory, who's my godfather, by the way, hated the outdoors, too and refused to come along. So, most of the time it would be just me and my dad."

"The important part is that my father got Uncle Gregory to partner with him in a scheme to sell property up here on Lake Vermilion, like those lots in Canfield Bay over there. They bought up a bunch of land, laid out plans for a gargantuan year-round community, created sales brochures and advertised in the big city newspapers and sporting magazines. Big ideas. Big dreams. All set to go."

When Stark leaned forward, elbows on knees, and hesitated for a long time, lost in thought, Carl gently prodded, "What happened to their plans?"

After a long swig of his drink, Stark looked up and said with surprising bitterness. "Well, nothing really. Until now."

He paused again, looking back and forth between Carl and Elsa before continuing, "Twenty years ago this summer, my father and Uncle Gregory, who hadn't even been up here before, came to Pine Island to hold a property sales extravaganza. My mother and I stayed at home in Duluth. I think I was sick or something because I remember really wanting to come with but wasn't allowed to. Anyway, over forty interested parties, mostly married couples, some with their children in tow, were ferried over here from Tower, almost to this exact site, for a weeklong camping experience."

"It was a gala affair. Wealthy people exploring the wilds, thrilled with the possibility of owning a part of it. They were housed in tents like these," Stark said, gesturing around him, "Elegant tents, cooks and servants to tend to their needs. Crystal stemware and oriental rugs. A few daubs of 6-12 lotion for the mosquitoes, and there was barely any disruption of their daily life at all. After a few idyllic days of fishing and gourmet dining, a huge storm came up during the night, and most of the tents were blown down while people were sleeping. It was chaos with some people trapped inside, screaming for help. No one was actually hurt, but after a horrible night exposed to the storm and the elements, everyone wanted to go home. The dream was over for most of those people."

"But for me the nightmare had just begun. My father went missing during the storm and was never seen again. The sheriff back then thought he must have slipped on the shore, fallen in, and drowned. With the negative press about his disappearance and the reports of the horrific storm, people wanted to cancel their contracts. When he got back to Duluth, Uncle Gregory found the company's bank accounts had been emptied. My father had taken all the money, and there was nothing to be done. There was no money left in the company to make any refunds. Only a few of the campsite purchases actually went through. You can see what came of those back there in Canfield Bay. But hundreds of other people lost their investments."

"There was a warrant for my father's arrest for embezzlement and fraud. But he was never found, and neither was the money. They speculated he'd had it in cash with him that week and just got in a canoe and left for Canada. All the evidence pointed to my father, but Uncle Gregory had to face a lot of bad press and scrutiny. It wasn't long before he closed the company and moved to Florida. And that was that. I don't blame my godfather. He's rather clueless, if you know what I mean. I can't see him ever doubting my father. He worshiped my father."

"My mother, sister and I had to leave Duluth in shame and went to live with her relatives in Wausau, my father's name in disgrace," he paused for a draw from his glass. "But life goes on, you know. I graduated from high school, went to the University of Wisconsin, and became an architect. My mother passed away three years ago. I've been very successful, you know. I certainly didn't need the money I received from her life insurance, so I decided to use it to build a real house, one which will last. My father's land had been confiscated, but I bought back this piece, which is where the grand opening was held," he said with a smug upward thrust of his chin.

"My father's vision was for a bunch of paltry cabins stuck back there on tiny lots with no view, all crowded together just like in the city," Stark gestured toward Canfield Bay. "But he even reneged on that. He was a liar and a cheat. He cheated all those people, and he cheated his best friend and he cheated my mom and me. I hated him while I was growing up because he humiliated all of us and left us poor. But I'm over that now. Now I just want to build my new cabin, my grand house. I know what grand means and my place is going to be grand."

"Now you know why it's so important for me to build this place. I'm doing it because I can. And I will. You can bet your life on it," Stark said. "My place here will show what I can do. It will be spectacular."

Stark stopped there, eyes wide with bitter excitement. He gathered himself and, after a short pause, moved close to Elsa to offer her a refill. She declined with a head shake, as did Carl. Stark poured himself another one and stayed quiet, staring into the ice as it clinked in his glass.

"I don't mean to pry, Stephen," said Elsa, "It's going to be absolutely wonderful when it's done. But do you have any idea what's going on? Why would anyone not want you to build this house?"

Stark looked at Elsa with stormy eyes, "I don't know and I'm sure I even care. What I do know is that I'm not going to stand for it. I don't know who is doing this or why." He stood and turned away from his guests to look out at the unfinished mansion. "But I'm going to find out who it is and, believe me, they are going to be really, really sorry," he said with a quiet fury in his voice.

At the turn of the century, snake oil salesmen and phony real estate deals were common. Lies and scams were so egregious that advertising Vigilante Committees began exposing bad business practices. The Better Business Bureau was founded in 1912, and Blue Sky Laws were crafted in many states to keep people safe from unscrupulous businesses using untruthful advertising. Minnesota's Blue Sky Law was enacted in 1915. But with the end of World War I, the United States was prosperous, and, in general, life was better. More people had more money to spend, which again led to the exploitation of people's gullibility.

With more discretionary money and free time, people wanted more interesting and exciting ways to spend it. Vacation real estate became available all over the country in both ideal and less-than ideal places. Swampland in Florida, desert lots in Nevada, and the wilderness of northern Minnesota were all advertised as paradise get-aways in magazines and big-city newspapers.

A few real estate investment companies bought up vast areas of Lake Vermilion shoreline, plotted it into thousands of fifty-foot lots, and began to sell 'the dream .'The Star Investment Company sold lots in a platted vacation community on the southwestern tip of Pine Island. Grey and

Morgan also successfully advertised lots in several places on Lake Vermilion. Their brochure had hundreds of vacation or permanent resident sites available on Birch Point, Daisy Island, and in Canfield Bay on Pine Island. Without these reckless entrepreneurs, Lake Vermilion might appear quite different than it does today. As it is, for the past one hundred years, families have enjoyed vacations on the lake, albeit on fifty-foot lots.

1928

CHAPTER 19

In the post-WWI era, when the economy was growing exponentially and exuberant optimism was the norm, opportunities for wealth abounded for those with the nerve to step up to the proverbial plate. In 1923, after yet another fishing trip to Lake Vermilion, Nathan Stark approached his friend, Gregory Morgan, with his idea for land development. Morgan hemmed and hawed and put his friend off for several weeks, during which time he secretly investigated the area and its potential value. Finally, he reluctantly agreed to partner with his friend, with the stipulation he would not have to put in any money up front. Nathan agreed and used his life savings to get the project started.

They both continued to work their jobs. Nathan traveled up to Lake Vermilion many times, but Gregory refused to go. He preferred to take care of the paperwork. They spent several years acquiring the land on Pine Island by leveraging Nathan's money and using their business idea as collateral. Then they hired surveyors to subdivide the lots and lay out the common areas – a community center, roads, boathouses, docks, and lake accesses. When they thought they were ready, they cautiously placed small advertisements in the major newspapers in Milwaukee, Minneapolis, St. Paul, Chicago, and Des Moines. Little came of it, and Nathan was worried. They discovered another company in Duluth, the North Country Outing Company that had the same idea and ran more prominent ads in Field and Stream Magazine.

In 1926, at Nathan's insistence, they took a huge gamble. They invested in an advertising campaign that almost emptied their bank account. They hired a Saint Paul advertising agency to create a twenty-four-page brochure with professional photographs and drawings. The brochure touted the glory of the Northwoods, Nature's pristine offerings for the busy man's get-away. It promised the best vacation sites for reasonable prices.

"You owe yourself and family a real outing each season. Get away from the heat of your hometown, away from business and household cares, camp in the fashion your forefathers did, and return brown as a berry, full of vigor, ready to withstand the rigors of a winter season."

They placed large photo ads telling people to write in for a copy of the brochure. The Stark-Morgan target audience consisted of three types of wealthy people. Couples who wanted to get their children out of the city into the clean northern air, businessmen who wanted a fishing get-away, and the ultra-wealthy who already had second or third homes and wanted yet another diversion for their copious free time. Within weeks, reservations and payments started coming in. People purchased, sight unseen, fifty-foot lots for camping with rights to use a communal dock and lodge. Buyers could build cabins on their site if they chose, under the supervision of a builder provided by the management.

The much talked-about beauty of the Northwoods with its unlimited fishing, crystal clear waters, and long pleasant summer days lured hundreds of people to put their money down. In early 1928, Stark-Morgan Co. announced a Lake Vermilion Camping Paradise Grand Opening to be held in July.

People from all over the country came, about forty families, mostly with children. A few couples had left their children at home, and there was one single man from Des Moines. The arrangement had been for all the interested parties to meet in Duluth and take the train to Tower together. Nathan met them at the station, checked their names off the reservation list, and directed them into the club car. A banner had been hung above the windows, and champagne and finger sandwiches were served. The women were dressed in fine traveling clothes and carried colorful bags. The children were boisterous and played in and around the seats and adults.

When they arrived in Tower, Gregory met the train with the music of a local trio, which included an accordion, drum, and a horn. He had also hired an Ojibwe Indian in full ceremonial dress to stand by and welcome the jovial party of investors. It was a short distance from the station to the ferry where the travel party continued. The little band joined the group on the ferry and played all the way to Pine Island, where everyone disembarked. Gregory had expected the Indian to mingle and entertain the people on the ferry as well, but for some reason he slipped away as they were boarding.

The steam-driven ferry boat made the trip in just twenty minutes. The passengers were enthralled by the beautiful expanse of water and sky, fringed by a rugged shoreline of dark and light greens of the endless trees and streaked with white and grey rock. When they arrived in Canfield Bay, they saw an array of large tents in a flat open area. They were assisted onto a floating dock by a staff of maids and butlers who helped with their luggage. There was a delicious smell in the air as the kitchen staff had prepared a hearty welcoming meal. Each family was assigned to a tent and given some time to settle in.

At the designated hour, they gathered together and were given a tour of the property. With grand gestures, Stark and Morgan described the plans for a community center, a playground, a store, and a marina. Everyone was duly impressed, and after a gourmet meal served on china and silver, they retired to their tents. It was a great success, Nathan thought. Still, he had some concerns, so he went to look for his partner to discuss some details.

* * *

The weather during July of 1928 was excellent, making for a vacation paradise just like the brochure promised. Gregory sat on a camp chair outside his tent, sipping a Campari and soda from a crystal tumbler. The week was going well so far, he thought. The families who had come to see their new campsites were happy, although they voiced concern things weren't as far along as had been promised. There was no permanent dock yet, only the floating barrel contraption that Aronson's Marina had rigged up for him. The buyers loved the big tents and the wonderful food; having wait staff and maids made all the difference. It didn't occur to these pampered jerks, Morgan thought, that all the hired help would be gone next time they came up to their own campsites, if that ever happened.

Fortunately, too, the fishing had been great. He congratulated himself on his idea to hire the fishing guides. It kept these city people from getting lost, saved the cost of boat rentals, and guaranteed some big catches. He laughed to himself. These fools thought they were on a real safari just because a few of them had sighted a mother bear and two cubs swimming across from Pine Island to Spider Island.

Gregory smiled as he thought about his escape. He was so disgusted with the dirty, hilly streets and bone-chilling cold of Duluth. He was tired of stupid, poor people. He hadn't planned it this way at the beginning. Out of college, he had resigned himself to working at the law firm of Washburn and Weinstein until he retired as an old man. It's what was expected. He would be just barely comfortable, maybe even have a wife and kids, and die some cold day slipping on the ice and having a heart attack when he hit the ground. Even when Nathan brought this crazy campsite vacationland idea to him and realized there was money to be made, he hadn't considered any other options but to live and die in Duluth boredom. He remembered thinking he would use his profits from this venture to buy a house on London Road where the Duluth wealthy maintained their primary residences.

All his plans for making small steps up the social ladder of Duluth changed when the law firm he worked for sent him to Miami. Morgan was listed as executor of the will of a childless lumber magnate from Hibbing who had died at his winter home on Key Biscayne. As executor, Morgan was required to go to Florida and see to the dispersal of the property there. At first, he was resentful about being torn from his routine. He opted to stay at the deceased's residence in order to complete his inventory of the possessions and property more quickly. But it wasn't long before Morgan fell in love with the place – the luxurious house, the heat, the ocean, the self-indulgent nightlife.

Miami was warm, wonderful, and welcoming. He found that old money didn't look down on new money there. There were opportunities for clever lawyers, and indulgence was not only acceptable but expected. The women he met didn't care if he was handsome or athletic. He knew it was because he had money to spend. It didn't matter that it was the firm's money, of course, but no one cared.

But now, he thought as he sat on the rocky shore of Lake Vermilion, if he could just finish his plan quickly, he would be spending these fools' money on his new lifestyle far away from the pitiful life he was living in Duluth. He just needed the next round of payments to come in, and he would be on a train to Florida. He could tell that half of the people here this week would be hooked on the place. God's Country, they called it. God Forsaken Country – that's what it was. He was confident he already had most of them convinced to send the entire purchase amount when they got back home.

He was still smiling to himself, thinking about sitting in a chair like this one but on a Florida beach with its warm bodies – both water and flesh - when Stark came up from the dock. The worried look on his face made Gregory sit up.

"What's the matter, Nathan?"

"Let's take a walk. I want to talk to you."

As they walked along the shoreline toward Canfield Bay, they passed by the small tent city spread out between the hill and the lake. People lounged on camp chairs, drinking and watching a few children play. Nathan greeted the vacationers and paused to ask how they were enjoying their stay. The replies were consistently positive, with minor concerns thrown in to show they were discerning people, not to be dismissed as easy to please. Nathan responded with promises to have things corrected. Gregory nodded and smiled.

A short way beyond the tent area, they moved away from the water and followed a deer track at the base of the hill which led into the woods beyond. They came to a spot where the hill's rock formation had been dramatically disturbed by dynamite blasting done some sixty years before, during the Lake Vermilion gold rush of 1866. Instead of the huge smooth mass of solid rock pockmarked with lichen and small bushes and trees, there was in front of them an area the size of a house strewn with jagged rocks of all sizes. The hillside, cracked and split into giant shards of granite by the blast, was disfigured by a huge gouge in it as if a giant mythical animal had clawed it, laying bare sharp shards of ancient granite. Like my friendship with Nathan, thought Gregory, all smooth on the outside, but my hatred digs jagged spikes deep inside me that only I can feel.

They both knew what had happened there - it was a man-made event that took place many years before that had created this havoc of stone. But it was still an awesome thing to see, incongruous in this sublime natural setting. They stopped for a moment to stare at the massive disarray. Then Nathan turned to Gregory and spoke.

"I've had some serious concerns, Greg. I thought we'd be so much further along than this. I didn't say anything the first few days we were here because I've been so busy entertaining and taking new owners out on the lake. And I assumed you even planned for the work to start while we were here. It would impress the buyers. But this morning, when I went into Tower, I stopped at Bystrom's lumber yard and they said there's nothing on order for us. No lumber, no supplies, no gravel, no nothing," Nathan sputtered. "So, I figured you must be using another lumber yard. No big deal. On my way out of town, I decided to stop at Aronson's Boat livery to ask when they had our deliveries scheduled. I knew they'd have to be the ones to bring over the bulldozer on their big flatbed barge. When he told me nothing was scheduled for delivery to Pine Island, I backtracked to Soudan and talked with the builder you told me you had hired."

"And you know what he said? Huh?" he continued angrily, pacing as he talked. "He said he hadn't even heard of you. What is going on, Greg? This is really messed up. How can we possibly have the campsites leveled and ready and the lodge built by fall if we don't get started now? Tell me what's going on! You told me construction would be going full steam by now." Nathan was pacing now, getting angrier by the minute.

"Well, Nate, I've been meaning to tell you, but you know me, I can't stand making you angry or disappointing you," Gregory said calmly, looking down to hide his attempt to think of a way out of the situation.

"So? What's going on here? I've got my life savings on the line here. What is it? Why hasn't anything been done here?" Nathan demanded.

"Well, for one, we don't actually own all the land yet, so we can't really sell it. I'm working on a deal to get it all straightened out by August 15th. I just need a little more time. And we need the money from these new buyers to secure the rest, the pieces we don't own. We'll still have to make some payments through the next two years but after the 15th, we'll have title and can start the improvements and actually sell the individual plots."

"What? We don't own the land? All this? And, we don't own the land?" Nathan shouted, waving his arms around him. "Why? What happened? You told me we bought it already."

"Lower your voice, Nate. This will all work out. What happened was I missed a deadline for the auction of some of the property. We do own some of the land, but it isn't contiguous, so we can't do much with it until we get the rest. I've got it under control. I'm meeting with representatives of the owners in a couple of weeks. They've already told me it's a go, just a few more hoops to jump through. So, stop worrying. I've got it taken care of," Gregory said calmly, pleased with his impromptu and reasonable-sounding excuse.

But Nathan wasn't backing off. He was pacing faster now, getting angrier and angrier. "How could I have trusted you? What on earth was I thinking, giving you my life savings? You've never done a successful thing in your life without my help! I could have done this project without you, you know. You're nothing but a loser, and I felt sorry for you. Felt like I should bring you along on this great idea because we're like brothers. Now you're going to completely ruin my real family's future. How could you do this?" He was ranting as he paced. He turned to throw another barb at his partner and suddenly, he tripped, his ankle turned, and he fell onto the rocks.

Gregory was looking at Nathan's face as he fell and saw the surprise register there. He saw his friend's head hit and bounce like a small cushion flung onto a sofa – just bouncing enough to make a whoosh of air blow the fringe for a second. He saw it all in slow motion, the trip, Nate's arms flinging, eyes wide in surprise; his friend's head hitting the rock, then coming up just slightly and, as it fell back down, his hair flying, finally settling splayed out around his head.

Joy filled Gregory. He stood totally still for several minutes, flooded with relief and effervescent joy. The man who had so totally dominated his life was finally gone. He had been compared to him, forced to share with him, patronized and pitied by him, humiliated by his very existence for as long as he could remember. Gregory had been jealous of Nathan his entire life, knowing he never possessed any of the traits that made Nathan the strong, handsome, loved, successful man he was. And other than his mother, Nathan was the only person who was always there for Gregory, always positive and supportive. He knew he also didn't have the power to walk away from Nathan – at least until the trip to Miami. Now, as he calmly thought through the repercussions of this amazing turn of events, he realized he had an unusual opportunity, one which, with his newly found strength of will, he would not let slip away.

He carefully stepped over to where Nathan lay, blood streaming from the back of his head onto the sharp rocks. He squatted down and watched the shallow rise and fall of his friend's chest as he breathed for several minutes. Then he gently pinched Nathan's nose and held it shut while he put the other hand softly over his mouth. He watched the small movements of Nathan's chest as he struggled briefly and then subside. He went back to where he had been standing before and, looking at Nathan's lifeless body, took his time deciding how he would proceed. Years of being a lawyer had taught him he needed to consider all possibilities and make strategic plans.

He decided the best course of action was to do nothing. He would walk back the way he came. If anyone asked where Nathan was, he would say he didn't know, that he had wanted to come back to camp, but Nathan had said he wanted to explore further around the bay. Gregory decided once the body was found, it would be deemed a tragic accident. He would appease everyone with a small discount or some such trivial gesture to ease their discomfort, and then they would go home. He decided he wouldn't wait for August 15th. He would take what funds he had accumulated already, which was a significant amount, he reminded himself pleasantly, and leave for Florida. He would monitor the Duluth newspapers from the ubiquitous newsstands around Miami Beach which catered to tourists from all over the country, just in case any suspicions were cast in his direction.

He had already secured a small apartment in Coral Gables on the last trip he made there on law firm business and had had enough foresight to do it in an altered name. He knew he wasn't a mastermind criminal, but he was a devious, cautious lawyer who could throw a curve ball and cover his bases. He laughed out loud suddenly, thinking of the irony of the baseball reference used by the klutz of all-time standing here before the body of a fallen college baseball hero. As he laughed, he looked up and saw a man standing half-hidden behind a tree. He was in shadow, but the sun came out from behind a cloud for a moment, and he could see the man's face. Their eyes met briefly. It was someone he had never seen before.

Gregory's self-preservation instincts kicked in and even though he wasn't sure the man could hear him, he said, "Oh, my god, Nathan! You're hurt! Don't move. I'm going to get help."

And turned and hurried back toward the shore.

When he got there, he stopped for a moment to compose himself and concluded there was no need to change his plans. He would not mention Nathan unless someone asked him. The man in the woods was definitely not a member of their party and, come to think of it, perhaps he had even imagined him. Who would be walking around in the woods there, anyway? And if the man ever came forward, it would be easy to refute anything he said. After all, it was one person's word against another, which, as any good lawyer knows, proves absolutely nothing.

He casually walked back to his tent, again passing the happy vacationers, greeting them pleasantly as he went.

That evening, after a meal of fresh-caught walleye, the group was sitting around their campfires, laughing and drinking cocktails made with smuggled Canadian whiskey when the stars disappeared and the skies began to rumble. Many people were already in bed when the rain started, but no one stayed asleep once the storm hit full force. They huddled in their tents, which flapped and banged loudly against the metal support poles. Rain poured down in sheets, and broken tree branches flew by, scraping against the canvas. The floating dock made horrible screeching noises as the barrels rubbed and strained against the ropes holding them together.

Then the straight-line wind hit. In just a matter of seconds, tents were torn from their guy lines and tumbled away to end up strewn in the trees like so many napkins blown off a picnic table. It didn't last long, perhaps just a few minutes, but it seemed an eternity to the people in their nightclothes, now exposed to nature's violence. When the hurricane-like wind was over, there was little to be found in the open area where all the tents had been standing. In the continuing rain and pitch black, lit only by lightning, people called to one another and gathered together in the open, afraid to be under the trees for fear of a lightning strike. Some dragged any oriental rugs they could find to use as cover, wrapping them around the women and children.

The storm raged for another hour. Finally, the rain subsided, and the storm passed by. It was still desperately dark, and everything was soaked. Some men found enough dry wood to get a small fire going, and people gathered around it, glad for the light even if not everyone could get close to it for warmth. The waiters and maids scurried to try to please the campers, but there was little to be done except pass around the contraband brandy.

As soon as day broke, one of the local fishing guides pulled up to the dock in his Lund boat. He realized it had been a bad storm, and he came to see if they needed help. Some people who had managed to gather up a few of their belongings insisted he take them to the train in Tower. Even though his boat was only big enough for six people, the guide took two mothers and their five children on the first trip, promising to return as quickly as possible. Morgan, besieged with questions and demands, hailed the guide before he left and arranged for him to go to Aronson's instead and have the ferry come out to get them.

While the ferry took the traumatized vacationers to Tower, the staff laid out pieces of tent canvas and literally threw onto them anything of value they could find strewn about in the woods or on the grass or floating on the water. When the ferry came back for the last group, they gathered up the corners of the canvas pieces and dragged them onto the ferry. Everyone was exhausted when they finally left. One of the maids said to Morgan, "Have you seen, Mr. Stark, sir?"

Morgan was prepared with his answer and replied confidently, looking thoughtful, "No. No, I haven't. But I'm sure he must have gone on the ferry the first trip to get things ready for us in town. He's so resourceful that way, always thinking of others."

CHAPTER 20

Pittella had been Deputy for ten years at that point and had dealt with every crime in the book. But this was his first missing persons case and the only one that went unsolved. There had been several instances of people disappearing. Still, most of them involved berry picking, and the people were found wandering in the woods or at the Marjo Motel on the outskirts of Tower, enjoying a bit of extra-marital fun. He had taken the initial missing person's report from Gregory Morgan two days after the storm. Morgan had come to the Deputy Sheriff's office to report his partner, Nathan Stark, had not been seen since the afternoon of the storm. Pittella had called the various branches of law enforcement, including his Canadian counterparts, and enlisted their help to find the missing man. Pittella was the point person on the case and coordinated the efforts of the various agencies and volunteer search parties. Morgan was relentless in insisting the search continue, but after a week with no sign of

Stark, the search was called off. Stark's body was never found.

The question which remained on everyone's mind was whether he took the money and made it to Canada undetected or if the money was lost with him during the storm. If he had had a canoe stashed strategically on the north side of Canfield Portage, Stark could have easily paddled to the Trout Lake portage and carried his canoe into Trout Lake. From there he could paddle and portage to the Vermilion River, which led to Crane Lake on the US-Canada border. Crane Lake connects to Lake of the Woods and other border lakes with plenty of resorts and road access points on the Canadian side. People could only speculate how far Stark might have gone before the storm hit and if he would have survived if he had been on the water at the time.

Pittella felt confident an experienced outdoorsman like Stark could have made it through the storm. He felt the man was just clever enough to have gotten away, but the question which stayed in his mind was why. Why would Stark have abandoned his family, job, and new lucrative endeavor when all those things seemed to have been going so well?

It was a few years before the Vermilion Paradise scam was sorted out. Immediately after returning to Duluth, Morgan, with exceptional foresight, began to hint even more money was missing, always trying to seem like he was sure Stark wasn't guilty of any misdeeds, always appearing devastated by the betrayal of his best friend. Only a dozen or so buyers ended up owning property on Canfield Portage Bay. The rest lost their money, and there was nothing to be done about it. Morgan gladly turned over the books for the company, which showed sums of money missing over time. His clever planning and manipulation of the documentation provided evidence that he had not taken the funds. He was a lawyer, after all, he exclaimed, not an accountant, and he had trusted his partner.

The only logical assumption was that Stark had taken the money and fled. No Northwoods vacation paradise was ever developed. Morgan, impervious to the negative publicity and rumors of his complicity, waited out the furor. There was no money in the company coffers, and his efforts to hide what he had embezzled were very successful. Any parties with claims to make had no recourse. He kept a low profile for a few years, then quietly moved to Florida as he had planned. The partners at the law firm had deemed it prudent not to fire Morgan as it would imply their firm had been employing someone involved in a scam. They were delighted when he left.

Morgan kept in contact with his godson, Stephen Stark, and Stephen's mother, Nathan's widow. Every few years, he sent money for them to visit him in Florida. At first, the contact was somewhat awkward as he felt pangs of guilt for depriving the boy of his father. In time, he deluded himself that he had replaced Stark in the boy's eyes, even though their time together was minimal. He was, in actuality, only interested in the boy as a reminder of his old friend, a tenuous connection with the man he was so perversely connected to. Still, this relationship with Stephen was one in which he had the power. Sometimes his guilt overwhelmed him, and he wept for the friend he had lost and for the guilt he felt, but it didn't last long and was usually assuaged with an 18-year-old scotch on the rocks. It happened less frequently as the years went by. He even came to think his friend would understand his drastic measures to get away from his horrid life in Duluth and would even congratulate him for his cleverness. Ultimately, he knew he was smarter, and he had won. He got what he wanted, and Stark got his comeuppance. And that was that.

1948

CHAPTER 21

They took off from Stark's dock slowly. Bruno curled himself on the life jackets up front again. Carl and Elsa waved to Stark standing by his tent with yet another refilled glass in hand as they headed home. The weather had changed, the wind much stronger now. Big Bay was rough with whitecaps. Carl cranked the handle when they were away from the dock, and the Evinrude switched from purr to roar. But he immediately had to reduce speed to avoid getting drenched with each wave.

Carl aimed the boat directly perpendicular to the waves and rode up onto the crests, down into the trough and up the next one. If they kept on their southwesterly course, they would end up on the south side of Birch Point, missing Daisy Bay altogether. So, every ten minutes or so, Carl would guide the boat into a trough and immediately turn into it, heading north. They would ride parallel with the wave for several minutes in the wrong direction, then go back to riding through the waves again similar to tacking a sailboat. Carl could read the concern on Elsa's face and his heart was racing each time they changed course and the boat came perilously close to capsizing. All three of them were soaking wet. Carl continued this zigzag maneuvering until they came to Comet Island and could get to the calmer water between the two islands, Comet and Pine. The rest of the trip was much less stressful. They made their way into Daisy Bay past Isle of Pines and further on into the tiny bay where their boathouse waited like a grandmother with open arms. It was almost dark by the time they pulled up to the dock and backed into the boathouse.

"Well, that was quite a day," said Elsa as they finished securing the mooring lines, "How about we skip dinner? And maybe have a brandy to warm us up?"

"Sounds wonderful," Carl replied. "I'll be up in just a minute. Bruno and I have to attend to some business first."

Carl and Bruno walked to the end of the dock as Elsa went up to the cabin. "What do you say, big guy, did you like the boat ride?" Bruno pushed his nose up hard against Carl's hand, then he took off into the woods. "Don't go chasing any skunks!" Carl called after him.

As Carl climbed the steps to the cabin, Bruno came bounding up and pushed himself inside in front of Carl. He went to the dog dish at the end of the sink counter, sat down, and looked back and forth between his humans, communicating his need for dinner. Elsa obliged him with a generous scoop of dog food and some good pats. Carl started a fire in the cast iron stove, adjusting the draft on the stove pipe after it was lit, encouraging the fire to roar in its confined space. They changed into dry clothes and hung the wet ones near the stove.

They settled on the couch next to each other with a simple meal of sandwiches and tea laced with brandy. Elsa broke the silence. "You don't think Ike could be the saboteur, do you, Carl?"

"He certainly seemed upset with the construction taking place so close to his cabin. I can't imagine him being malicious though. But then we really don't know him all that well. Living by himself like a hermit for so many years, I doubt if anyone really does know him very well."

"Hmm," said Elsa, "I have a bad feeling about this."

"Let's go back out and see him again soon. Maybe we can talk to him and get him to make peace with his new neighbor," said Carl trying to ease her mind.

"Good idea," Elsa said.

They listened to the radio for a while, then went to bed.

* * *

Bruno made a couple of tail circles and uffed loudly as he lay down beside the bed. He listened to the intimate noises his humans made at night under the bedcovers. Sometimes they moved around so much the blankets would fall off and land on top of him. When they finished moving around, they would retrieve the covers, talk and laugh for a bit, and finally settle down to sleep. Only then would he finally go to sleep himself. He didn't know what it was they were doing, but he knew they enjoyed it, and that made him happy.

CHAPTER 22

They spent the next two days close to home and went fishing after dinner.

The first evening, they went down on the dock and cast using heavy lures like the Red Devil and the Swedish Pimple. The weight of the lure meant they had great range on the throw, but as soon as it hit the water, they had to reel in quickly or it would sink and catch on the bottom. The fast-moving lure was very tempting for the fish, and they caught several small-mouth bass. Bass were energetic and fun to land, fighting every inch, but they were harder to clean, and not all the bones could be filleted off the flesh. Walleye, on the other hand, was bone-free when filleted and gave almost no fight when being landed. Sometimes it was even difficult to tell if a walleye had taken the bait.

The next evening, they trolled the reefs across Daisy Bay near Horseshoe Island. The maps called it Rainbow Island, but the old timers they met on the lake referred to it as Horseshoe. First,

Elsa caught a nice eating-sized walleye. Carl caught a bass, but it was too small, and he threw it back. Next, Carl caught two sunnies in a row, which he also threw back because they had too many bones for his taste. Just before they quit for the evening, Carl hooked a medium-sized northern, and Elsa caught another walleye.

Each time they caught a keeper, Carl put it on the stringer. He preferred the clip stringer, a chain with a series of large dull safety pin-like clips attached along its length. The stringer was always attached to the boat by looping one end through the gunwale and hooking it onto itself, ready for the next catch. It was attached far enough forward so it wouldn't be sucked into the motor as they drove. Carl pulled the stringer inside the boat, opened a clip and pushed it through the upper and lower jaws of the fish, then closed the clip and tossed the stringer overboard. When they were trolling, the stringer was left in the water. If they needed to get somewhere faster, like to go across open water to the next fishing spot, Elsa would hold the stringer, with whatever fish was attached to it, up outside the boat but out of the water, and Carl would open the throttle.

When they got home, Carl took the stringer to the live box and released the fish into the protected environment.

The first year they had the property, Carl had worked waist deep in the water for several days digging and moving rocks, cementing them together in an eight-foot circle and lining sections between the stones with heavy metal, large-meshed screening to create a live box that could hold dozens of fish. The lake water and even minnows flowed in and out freely through the openings. Over the top of two-thirds of it was a dome of concrete, keeping the water below cool and shaded, almost like it was deep and not right up against the shoreline. A removable window-screen dome over the final third kept the trapped fish safe from land-based predators like the mink, which made their home along the shore, or herons which would stand statue-like along the water's edge, waiting for a fish to appear near the surface.

On days when Elsa wanted to fry up some walleye for dinner, Carl would move the screen dome aside. He'd kneel down with a long-handled fishing net, scraping it around the back of the dark, calm waters inside the live box, bring up a fish, and put it in a five-gallon bucket of lake water. He'd repeat the process until he got the perfect combination of fish for dinner and throw the ones he didn't want for that meal back into the live box, leaving them for another day. In his head, Carl kept track of each fish he put into the live box and how long they'd been in there. If needed, he would throw some worms or bugs into the water to feed them.

Cleaning the fish was Carl's job, and it was like a sacred ritual for him. First, he would get a bucket of lake water and place it at the base of the tall wooden table he had built for just this purpose down by the shoreline. He would use one of the boning knives his brother had given him. His brother was a butcher in Chicago, and after he had sharpened a butcher knife every day for a few years, it would end up being so narrow and pointed that it was no longer useful to him. But that shape made an excellent fillet knife, and he had given Carl several. Carl would hold the fish upright, its belly on the wood, and pierce its head straight down through and through with the sharp pointed blade, killing the fish quickly, but even so it still flapped and squirmed for a bit. It made Carl feel better knowing it was dead before he started to gut it. Then he laid it on its side to trim away the fins on the belly, slit it open, and scrape out the guts, taking care not to pierce the liver bile sack.

He'd rinse the gutted fish in the bucket of water. Then he turned the fish around so the mouth was facing him, and he would slide the knife along the backbone, carefully working his way on the outside of the ribs all the way down to the belly, then turn it over and repeat the process. The result was a three-part carcass connected at the tail. The center section was the head and backbone with all the ribs still attached. The outer two were fillets with no bones but with the skin still intact.

Carl would then lay one fillet skin-side down and flip the other two parts back, using them as a handle to steady the fillet process. Ever so carefully, he would slide the knife between the skin and the flesh of the fish, starting at the tail. Careful not to cut into the skin or hack up the meat of the fillet, he would first slide the knife smoothly left, then smoothly right, back and forth, until the fillet was separated from the skin. He'd drop the fillet into a small bucket of clean water, then flip the fish over and skin the other fillet. When he was done with all the fish cleaning, he would choose one of the smaller fish heads, detach it from the bones and skin, and give it to Bruno, who waited for this special treat.

Carl cleaned the two walleyes they caught and brought the fillets into the kitchen. Elsa was a good cook. Carl thought she was a great cook and pan-fried walleye was a favorite dish of his. Elsa mixed flour, salt, and pepper together on a pie plate. She rinsed the boneless fillets one more time, then laid them in the flour mixture, first on one side, then the other, dusting them with the three simple ingredients. Then she sautéed them in butter in a cast iron skillet. The pan was nice and hot, and in just a few minutes, the fish was done. And that was all there was to it.

She had peeled potatoes while Carl was cleaning the fish and boiled them. Fresh walleye, boiled potatoes with lots of butter, a can of creamed corn, and a piece of hardtack, and Carl was a happy man.

The next day was Tower's Fourth of July celebration, and they were anticipating a day of good food and casual hometown entertainment. They went to bed early after listening to a concert in Carnegie Hall on the radio, sitting close together on the sofa.

As they snuggled to sleep, Elsa said, "I'm a happy woman, you know."

"How's that?"

"I'm safe and sound in a good man's arms. I've got a good dog next to the bed. What more could I want?"

"You?" he said, "You always seem to want another adventure."

"Maybe tomorrow," she murmured as she drifted to sleep.

Patriotism was high all through World War II with the help of newsreels, patriotic movies, print propaganda, and, on a local level, parades. Since the war ended in September 1945 and everyone was finally home who was coming home, anticipation for the 1946 Fourth of July parade in Tower was high. But the spectacle, when it took place, left everyone feeling hollow— too many missing family members. The many losses seemed too fresh to celebrate the sacrifice.

So, Tower decided there would be no Fourth of July parade in 1947. However, the community leaders had second thoughts in 1948 and reconsidered, holding the parade on the 3rd for economic reasons.

CHAPTER 23

The guys down at VFW Post #1209 knew it was a disgrace. Not having a Fourth of July celebration in 1947, just two years after the end of the War to End All Wars, was just wrong. Although the VFW Post had held its own parade with a couple of decorated pickups filled with grandkids throwing candy, few people showed up except members' families and a few guys from the American Legion. Patriotism had been high during the war years. But in the glow of peace and prosperity, people were blasé. No longer called upon to sacrifice and make do with less, they had become more interested in their personal comforts than in standing around waving little flags. They wanted to forget and move on. For others, the sacrifices had been too much to celebrate.

When 1948 rolled around, the Tower businessmen started discussing it again. For them, the issue seemed to be black and white. You either thought it was worth the effort, or it wasn't.

But the one thing they agreed on was that it was a real dilemma. If they didn't host a parade and all the trappings that go with it like the special sales, door prize drawings, and kiddie games, all the people who like to attend parades would go to another town. That is indeed what happened last year. Tower had been a ghost town on the Fourth.

"We might as well just close every shop in town for the day, eh?" said Martilla, "No need to pay the soda fountain kid if we won't sell one hot fudge sundae. There won't be any business at all, nope, not at all, if we don't have the parade."

The naysayers said it was too much trouble, that it didn't generate enough profits, what with all the extra expenses they had to cover. The argument had been carried on at every monthly meeting with no decision made. The newspaper ran articles pleading for a decision from the committee. The mayor gave a deadline - which was ignored. Finally, at the meeting the first week of June, a vote came down with a shaky 'Yes.' A Saturday was sure to bring more people and more revenue, so a compromise was made - a Fourth of July Celebration in Tower would be held on July third.

And so, the event was on. People from the surrounding areas and other small towns drove in and parked their cars on the elementary school playground. The high school athletic field was the staging area for the parade. Starting at 9:00 a.m., a steady stream of people began to fill up Main Street. Stores were open, and each one had some kind of kiddie game going on before the parade started.

In the late 1800s, the East Two River had been dredged and widened during the lumber boom. Retaining walls had been built in the water to guide the timbers upstream to the waiting railroad cars where the tracks from Duluth to Tower ended near the river. After all the tall timber had been cut down, it became safe for private boats again. People with cabins on the lake who liked an adventure would take the river into town despite the slow speed required because of all the S-curves and deadheads. Hitting one usually just pushed it out of the way, but it could cause major damage to a motor. It was a beautiful trip through a wilderness not accessible to many people. Turtles lined up on logs in the sun. Waterlilies, white and yellow, spread across the calm dark water waiting for dragonflies to land. Frogs called out to their compatriots. If you were fortunate, you might spot a moose.

A small marina and a number of boat houses had been built along the water's edge where the rail cars used to be loaded. There was a small public dock there, too, where anyone who boated in from Lake Vermilion could tie up for an afternoon of shopping or dining. On the third of July, many boaters came early and occupied all the dock spaces in town. McKinley Park was the only other public place boaters could land. Located on the south side of Big Bay just east of the Narrows, the entrance to Pike Bay, the large public park was a remnant of grander days. The long stretch of sand beach and the huge, flat grassy park created when the mines were flourishing gave the thriving community a place to gather with their families after church on summer Sundays and for various celebrations and holidays. Enlargements of old photos of the park hanging in city hall showed a beautiful Victorian band shell, several pavilions, a gazebo, and other small buildings. Most of these had fallen into disrepair and had been destroyed for safety reasons, replaced by a few uninspired cement-floored pavilions and lots of picnic tables. In the early 20th century, there had been a long wide dock used by several ferry boats that regularly serviced the resorts, islands, and remote areas of the lake with no road access. By 1948, only resorts with road access remained in business, and steam-engine ferries were no longer needed. Over the years, the dock had been replaced several times, each time with a shorter, narrower version.

On this glorious July day in 1948, boats lined both sides of the dock, and the rest were just pulled up on the sand of the public beach. A farmer from Embarrass had volunteered his flatbed hay wagon and team of horses to take the people arriving by boat the mile or so into town. People crowded on for the ride, some sitting on hay bales, most jangling their legs over the side.

At the end of Main Street by the public marina and train station, food vendors had set up tents and tables in the grassy triangle. The VFW and American Legion had dueling grills, making similar brats and hamburgers. The only difference between the two groups' menus was that the VFW coleslaw was creamy, while their friendly rival served the vinegary kind, with little bits of grated carrots in it. The smell of grilled onions and nearly-burnt meat was enticing.

Cold beer and pop. Pretzels, giant cookies, cotton candy, and ice cream. One vendor was selling a local version of the Pronto Pup, a breaded hot dog on a stick introduced at the Minnesota State Fair the year before. The Old Settler's committee served its specialty - bouya stew. They had fifty-gallon pot, hung over a wood fire, which had simmered for two days, full of chicken, carrots, rutabagas, celery, potatoes, and a bag of secret spices. The old folks stood in the long line waiting to get a bowl, chatting about if the stew would be as good as last year's or any number of years gone by. There was coffee and potica; the sweet coffee cake rolled with honey and walnuts the miners liked so well.

People started claiming their territory on the sidewalk of Main Street around 10:00 a.m. The street had been blocked off at both ends by law enforcement vehicles and sawhorses. By 10:30, people of all ages filled the curb. By 11:00, the length of the sidewalk, all four blocks of it, was lined three and four deep. Not crowded close together, of course. This was Minnesota, after all. There were family groups with little ones showing off, running around in circles on the street in front of mom and dad, grandma and grandpa, the older generation seated on aluminum folding chairs. Groups of high school kids laughed and chummed around, jostling one another loudly and smoking cigarettes. Loners stood back against the buildings, allowing pedestrians a space to walk between them and the crowd along the curb.

The mayor was determined to start the parade on time and since his car was first, he did just that. Sitting in the passenger seat of a 1929 Hupmobile with the top down, the mayor waved judiciously at his constituents while his friend, George Knaeble, who owned the old car, drove. After the mayor passed by, it was a full ten minutes before the first float appeared. It was the official float of Tower, a real beauty. Mel's flatbed lumber truck had been gussied up with fabric and flags and homemade paper-mâché representations of a duck, a fish, a pine tree, and a miniature wooden version of the Tower-Soudan mine shaft rigging. Miss Tower, hastily chosen the week before from all of the business owners' daughters of the appropriate age, sat in the middle waving and smiling. The rest of the parade, despite having only four blocks to cover, took over an hour.

After the Tower float came the Quarter Horse Association riders mounted on shiny horses with equally shiny saddles and bridles. Then there were several different ethnic groups, carrying signs in their native languages and waving their flags – Slovenes, Italians, and Finns followed each other in colorful costumes. The children were always so proud to be part of something so important. The Swedes and Norwegians came next – mixed together. Their people had intermarried so often that they had given up on keeping their parade groups separate. It confused their children too much.

Next came the guys from the various volunteer fire departments around the county. They were dressed as clowns or, with balloons under their shirts and outrageous makeup, pretended to be busty-looking women carrying toilet plungers and giant flyswatters. They were followed by an antique fire engine which retired firefighters spent endless hours restoring while drinking endless bottles of beer. Children from the Tower Elementary School came next, riding tricycles decked out with balloons and colorful stringers, playing cards fastened to the spokes of their wheels with wood clothespins, clacking away like a flock of cartoon ducks.

Floats separated the high school band and the accordion polka band to allow the curbside audience to listen to the music without their sounds overlapping. The music was often off pitch and even more frequently out of rhythm, but no one seemed to mind.

The Shriners' drill team was the coup de grace of every Iron Range parade. Of all the people in Minnesota who love parades,

Shriners take the cake. A parade wasn't really worth its salt if it didn't have a Shriners' precision drill team. Each member of the drill team rode something motorized. They practiced various routines of such complexity as to amaze the onlookers. In the past, they had ridden mopeds or lawnmowers. This year they all had small go-carts decorated as canoes. The Shriners, in their red fezzes with black tassels, drove intricate patterns down Main Street to the hoots and cheers of the crowd. The tiny canoes with big men's torsos sticking out wove between and around each other so quickly and closely that it caused the crowd to hold their breath. This was the big time. Almost as good as a circus. Just like the big city – only better, thought the mayor.

* * *

Carl and Elsa arrived in Tower early and parked on the shoulder of the road just outside of town knowing they would be able to get away easily should they choose to leave before the festivities were over. As they neared the festivities, Elsa stopped to put on Bruno's leash. He walked calmly next to her until they stopped at the barricade at the end of Main Street where Deputy Sheriff Pittella was keeping an eye on the crowd. Bruno pulled on the leash to the reach the big man and was rewarded with rigorous scratches and worthy pats. After a pleasant bit of conversation, they walked down the street and found a nice vantage point from which to see the parade on the north side of Main Street. Across. Across from them was a large family group with several generations happily enjoying the occasion. Elsa found it as much fun to watch the kids playing around as it was to watch the parade.

As the marching band began to go by, her gaze again scanned

the people on the other side of the street, seeing them through the passing rows of the marching band like watching a choppy silent movie. There, at the back of the crowd, she saw Stark and a tall, older man talking animatedly. The man was pointing at something across the street from them. At first, she thought he was pointing at her, but she quickly realized whatever he was agitated about was to her right. She turned her head in that direction to figure out what was so interesting. That's when she saw Ike to her right about twenty feet away. He, too, was looking across the street, directly at Stark and the tall man. She could clearly see that Ike was distressed. She quickly returned her gaze to the other side of the street where the two men were still talking excitedly while looking in Ike's direction.

Elsa turned back to look again at Ike, but he was gone. She craned and stretched around to see everyone in the crowd, but no sight of Ike. She leaned close to Carl and said, "I thought I saw Ike a minute ago."

"Oh, that's nice he came into town to see the parade. I'm surprised. It doesn't seem like something he would want to do," said Carl close to her ear so she could hear over the marching band.

"He didn't look happy," said Elsa in response. "He looked weird and far away and a little scared, like he'd seen a ghost."

Carl turned to her with an incredulous look, "Seriously?"

She nodded, concerned. "I'm not kidding. I hope he's okay," she said.

* * *

The docks at the Tower public marina were almost completely filled, but Ike found a space close to the short where he could tie just the bow rope to the end of the dock. His boat would float against the shore, but there were no rocks in this part of the river and no waves either unless someone defied the no-wake sign. He thought it strange there was no space for his boat at the public dock and wondered why there were so many boats. He knew it was the Fourth of July weekend because last night when he decided he needed to come into town, he had looked at the calendar he got every year from the Standard Oil Station. But the holiday hadn't concerned him because earlier in the summer he had heard there wouldn't be a celebration again this year and besides, it was only July third, he was sure of it.

Ike walked across the bridge and past the train station. He saw the crowd and the mayor's car starting down Main Street. He wanted to get back in his boat and head home, but he stood for a few minutes, trying to concentrate on what was important. His lips moved as he talked to himself. What had he come to town for? Coffee. Yep, he couldn't believe he had let himself run out of coffee. There was always an extra two pound can of Folgers under the sink. But not this time. He wondered if someone from the new neighbors had snuck in and stolen it. Horrible, noisy neighbors, probably thieves. He fumed for a few moments, then ticked off the things he needed at the grocery store on the fingertips of his hands, struggling to remember what the six or seven items were. He finally decided to go on down the street to Zup's, buy his groceries, and get back home as quickly as possible. He sure as heck didn't want to be without coffee or, even worse, waste the trip.

He crossed over Main Street at the barricade, nodding at Deputy Sheriff Pittella as he did so. The parade route was full now of people dressed as cowboys on prancing horses and kids on tricycles as Ike made his way through the crowd along the north side of the street. The people along the sidewalks were waving and laughing and talking, kids dashing to pick up candy thrown from an open car decorated like a flowerpot full of daisies. The daisies being a half dozen kids in green leotards, giant white petals coming off their shoulders and yellow beanies on their heads. The St. James Presbyterian Church's float was passing, adorned with flowers, the church's name, and a scripture verse written in curly handwriting on a bed-sheet banner.

Ike was halfway to Zup's when a burst of laughter made him stop and look at the parade. The firemen clowns were dancing their way down the street, and the last one of them had just done something the crowd thought was really funny. As he watched the mop-wigged man in a short skirt and striped leggings fondle his balloon breasts, his subconscious was registering the sounds of the approaching high school band with increasing alarm.

His gaze fell across the street to the crowd on the other side as the boom, boom of the bass drum and the ratta-tat-tat of the snare drums grew louder. His heart started to pound, his breath came faster. His eyes tried to adjust as the people were transformed into soldiers, moving around agitated and firing weapons, screaming and crying out. Red shirts on people in the crowd became bloodied uniforms. Children jumping and running seemed to have been flung by bomb blasts. The bombs and bullets were devastating. The noise. The confusion of war was overwhelming. Ike saw a man across the way he recognized from an earlier skirmish. Ike remembered seeing him kneeling by a fallen soldier. The ground was covered with blood from the back of a soldier's head where shrapnel must have hit him. The man looked at Ike, and Ike knew he recognized him too. He knew he had to get into a bunker, the bombs were so loud. Boom. Boom. Boom. The bullets were flying everywhere. Ratta tat. Ratta tat. His heart was pounding so hard he panicked. He ducked his head down and started to run, pushing through the crowd of soldiers and screaming wounded, confusion overwhelming him. People yelled at him as he pushed onlookers out of the way. He cried out to them, "Run! Seek shelter! Hide! They're coming!" He ran, panicked, finally turning off Main Street.

The noises of the war lessened as he ran, and after another block, a shaky version of sanity began to return. He was sweating and out of breath. He sat down on the curb, disoriented and shaken, his head in his hands. He sat there for some time until a young couple walking to their car stopped and asked, "Are you okay, mister?"

He looked around and saw the small, neat houses, the street lined with stately ash trees. He shook his head, then nodded slowly and replied, "Yah, I'm fine. I'm okay. I just had to get away from the bombs. I'm okay now. Yah." The couple hesitated but then moved on, thinking the old man was just a little confused but not hurt.

When the far away sounds of the marching band from the end of Main Street finally faded away, Ike realized he was safe. People passed him, making their way to their cars or down to the west end of town to where the food vendors were stationed, and the polka band was playing. Still feeling shaky, he hurried to Zup's and bought the few staples he needed. With a bag of groceries in his arm, he gave the crowd watching the accordion

band a wide berth as he hurried back to his boat and started the
two-hour ride home.

CHAPTER 24

The morning after the celebration in Tower, Elsa was still feeling disturbed by the incident during the parade. Over breakfast, she told Carl her lingering concern about the look on Ike's face. Carl tried to convince her there was nothing to it.

"Ike's fine. I'm sure what you saw was just his reaction to being around all those people. You know," he said with raised eyebrows, "I'll bet I know what happened. He needed supplies and thought he'd go to town, not realizing the Fourth of July was being celebrated on the third this year. When you said you saw him, I really couldn't believe he'd be in town when he knew there would be so many people. Yep, I'll bet that's it. He was just upset at the situation and rushed on down to Zup's to get his groceries."

"That's probably true, but I just can't shake this feeling Ike was really upset about something else," Elsa said. "Golly days, I'd hate to think my sixth sense is off. But in this case, I'd hate to think it's on! I want everything to be okay with Ike. You know, I'd just feel so much better if I knew he was okay."

"Well, how about this?" said Carl. "Let's head over to Pine Island, visit Ike, then we can head up to Armstrong Bay to fish and maybe fish the reefs around Gull Island on the way back home if we have time."

Carl got the boat ready while Elsa packed a picnic lunch. She put in some hard-boiled eggs wrapped in wax paper, a couple of beers, and a bottle opener, along with the sandwiches she had made from the leftover meatloaf. She packed it all into the picnic basket and added a tin of homemade cookies to give to Ike.

The boat ride down the length of Big Bay was pleasant, with only small waves, lots of sunshine, and a few fluffy clouds in the blueberry-milk sky. They passed the point of land where Stark had been sitting on the cement pad. The chair was still there, but it was vacant. There was a bustle of activity on the construction site, but they didn't see Stark. Carl kept the boat out from the shore so it wouldn't appear they were being nosy or look like they were hoping to be invited in again. They continued past Canfield Bay and around the corner to the small cove where Ike's cabin stood.

Ike's boat was not there. His canoe was pulled ashore and overturned to the left of the dock in its regular place.

Elsa and Carl tied up at the dock. Bruno hopped out before they were finished and sniffed around, lingering at the shore end of the dock. The three of them went around to the back of the ccabin, stepped up onto the long narrow porch, and Elsa knocked on the door. There was no answer. They stood for a bit, looking around. The construction noise was muffled but annoying, like a wasp searching for a way in along the edge of a kitchen window screen. They sat on the steps for a while, looking into the thick woods behind the cabin. Bruno was pacing and sniffing along the edge of the trees, stopping every now and then for an in-depth sniff.

"The construction crew must have had yesterday off for the holiday and they're making up the time today. Why else would they be working on a Sunday?" asked Carl.

"I wonder how far it is to walk over to the construction site from here."

"Well, it certainly isn't that far. But why would you want to walk through the thick woods when you could take your boat over there in just a few minutes," answered Carl.

They sat quietly for a while longer, then Elsa asked, "What do you want to do?"

"Well, his boat is gone so there's no telling how long he'll be. But then, we could wait a while longer. We're in no hurry, are we?" replied Carl.

"No. No hurry on my part." Elsa glanced around, thinking about Ike and his solitary life, taking in the details of the porch and the back side of the cabin. "Looks like he finished the paddle. It's not there anymore," pointing to the spot where it had been resting against the wall the last time they visited.

After a bit, she said, "Let's go inside and leave him a note."

She stood up and brushed off the seat of her pants. They knew the door would be unlocked. No one locked their doors in the Northwoods. As she opened the door, Bruno pushed his way inside in front of her, sniffing as he went. He kept circling the room, nose to the floor, back and forth.

Even though he knew they would be welcome inside, Elsa was uncomfortable, standing awkwardly in the middle of the room, not wanting to be in someone's home without their knowledge.

"Look," Carl said, pointing to a framed photo on the far wall next to the windows looking out on the lake. "I guess he must have liked it," he said with a shrug, a smile on his face. "He hung it up, anyway."

He walked over to look at the picture he had taken of Ike and the fox. Elsa joined him, looking at the photo, and said, "That was one terrific shot, Carl. The connection he had with the fox was amazing, don't you think? It's like they really knew each other."

"Yeah, I know what you mean. It was really special," said Carl.

Elsa looked around for paper and pencil to leave a note next to the tin of cookies she had placed on the pine table. With nothing to write on in sight, she started opening drawers, briefly inspecting the contents. When she found a pencil but no paper, she started looking on the shelves under the front windows. She pulled out what she hoped would be scrap paper and stopped where she was.

"What is it?" asked Carl.

"It's a map. A map of Lake Vermilion. But a really old one. And it's got all this scratching and some writing on it. It's strange looking. Like a treasure map."

Elsa brought it over to the table in the middle of the room and smoothed out the folds. They both leaned over to see it better, but the light was dim in the cabin.

"Let's take it outside," Carl suggested.

Bruno stretched out on the grass nearby. They sat next to each other on the steps and spread the map across their knees, pointing to places they recognized or parts that looked interesting. They speculated about all the scratchings, cross hatches, and cryptic notes. As they talked, they became convinced the map showed someone's efforts to find something - like a treasure map.

Printed in dark blue on a large piece of linen type of material, the map appeared to have some sort of waterproofing on it. But it was soft from having been folded and rolled many times. The edges were frayed like a worn-out dish towel, and along the top left-hand corner, a piece of the fabric had been cut away. A few little lines of ink like the bottoms of letters on the cut edge implied there had been a name or more information written there on the missing part.

Other than the names of a few places on the map, there was no legend or any other words printed on it. The outlines of Lake Vermilion, the islands, the rivers and streams, and other lakes around it were not drawn to scale. Many details were left out, as were most names. There were no roads, only the railroad ending in Winton. There were some random dots with small circles around them on Pine Island. But those dot circles were also at various other places around the lake, even some on Daisy Bay's north shore where their cabin was. Handwritten markings and cryptic notes covered a large part of Pine Island. Pencil lines crisscrossed much of the island.

"What do you think these pencil marks mean?" asked Carl pointing to the crosshatch marks.

"It looks as if someone was keeping track of where they had been and how many times. They definitely cover where we are right now," Elsa replied. "I wonder what the circled dots are," she said with a finger on a cluster of them in the crosshatched area.

"Look here," Carl said, pointing at Daisy Bay, "these circles look like they're in about the same spots as the gold mines they blasted back in the 1860's on our backland. Remember? The plat the Nelsons gave us when we bought our land from them has marks in the same spot."

They sat silently for a bit, contemplating the map. Suddenly, Bruno jumped up and stood next to them, staring at the edge of the woods. A flash of red fur was visible briefly through the leaves. Then the fox stepped out of the trees and into the open area by the cabin. It stopped for a few moments, looking straight at them before it retreated into the shadows of the woods. Bruno gave a subdued woof.

"I don't like this," Elsa said, "I feel like we're snooping. I'm curious about this map but I'm not comfortable looking at it anymore. It's Ike's business. Let's put it back. I'll tear just a piece off the top of the bag of flour he's got sitting on the counter to write the note on. I'm sure he wouldn't mind that."

"Okay. I agree. You write the note however you can and let's leave. We'll head over to Armstrong Bay like we planned," said Carl.

Elsa went inside and returned the map to where she had found it. She wrote a note on a scrap of flour bag paper, tucked it under the cookie tin, walked out, and closed the door.

CHAPTER 25

The day was sunny and bright. The chop on Big Bay was minimal, and they made good time boating over to Indian Point, where they had decided to have their picnic lunch again. They tied up on the south side of the point with their usual routine. Today it was exceptionally calm as the wind was from the north-northwest.

"Hey, we're really getting good at that," Carl said, with a smile aimed at his wife's backside as they climbed between the towering pines, "too bad they don't have rocky shore boat landings as an Olympic event." Elsa laughed. The three of them made their way up onto the high point with the grand view of Big Bay.

Sometimes, especially if the weather was good, Carl would bring along his camera, an Argus C3, in case they saw a bald eagle perched in a tree or anything else interesting while they were boating. Now looking over the expanse of Big Bay from the height of Indian Point, Carl was glad he remembered to put the camera case in the picnic basket. He used the light meter and took some shots of Big Bay while Elsa laid out the simple meal on the small tablecloth spread on the massive rock. The two boats close together near Spider Island made for a nice photographic composition, Carl thought. He set the range finder to infinity, adjusted the exposure, and framed the shot.

Bruno had started out to explore the woods but came back quickly when the food came out of the picnic basket. He waited patiently for whatever scraps would end up being his. They noted how peaceful it was and agreed that the construction crew must have had a short day. They ate in congenial silence, looking out over the shimmering blue waters of Lake Vermilion.

When they finished lunch, Carl said, "How about we skip Armstrong Bay. I think it's too far at this point in the day. Let's troll the reefs around Gull Island. We can hit Potato Island, too, if we don't have any luck at Gull. Then we can stop back at Ike's before we head home. I'm sure he'll be home by then."

They packed up and made their way back down to the boat, which was floating peacefully on the calm water of the lee side of the point. Carl untied the rope from the tree and pulled the boat as close to shore as he could. Bruno and Elsa hopped on and moved back. Carl jumped in, bringing the front rope with him, and the boat moved away from shore, pulled by the tension of the anchor line. He made his way to the back of the boat and started the motor.

They rode out toward Gull Islands, which was really just a section of the reef extending above the water like the tips of icebergs. They had to pass another would-be island, lurking just under the surface, part of the long chain of rocks which ran down the middle of Big Bay. Red and white buoys marked this one. Carl slowed the boat as they approached, and Elsa brought up the fishing rods, handing one to Carl. Before they left home, he had affixed the lures appropriate for casting the weedy, shallow water of Armstrong Bay but not for trolling the rocky reefs. As the boat drifted, he opened the tackle box near his feet. He took Elsa's rod, removed the lure, and set it in the open tackle box. Then, his hand hovering over the array of possible choices, he pondered which one to use. He picked a medium–weight, shiny, minnow-like lure that he thought would tempt the fish lurking in the deep water and attached it with the safety-clip swivel. Then he did the same for his rod. They lowered their lines as Carl took the motor out of neutral. They circled the reef a few times without so much as a nibble.

"Let's pull up and head over there," said Carl, pointing his rod. They both reeled in their lures. Carl sped up and steered toward the tiny rock islands, each about the size of a large front lawn, spaced a quarter mile apart. They were home to many hundreds of seagulls. The rocks were whitewashed with guano and barren of any plant life. A few birds flew quietly around in tight circles above the first island they approached. It seemed to be painted white with flecks of light and dark grey. The illusion shattered when the boat came closer, as hundreds of gulls took to the air en masse with loud piercing cries, creating havoc of both sight and sound. The gulls were everywhere, on and above the island, which seemed to be in constant motion. It seemed as if there wasn't enough space for all of them who, in turn, circled, then landed, and so on, all the while screeching wildly, beaks open.

They trolled twice around the pile of rocks, the air above it constantly swirling with gulls like the debris in a tornado. Carl suggested they move to another Gull Island. As before, he and Elsa reeled their lures up out of the water holding the rods upright so the lures skimmed above the surface as they sped across the distance to the next giant rock. There were fewer birds, but the reaction was the same. The furor of the white and grey birds increasing as they approached.

Elsa noticed a tad of color at the edge of the rocks, dark blue and brown that moved with the waves. She pointed at it and yelled to Carl over the cacophony of the circling birds. "Someone must have lost their jacket overboard. See. Look there."

As they came closer, it was evident it did indeed look like a jacket, but with the sleeves extended out, and somehow, there were even brown pants where pants should be. They were both puzzled and exchanged questioning looks. Carl slowed and put his rod down along the edge of the seats, Elsa did the same. When they were some yards away, Elsa gasped a sharp intake of breath and said, "It's a person. They must be hurt. Oh, my god. Hurry and get close. Maybe we can help."

"Elsa, tie Bruno to the back here, will you?" Carl said, pointing to the rear rope. She quickly went to the back seat next to Carl and called Bruno to come to her. She tied the mooring rope to his collar so he wouldn't be able to jump out of the boat. Then she returned to the front just as they came up close to the rocks. The noise of the shrieking gulls was horrific, many of them diving at the boat to protect their rookery.

She swung her legs to the front and got on her knees on the first seat, leaning forward to see better. Carl steered to the right and gently bumped the nose of the boat into the rocks. The smell of the bird shit was overwhelming, and Elsa gingerly stepped onto the rocks, fearing they would be slippery. The boat was gently turned sideways by the movement of the water and rubbed against the rocks. Carl raised the motor to save the propeller and realized there was nowhere to tie up, but with the waves coming from the northwest, the boat couldn't go anywhere. He patted Bruno and commanded him to stay. Then he too stepped out onto the rocks without a rope, leaving the boat to bump gently against the shore.

He took Elsa's hand, and they supported each other as they made their way over the slippery rocks to what they could now clearly see was a body face down in the water. The seagulls were screaming a terrible noise overhead, diving to scare the intruders away from their nests.

The dead man's white hair floated back and forth in rhythm with the fabric of his clothes with the lapping of the waves. It appeared as if he was holding himself at the shoreline with his arms spread, bent at the elbows, hands on the rocks, legs floating freely perpendicular to the shore. His face was aimed directly down as if he was searching for something in the water on the bottom. The back of his neck showed a fresh injury between the collar of the jacket and his hairline. There was little blood, but a vivid mark ran from side to side, like a slash of red lipstick hastily applied without a mirror to grim lips.

"Oh, my god," Carl said, "it looks like Ike."

He kneeled down to turn the man's head so they could see his face. Then he gently set it back as he found it. Elsa was crying quietly as she stood back, arms tightly wrapped around herself. She had never seen a dead body before, lots of dead animals back on the farm in Canada where she grew up, but this was something altogether different. She didn't wipe away the tears that rolled off her cheeks.

Carl had seen many bodies during the war, most in much worse condition than this one. A wave of sadness, futility, and anger washed over him as unwanted scenes of fellow soldiers with wounded and torn bodies screaming for help flooded his mind. They're just sea gulls' screams, he realized. He forced himself to concentrate on the present. He shook his head, stood, and faced Elsa, putting both hands on her shoulders.

"Are you okay?" he asked.

She nodded and wiped her cheeks, pulling herself together. "I wonder where his boat is. He must have lost his balance somehow, hit his head and fallen out. Oh, how awful!"

"He can't have been here long. The birds haven't even started…" Carl let the thought trail away as he looked at Elsa, realizing how shaken up she was. "We need to get help. We've got to call Pittella. I wonder which place would be closer, Isle of Pines or Glenwood Lodge. I'm sure both of those resorts have telephones," Carl said.

"But we can't leave him here like this," she replied, visibly upset, looking around at the circling scavengers.

Carl pulled her closer and put his arms around her while still looking at the body. "Do you think you can take the boat yourself? I'll stay here with Ike. It'll be okay."

Elsa nodded again, her cheek tight against his chest. Then she pulled away with a thin smile. "Of course, I can run the boat myself. I think Glenwood Lodge is closer. I'll head over there and be back as quickly as I can," she said, looking northeast back the way they had come.

They made their way carefully to the boat. Bruno sat stoically in the back, his tail making a hollow sound as it thumped against the hull. Elsa climbed in, grabbed the picnic basket, and handed it out to Carl. "Just in case you need a drink or something," she said.

Carl gave the boat a strong push to get it away from the shore as Elsa lowered the motor and started it with just two pulls. She aimed it away and gave a single wave to Carl. He waved back, then made his way to the floating remains of Ike Iverson. He carefully lowered himself on the slippery rocks to a sitting position next to the body and put a hand on it protectively.

CHAPTER 26

Elsa cranked the motor as fast as it would go and sped north away from the reefs, then aimed east once she had passed the dangerous rocks. The tears came back as she looked to her left and saw Ike's dock in the distance. She made the two-and-a-half-mile trip in twenty minutes or so, not that she kept track. The bay at the east end of Pine Island is cluttered with small islands, and under normal circumstances, she would never have driven the boat full speed through the maze of reefs and markers, but she did now.

She reached the main dock at Glenwood Lodge and practically slammed into it. She managed to slow at the last minute by aiming across the end of the dock and latching a rope on a post as the boat was moving past it. She wrapped the rope around it several times, shouted at Bruno to stay, and leaped onto the dock. She ran up to the lodge building, past a few people outside on the broad lawn. Swinging the screen door open, she trotted into the big communal room and looked around. It was empty.

A ping pong table was in one back corner. Various clusters of couches, stuffed chairs, and tables for playing card games were spread throughout the room.

"Help! Anybody?" she cried out.

A teenage girl came out of the back and said, "What's the matter? Are you hurt?" When Elsa shook her head no, the girl said, "Wait here, I'll go get my dad." She went back the way she came, calling out, "Dad! Dad!" The girl returned in a minute with her father close behind.

"Are you okay? What do you need?" he asked.

"We found a body floating on Gull Island. I need to call Deputy Pittella. Where's your telephone?" Elsa said frantically, all in a rush. She took a deep breath and calmed herself. "I'm sorry. I'm kind of upset. My husband is waiting with the body and I need to get back out there to him."

"C'mon," the lodge owner motioned for her to come into the office. He went around the back of his desk, sat down, and picked up the handset of the big black desk phone. He ran a finger down a list of names and numbers he had under the glass covering his desk. Each number dialed on the rotary phone seemed to take forever, tick-tick-ticking for each digit, clicking its way around the dial. Phil Newsom waited for the ring as the connection went through, looking back and forth between his daughter and the distraught woman.

"Honey, why don't you get the lady a NeHi," he said to the girl.

"Hello, Deputy Pittella? I'm sure glad you were in. Say, this is Phil Newsom out here at Glenwood Lodge. There's a lady here who says she and her husband found a body out in Big Bay," the man said. He listened for a minute, then handed the phone to Elsa.

The ten or so people she had run past outside on the lawn had gathered in the hallway outside the office, curious to know what the emergency was. They craned and pushed to get closer to hear what was happening inside.

Elsa glanced at them as she took the phone. Pitella asked her what was going on. She first told him who she was, then explained how and where they found the body. "Uh, huh. Yes, we do," she said after a pause while she listened, "It's Ike Iverson. His boat wasn't anywhere around we could see. It looks like he hit his head and fell out."

The crowd in the hallway murmured, and she looked at them again, taking in each face this time. She didn't recognize any of them except the tall, somber-looking man in the middle of the group who was staring intently at her. Pittella explained what he was going to do and what she should do. "Okay. I'll start back and let Carl know you're on your way. We'll be there on the north side of the larger of the two Gull Islands," she answered and gave the phone back to Newsom. "The Deputy wants to talk with you."

The girl pushed her way through the group of onlookers into the office. She handed the bottle of orange pop to Elsa, who sat down heavily on a chair by the desk. She thanked the girl and took a big swig. Newsom listened as Pittella told him what preparations to make, repeating them out loud for verification. He was to clear all boats from the launch area and have someone ready to guide the ambulance, which would arrive from Ely, down to the ramp to load the body. Then he was to gas up all the resort's rental boats and find volunteers to be ready to take them out as part of the search party to look for Ike's boat when the Deputy got there. Newsom agreed he would do all that and added he would have coffee and cold drinks available for the search party.

By the time he hung up the phone, Elsa had finished her pop. She set the empty bottle on the desk as she got up to leave. "Thank you so much," she said. The crowd outside the office dispersed, some going out the front, others mingling in the community room, discussing what they had heard. She looked around for the tall man, but didn't see him. It came to her that he was the person with Stark at the parade when they were looking across the street at Jake and again wondered who he was.

Newsom walked with her down to the dock. "Would you like someone to go back out there with you?"

"No, I'll be fine. And I'm sure the Deputy will get there in short order. I know he has a much more powerful boat than we do. So even though he's coming from Tower, we'll probably get there about the same time. Thanks again," Elsa replied. She climbed in and started the motor as Newsom untied and tossed the rope into the boat. She waved her thanks as she took off.

* * *

The birds continued to circle, but some of them landed and stayed on the ground, now there was little activity near them, especially on the far side of the rock pile island away from where Carl sat still with his hand resting lightly on the body. Without hearing the noisy birds anymore, he gazed out over the lake and thought about the fragility of life. Ike had spent the last thirty-some years of his life living alone on this lake and now he had died alone in it. His thoughts wandered to his friends who had been killed in Italy - Henderson torn into pieces by a booby trap bomb; Winter slumped in the Jeep with a bullet hole in his chest, blood running in a neat stream down his shirt front as Carl drove; Smythe dying in the hospital, never waking from a coma to find he no longer had legs. There were so many more, some friends, some enemies, the scenes of death began to consume his attention and the present.

Carl jerked from his gory reverie when a large, fearless gull landed on the body and started pulling at the jacket sleeve. "Dra helvitt!" Carl shouted at it in Swedish, waving his arms. It flew away with a loud raspy squawk.

He glanced down at the body and realized it had begun to change already and that the legs had skewed to the side with the movement of the water. What if the wind changes and the body shifts? He quickly decided to take some photographs. Now, for the second time today, he was glad he had remembered to put the camera in the picnic basket. He got up carefully, making sure the body wouldn't float away from shore, and made his way to where the basket sat perched on a large flat, whitewashed rock. He dug around in it and pulled out the zippered leather case which held the camera and its accessories. He put the camera strap around his neck, held the light meter out toward the surreal scene there on the rocky shore, then adjusted the shutter speed. He put the light meter in his pocket and took several shots. He carefully walked on the slippery rock in a wide semi-circle and took photos from different angles as he went, finally going back to where he started.

Leaning over the body, Carl could see the light was different, so he used the light meter again and made the shutter change. Then he took shots of the head and neck. He got as tight a shot as he could on the bruise, using one finger to hold the jacket collar back for a complete view of it. It had already begun to change color, and the edges of it had started to blur. He thought it best not to move anything, even to see Ike's face again, so he returned the equipment to the picnic basket and sat back down by the body, resuming his vigilance.

The birds were getting aggressive, the cacophony impossible to ignore. Carl swatted at another gull that had landed near the body. As soon it landed, another one did too. When he waved his arms, they all took off, but each time he stopped, they got braver and landed on the body whenever they could. Carl wondered how Elsa was doing and when she'd be back. He hoped help would arrive soon.

CHAPTER 27

Elsa retraced her route back out to the island. The return trip seemed to go more quickly, she thought. Bruno, alert and staring straight ahead as if his concentration would get them there quicker. His big body leaned on her legs in a gesture of mutual comfort. She felt bad he was still tied but these were unusual circumstances, so she patted him frequently and told him he was a good boy.

When she got close to the island, Carl was waiting for her, waving his hands. He met the boat and gently pulled it alongside the rocks. Again, he commanded Bruno to stay and with the dog's arrival, the birds retreated to a safer distance.

After a comforting hug, Carl asked her how her ride had been and when help would arrive. They stood together near the body while she told him what had happened at Glenwood Lodge.

"Harvey should be here any time," she said. They decided it would be better to sit in the boat than stand on the slimy rocks, so they climbed in and sat next to each other on the middle bench seat, Carl's arm around her shoulder. They talked about Ike, recalling how Carl had introduced Elsa to him a few years ago on their first trip to the lake together, how they felt a kinship with him although he was so reclusive. Maybe it was their common Scandinavian background, maybe their mutual love of the lake and the Northwoods. Whatever the connection, Ike had welcomed their visits, and they had genuinely cared for the old man. Now he was gone.

They sat silently for what seemed like a long time, not even comfortable talking because of the noise of the birds continually squawking around them. Bruno barked at the birds whenever they started to land near them. Finally, they heard a motor approaching from around the end of the island. They made their way back to the body to wait for the Deputy.

A 24-foot launch, piloted by Deputy Pittella, came roaring into sight, Patrolman Korchenko was seated in the back. Pittella slowed to neutral directly offshore from where Carl and Elsa now stood by the body. Pittella looked the scene over from forty feet out before pulling up parallel to Carl's boat, pushed against the rocks. He tied on to the smaller boat's oarlocks, stepped onto its middle seat, and then onto the slippery rocks. With a wild swing of his arms, he gained his balance then carefully moved to the body which was moving vigorously in the waves the big boat had made. Pete Korchenko followed the Deputy Sheriff and tipped his hat to Carl and Elsa as they approached the body.

"You touch anything, move anything?" Pittella asked.

Carl answered, "No. Except to turn his head once to confirm it's Ike and to keep the birds off him."

"Good job, then. Some people would have just thrown him in their boat and brought him into Tower," said the Deputy. "Thanks. What you told me over the phone, Elsa, is probably just what happened, but we want to make sure everything is done according to Hoyle."

The Deputy squatted close to the body, examining every inch without touching it. He paid particular attention to the bruise on the neck. Finally, he stood and said, pointing, "Looks like he fell and hit the back of his head, on the neck there. Probably lost his balance and hit the gunwale as he fell out of the boat. Probably drowned. The Medical Examiner from Ely should be arriving at Glenwood Lodge in the ambulance anytime now and once he's out here and done what he's got to do, we'll take the body back there. The ME will take him to Ely, and then, hopefully, someone will come out of the woodwork and take charge of the funeral arrangements." He paused, shaking his head, "What a shame."

After asking Carl and Elsa a few questions, Pittella said, "You two have had enough of this tragedy for the day. I think you should go home. You did great, and I'm sorry for the loss of your friend. He didn't make friends easy, I know that about him. He was a strange bird," he said, looking down at Ike's body. "Speaking of birds, these gulls are god-awful! I can't believe you had to sit here in this stink and noise."

"I'll come over tomorrow and ask you some more details about how you found him, if that's okay with you," he said to them, "You go ahead and take off now. Thanks again, Carl, Elsa," Pittella said, nodding at each of them.

Korchenko helped them get their boat away from the cruiser and the rocks. They all cringed when both boats scraped loudly against the rocks.

"Sorry 'bout that," said Korchenko as he pushed the Sportland clear.

"Don't worry about it," said Carl, "Thanks for your help."

* * *

Once away from the rocks, he started the motor and quickly pulled away from the reef. The wind was picking up, so Carl aimed straight toward Pine Island in order to traverse Big Bay in the lee of the island. When they got near the shore and turned west to go home, Elsa stepped over Bruno, who was back in his favorite spot on top of the life jackets and over the middle seat to get close enough to Carl to talk without yelling. She sat next to him on the rear seat and said close to his ear, "I know this might sound weird, but do you think we should go get the cookies and my cookie tin? Ike won't be eating them, that's for sure," she asked.

"Sure, why not?" said Carl, a puzzled look on his face, and turned the boat eastbound. He followed the shore past Canfield Portage Bay. As they came around the bend into the cove where Ike's cabin was, Carl slowed down, and cut the motor as they pulled up to the dock. They secured the boat front and back and got out. Bruno took off up the path first, sniffing vigorously.

Halfway up the path, Elsa said, "Say, Carl, do you see this? How the dirt is all swooshed around like someone swept the dirt with something? It wasn't like that before."

Carl stopped, looked in front and behind them, and said, "Hmmm. Kind of a strange pattern, back and forth like that. Maybe a bear or some other animal made it, like the flat part of a beaver's tail, moving back and forth as he walks."

"Yeah, you're right. Must be something like that. What else could it be?" she replied.

They continued to the back of the cabin and stood at the bottom of the steps. "I can't believe we were here just this morning. Ike might have been dead even then," Elsa said thoughtfully. "Did you notice the pattern in the dirt when we were here earlier? I know I didn't, but I was carrying the cookie tin, and we were talking and looking around for Ike."

"No, I don't remember seeing it then either," answered Carl.

"What the heck!" Elsa exclaimed, pointing onto the porch. "Am I crazy? There's the paddle! Do you remember talking about it this morning? It wasn't here then. What is going on?"

They both went over to where the paddle was leaning against the wall, and Carl picked it up. It didn't appear to be finished. At least there was no varnish on it yet. "I don't think this is really done yet. Ike would want it sanded smooth even on the blade," he said as he looked it over.

"Hey, the blade has dirt on the end and, look, even some bits of grass. It will have to be sanded again or the stains will show through when he varnishes it." Carl stroked the long thin blade gently on one side, wiping some of the dirt away. "Oh, hmm. I guess it won't ever be finished."

They were silent as Carl put the paddle back where he had found it, and they went into the cabin. The tin of cookies was still on the table with Elsa's note. She picked it up and put the note in her pocket. They looked around, thinking of Ike.

"We should take the photo of Ike and the fox, don't you think, Carl? It really is a great likeness of him. We can hang it in our place in honor of Ike."

Elsa went to the bookshelf under the window and dug out

the map again. "Carl, do you think it would be terrible if we took this too?" she asked. "I'm so curious about it and, you know, someone is just going to come in here and empty this place out before it gets sold to some stranger. Ike didn't have any relatives. At least that's what he told us."

"Well, I can't see it has any value and knowing Ike, I'll bet if you had asked him for it, he would have given it to you," Carl answered. "He really didn't seem sentimental about any of his things. Sure. Go ahead and take it as far as I'm concerned. Actually, now that I think about it, I'm sure Pitella saw us head over here, so we should tell him we came to get your cookie tin and about the map, too."

"Okay. That makes sense. I'd feel better if we did. He said he was coming to see us tomorrow," said Elsa. She opened the cookie tin and offered it to Carl. "Here, have a couple cookies." He reached over and took three. She took one too, holding it in her teeth while she put the map in the newly made space in the tin and closed it up.

Outside on the steps, they paused to look into the woods, the view Ike preferred. "'Bye, Fox. Take care." said Elsa.

The trip home seemed to take forever. They ate leftovers and went to bed early, the sun barely having gone down. The emotional drain of the day had hit hard. They held each other a little tighter as they fell asleep, feeling a sense of sadness and vulnerability for how quickly time and life go by.

Elsa woke with a start, her heart racing. It was pitch dark, but she stared at the ceiling anyway, thinking things through. Finally, she reached over to Carl and gently shook his shoulder. "Carl. Carl, I know what happened."

"Uhhmmm. What, what happened?" Carl mumbled, then fell

back asleep.

"What happened at Ike's. About the paddle. I think someone killed Ike," she whispered to the ceiling.

CHAPTER 28

The sun woke them early as if it knew of Elsa's epiphany and wanted the world to know it too. The couple sat at the table drinking coffee, taking some solace from the warmth of the cups. The details of what had happened the day before were still clear and at the forefront of their thoughts. Elsa smiled when Carl told her he didn't remember she had tried to wake him.

"So tell me, then," Carl said, "what was so important that you had to tell me in the middle of the night?"

"I think someone argued with Ike on his porch, grabbed the paddle, and hit him on the back of the head. The mark on Ike's neck could have been made by the edge of the paddle blade. The body was dragged to the boat, and when the murderer saw the drag marks, he rubbed the paddle back and forth down the path to hide the heel marks. Then he took the body out into Big Bay and dumped it over the side hoping it would look like the deputy is assuming happened."

She paused and looked at him. "What do you think?" she asked him, "Makes sense, doesn't it?"

"Well, to tell the truth, no, not really. First, who on earth would want to kill Ike? Second, your crazy theory has a few holes. Like how come when we were there at 10 a.m. the paddle was missing but when we came back at 4:00 the paddle was back. Where was it and why bother putting it back? And where's Ike's boat?" Carl challenged her, eating an almond skorpa, the Swedish version of a biscotti. Crumbs dropped on the table as he talked.

"I don't know. There are more questions than answers, I guess. But somehow, I think the paddle is the key to what happened," Elsa said. "Do you think it's too crazy to tell Pittella?"

"Yes, it's crazy, but you should tell him anyway, and I'm sure he'll listen because he's a good guy. I want to tell him my theory about the boat, too. Speaking of which, I wonder if they found it yet. The boat, I mean," Carl said. "Maybe the Medical Examiner will even have found out if he had a heart attack or something. That's a much more realistic scenario."

"Hey, let's look at the map. Let me clean this up," Elsa said as she scraped crumbs into her palm. Carl held his cup of coffee up while she wiped and dried the table's surface.

She went to the shelf where she had put the old map they had taken from Ike's house and laid it on the table, running her hands over the fabric to smooth it out. "It seems really worn," she said. "Look, there's a piece missing at the corner. I wonder what was there."

Elsa leaned over the table with a knee on her chair to see more detail, her face hovering close to the faded map. The poor quality of the printing, the distortions of the drawings, and the lack of names made it difficult to figure out exactly what it represented. Carl looked at her, her hair falling over her cheek as she concentrated. He was taken aback at how much he loved her. She's so beautiful, he thought. Not saying a word, he leaned over and gave the back of her neck a long, luxurious kiss.

"My beautiful sleuth," Carl said. Elsa smiled at him through the waterfall of her hair.

She went to the bureau in the far corner of the room. She dug around a bit and returned to the table with a thin box of onion skin paper, a roll of Scotch cellulose tape, and a few pencils.

"What are you planning to do with the paper?" he asked between sips of coffee, "And, come to think if it, why on earth would you have a box of onion skin?"

"Remember? I got it last year so I could press some wildflowers. I made a few Christmas gifts with them, but they didn't turn out too good. Anyway, there's lots of it left and I'm going to trace a copy of the map. We need to give the map to Pittella when he comes today, but I think it's really interesting," Elsa answered. She taped pieces of the see-through paper together on the table, slid the map under them, and started to trace using a pencil.

"I'll bet you could use some help with that," Carl said, and he began to trace, starting from the opposite edge.

They worked together for quite a while, refilling their coffee cups a time or two. They had just finished putting the map and the supplies away when Bruno barked his 'there's someone here' bark. He went to the door and sat, nose to the door handle. Elsa let him out to greet the visitor.

Deputy Sheriff Harvey Pittella stretched his long legs out of the county vehicle, a burgundy Ford sedan with the St. Louis County official seal decal on the door. Bruno, who had run up to the car to meet him, wagging a friendly greeting, led him back to the cabin, up the steps, and squeezed in past Elsa who was holding the door open.

"Thanks again for all you did yesterday," Harvey said, taking off his hat and placing it on the sofa next to him. Elsa sat in the rocker facing him. Carl pulled out one of the chairs from the table and turned it to complete the triangle. Bruno lay down by the wood stove on his dog bed with an uff and a sigh.

"I know it wasn't an easy thing to do," he continued. "I hope you don't mind talking about it with me. I need to know as many details as you can remember."

Elsa offered Pittella a cup of coffee, which he gladly accepted. As she served him, she replied, "Of course, we'll be glad to tell you whatever we can."

"Okay, then. Let's start with your telling me how you started out the day."

Carl told him what they had done to get ready for their outing and how they had stopped at Ike's on the way to their picnic lunch on Indian Point. He turned to Elsa, and she picked up the description of how she noticed the paddle was missing from the porch.

"We saw it when we visited Ike last week and he said it wouldn't be ready for a while, so when we didn't see it, I thought he must have finished it quicker than he expected. I was happy for him that he had completed his paddle," she said, her eyes tearing up.

"We waited for a while on the steps but finally decided to go inside and leave the cookies I'd made for him. We wanted to leave him a note but couldn't find anything to write on. I was poking around on the shelves under the front windows looking for some paper and we found an interesting old map but no writing paper. In the end I tore a scrap from the bag of flour on the counter."

Carl picked up the story again and told Pittella how they continued to the picnic spot and, after lunch, started fishing the reefs near the Gull Islands.

"What time would you say that was?" asked the Deputy Sheriff.

"Must have been one o'clock at least by the time we started fishing," said Carl.

They were all quiet for a minute while they thought about what came next. "What happened then?" asked Pittella.

"We pulled our lures up out of the water when we went to the smaller Gull Island. We had just started slowing down as we approached to start trolling again, when Elsa saw the jacket on the shore. She pointed it out and I pulled the boat up to the right of it. We could see it was a person and we hurried over, thinking we could help," Carl continued. He lowered his head and paused. "There was nothing we could do."

Elsa sat quietly, arms wrapped tightly across her chest, feet and knees pressed together. "It was awful," she said with teary eyes, "We could tell right away it was Ike. It was his white hair floating in the water. And we recognized his clothes. It's not like he had much of a wardrobe."

"Then we decided someone should stay with the body so it wouldn't float away and…" She paused, then continued softly, "to keep the birds off him. So, Carl stayed, and I took the boat and went to Glenwood Lodge. I guess you know the rest."

"So, you were with the body for about three hours then, eh, Carl? From when you two pulled up to the island until Korchenko and I arrived."

"I guess that would be about right," Carl replied, "Although time wasn't really what I was thinking about, it really did seem to drag. The noisy gulls and the smell didn't help. They were getting pretty aggressive, too, just before Elsa and Bruno got back. Then Bruno kept them away with his barking."

"Did you see any other boats around?" Pittella asked.

"No. Not specifically. We saw a number of boats during the day but no one around the Gull Islands. We waved at a couple of fishermen heading toward Bass Lake Portage earlier. But most of the boats we saw were too far away to even wave at," Carl said, "Elsa, do you remember any boats?"

She shook her head. "More coffee?"

"Sure," both men replied. Carl held the cookie tin out to Pittella, then took a couple himself before he set it back on the table.

Elsa put the coffee pot down purposefully. She sat on the couch next to Pittella and looked at him thoughtfully.

"I need to tell you what we did after we left you yesterday. I know you told us to go home, but I suggested to Carl that we should retrieve my cookie tin, so we went to Ike's to get it," she said.

Pittella raised his eyebrows. "You did, did you? And what did you do at Ike's?" he said. "Something tells me picking up your cookie tin isn't all you did."

"Well, I know it probably wasn't kosher and all, but I was

curious about the map we had seen earlier, so we took that too. We all know Ike didn't have any relatives and it seemed too interesting to just have it get thrown out later by some strangers," she said, "Would you like to see it?"

"Yes, of course, if it's that interesting."

Elsa took it off the shelf and handed it to the Deputy Sheriff. He unfolded it, turned it over, and looked carefully at some of the printing and pencil marks. Then he folded it back up and tucked it into the chest pocket of his jacket. "I don't think it's anything important, but I'll keep it just in case it becomes relevant to the case, and in the end, it should go to whoever will end up with Ike's estate. I'll be notifying Ike's family. I know he had siblings. Some of them or their offspring might still be alive.

"Now, as Deputy Sheriff, however, I have to arrest you for breaking and entering and burglary," he paused, looking from Elsa to Carl and back. Then he broke into a smile and laughed. "But I think we have better things to do. Leave things alone next time, okay?"

Elsa breathed out loudly. "Okay. Yes, sir," she said with a smile. Carl laughed awkwardly and patted his hands on his thighs, a little embarrassed.

Pittella started to get up to leave, but Elsa reached over and put a hand on his arm. "There's more," she said holding his gaze. He sat back down.

He listened intently as she told him about the sweep marks on the path, the unfinished paddle being back on the porch, and the grass and dirt on the paddle blade. She took a deep breath and added, "I have a theory."

Pittella leaned back on the sofa and looked at Elsa for a moment. "Okay, let's hear it," he said.

She told him she thought Ike was killed with the paddle; hit on the back of the head with it, dragged to the lake, put in his boat, taken out to Big Bay, and dumped overboard. She suggested the paddle was used as a weapon and to erase the dragging heel marks.

He thought for several minutes. Then he said, "Well, that's quite a theory." He turned to Carl and asked, "What do you think about your wife's crazy idea?"

Carl didn't hesitate, "I thought it was a little crazy at first, but I don't know now, the more I think about it. The paddle was definitely missing in the morning and then it was back on the porch in the afternoon. There's got to be something to it, but I can't tell you what."

There was a silence while they all tried to find a reasonable explanation. Pittella was again about to get up, but this time Carl spoke, "And there's more. You know. I did a lot of thinking about how Ike died as I sat on the island with his body. His body there like that and the mark on his neck, it really looked like he hit his head and fell overboard and drowned. But to tell you the truth, what I couldn't figure out is how you'd hit the back of your head and fall overboard. I mean to hit the back of your neck right there," he gestured with his hand at the hairline on his own neck, "you'd have to have your feet on the far side of the boat. And if your feet were there when you fell, your body weight would drop into the middle of the boat, not over the side. And when you look at the wound, it's shaped like the edge of the paddle blade, not the double pieces of wood a gunwale is made of."

"Well, well. You two have made some interesting observations. I spoke with the Medical Examiner this morning and the only thing that's been determined so far is Ike didn't drown. There was no water in his lungs. In fact, the ME hasn't yet determined cause of death."

He stood and headed to the door. "Thanks for telling me all this. That paddle might just be important. I saw it yesterday when I went to Ike's after the ME left with the body. As soon as I get back to Tower to get my boat, I'll head over to Ike's and get the paddle. Bring it in for a closer look. Maybe some forensics."

"Oh, wait. I just remembered something," said Carl. "Wait here for a minute, will you? I took photos of Ike's body while I was waiting for help to arrive. The bruise on the back of his neck seemed to be changing as I kept watch there. I had put a new roll of film in the camera before we left home. I did take some shots from up on Indian Point while we were having our lunch earlier, but they're not anything important, so you can keep the whole roll." He had gone to the camera bag hanging in the closet as he was talking, then went to the table and unzipped the case. He took out the camera and clicked a small button on the top left to rewind the film. He lifted the handle on the top of the camera and began to crank it. He could feel the film moving inside the camera. When the handle moved with no resistance and the tiny whirring sound had stopped, he popped open the back of the camera and took out the small yellow canister marked Kodak, the undeveloped film safely inside. He dug around in the camera case, came up with a metal film container, and put the roll in it.

"Here you go," he said as he handed Pittella the film safe in its container.

"Thanks. I'll get this developed first thing in the morning.

I'm sure the Coroner will want to see the photos. Talk to you tomorrow."

He waved goodbye as he got into his car. Elsa and Carl stood at the cabin door, just as they had when he had arrived. Bruno followed the Deputy to his vehicle and was rewarded with a pat. He barked three times from the end of the driveway as the Deputy Sheriff drove away.

CHAPTER 29

When he hit Highway 77, Pittella turned on his roof-mounted rotating beacon and made it back to the marina in Tower in short order. He hopped into the department's launch and headed out to Pine Island. At Ike's, he tied up at the dock and sat for a minute absorbing details about the property. The canoe was upside down to the left of the dock, pulled up on roller logs, and flipped over in place. The same arrangement was on the right side of the dock, but no boat was pulled up there. The natural vegetation and rocks around the cabin seemed undisturbed. The Deputy figured Ike used a hand sickle to keep the tall weeds in check, like many old timers who hadn't embraced the idea of a lawn, let alone a lawnmower. He looked at the path to the cabin but couldn't see anything out of the ordinary, so he got out and stood at the end of the dock. From that angle, he could see what Elsa had been talking about, a rough sweep in small arcs back and forth across the path all the way up to where it went around back. The few weeds growing in the worn path had regained their upright position, but the pattern in the dirt was still visible.

Pittella took out a small notebook from his jacket pocket and wrote for a minute. Then he walked up the path to the corner of the house and turned around, looking back down to the dock. Nothing jumped out at him. He stood still again at the base of the steps to the open porch, then squatted to check the porch floor. He noted a lot of footprints mashed together, but nothing which looked ominous. Elsa and Carl had walked there yesterday for sure, and Ike probably had been on the porch frequently, so it was no surprise there weren't distinct marks or footprints. He examined the area around the chair where Ike had sat to whittle the paddle, lots of wood shavings and sanding dust lay around, much of it disturbed.

He saw the paddle leaning against the wall next to the chair and thought about its placement. Is that how Ike would have placed it after carving for a spell? He sat in the chair and reached back to the wall as if to lean a paddle. He stood as if to go inside and reached to the wall as if to lean the paddle upon standing. Neither scenario matched where the paddle actually was, which was to the left of the chair, too far to comfortably reach from a sitting position and not on the side where the door was.

Pittella again took out his notebook and sketched the placement of the chair and paddle and door. He nodded to himself in silent agreement with Elsa's determination that something wasn't right with the paddle.

Next, he picked it up by the shaft with his handkerchief. He scrutinized both ends. The handle end showed nothing of significance, but the paddle blade end appeared scratched and dirty, especially at the tip. There were even a few small remnants of grass at the very end, and the unfinished wood had dirt on it. There was no sign of blood or hair that he could see. He put the paddle back and went into the cabin.

He didn't like this part of the job - looking through other people's things – but knew he had to be thorough. He had done a precursory job yesterday, before Ike's death had become suspicious, hoping to find an address for a relative or someone who might know Ike's family.

Now, he perused every shelf and drawer, every nook and cranny, of which there were few, and every container of food, finding nothing out of the ordinary. When he saw the two-gallon jug of cooking oil, he wondered if Ike realized it would be rancid before he could possibly use it all up.

He even looked in the wood stove, poking around in the ashes, and moved every piece of wood in the small stack by the door. He pulled out a chair and sat, taking his time looking at every inch of wall, floor, and ceiling. Then he went into the bedroom and checked everywhere, including under the mattress and in the pockets of all the clothes. He really had not expected to find anything, but he would be remiss if he didn't look. What he did turn up did not seem to be related to the man's death. Nonetheless, he took the small stack of papers and letters with him to go through in his office.

Pittella left the cabin and checked the shed and the outhouse. The shed contained a few tools, two rusty soup cans half full of nails, a spare gas can, and a few pieces of cedar lumber leaning in the corner. Ike's tackle box and fishing rod and reel were just inside by the door. The outhouse had the usual box of lye, the expected empty soup can for spreading the powder, and a stack of toilet paper rolls. Again, nothing unusual. He went back to the porch and retrieved the paddle. As he walked down the path to the lake, he compared a few of the clear sweep marks on the path to the width of the paddle. It seemed to be about the right size. He also noticed the marks overlapped in the other direction, as if the sweeper were heading to the cabin, not away from it.

Suddenly he had a feeling he was being watched. He looked around slowly, listening for any noise. At the corner of the house, he caught a flash of red fur disappear behind the cabin – the white tip of a tail confirming it was a fox that had been watching him.

Pittella smiled. He remembered Ike's first fox. That one had adopted Ike his first year on Pine Island. Pittella saw her several times when visiting Ike during those early years. She had a distinctive white mark on the tip of one of her ears. One time, Pittella had asked him about the fox. Ike had told Harvey about his brush with death that late fall blizzard his first year at the lake when Harvey had lent him the compass. His retelling of the story downplayed the danger he had been in and focused on how the fox had encouraged him to keep going on the long trek through the deep snow. Pittella remembered lying in bed with his wife later that night when he told her the story. She was not surprised about the fox's help or presence in Ike's life.

"Ike has a broken spirit. Once he felt love and happiness, but his broken spirit could no longer bear the weight of love and happiness and so he came to the woods to wait for death. Sometimes an animal spirit feels kindred with an injured human spirit. It seems the 'waagosh' has decided to be the protector of Ike's spirit," Minnie said. "I think you will find there will always be a fox keeping watch over Ike until it is his time to leave this world for the spirit world. And there they will walk together."

He remembered that some years later, Ike told him the fox had brought one of her kits to Ike's yard. The young fox often visited with its mother. Then one day, it came alone, and he never saw the mother with the white mark again. The young one kept visiting him, though, and did the same as its mother, always keeping a distance and disappearing for long periods of time. And again, a few years later, the second fox brought a single kit to Ike's yard and disappeared when the kit was full grown. When Harvey told Minnie, she said, "Of course. The moon must set for the sun to rise. For all things, a cycle exists."

Pittella guessed this was yet another generation of Ike's guardian fox which had been watching him as he searched Ike's property.

Suddenly a powerful feeling of knowing overcame him. He stopped and closed his eyes, searching his brain for what it was he felt he knew. Was there a clue about Ike's murder hiding in his subconscious? Had he learned something here he couldn't yet put his finger on?

He stood there with the paddle in his hand and closed his eyes. A vision of the fox walking away presented itself at the forefront of his perception. Finally, it came to him. He knew with certainty that Ike was at peace - despite the violent death he had experienced, he was at peace. Whether or not the spirit world or the fox had anything to do with it, he knew, beyond a shadow of a doubt, Ike died content. He had never tempted fate. In fact, he had been a cautious, careful man, but he was prepared for his life to be over at any point in time. Now that Pittella thought about it, the feeling of the acceptance of inevitable death had been evident with Ike since the first time he met him. It wasn't until just now, however, that Harvey could comprehend the pain he had sensed in his reclusive friend.

He felt a sadness so heavy it weighed down his shoulders, and he wept standing there, resting on the paddle. Finally, he opened his eyes and wiped the tears away with the back of his hand. He continued down the dock to his boat and went to search for Ike's killer.

CHAPTER 30

It would still be light for several more hours, so the Deputy headed to Glenwood Lodge. He needed to see Ike's boat. As he tied up at the lodge's main dock, he heard someone call his name.

"Harvey. Over here."

Phil Newsom waved from inside the fish cleaning house, knife in hand. Pittella walked up the gentle slope to the small building and went in the screen door. There were a couple of empty buckets near the spigot right inside the door. The floor was a concrete slab with a big drain in the middle under the table in the center. The walls from waist high up were screened to keep the flies out while fish were cleaned. Newsom was working on a stringer of small to medium-sized walleye, moving the knife expertly between bones and flesh, then skin and flesh. He tossed the fillets into a bucket of clear water under the tall wood table and the guts into another.

"Our customers from the big city don't want to clean their own fish," he said quietly to the Deputy. "But I shouldn't complain 'cause I charge 'em an arm and a leg to do it for 'em." He smiled and continued, "You want a cold drink or a beer. Help yourself from the cooler over there."

Pittella shook his head as thanks for the offer and said, "Nope. I'd just like to ask you a few questions about yesterday and then I got to take a look at Ike's boat."

"Sure," Newsom said, "You mind if I keep cleaning these here fish, eh? Got about four to go."

The Deputy pulled one of the pair of high stools away from the wall and sat, his heels hooked on a rung. He asked Newsom a series of questions about the past few days and who his current guests were. He wrote a few things in his notebook and then asked Newsom about how Ike was recently. Glenwood Lodge was the closest resort to Ike's, and the Deputy assumed Ike would have gone there if he needed anything on short notice.

Most resorts had a store of sorts. Usually, it consisted of a large, glass-doored refrigerator with milk, eggs, and butter and a shelf unit with a few canned goods, toilet paper, matches, 6-12 mosquito repellent, soap, and bread. At Glenwood Lodge, the store was in the back corner of the big lodge room. There was also a beer and pop cooler. The ice cooler was around back on the outside of the building.

Newsom said Ike seldom came over to the Lodge. He stopped the knife in mid-air, thinking. "I think he came over a couple times this year," he said, going back to gutting the last fish. "Don't think there was anything out of the ordinary with him. He grumped about the noise of the construction but that was the last time I saw him."

Newsom finished the last fillet and scraped the table surface debris into the slop bucket. "There," he said, "that was a nice catch. Gotta clean this up and it might get kind of sloppy. You better wait outside." After Pittella stepped out, Newson filled another bucket with water, splashed some on the table, and scrubbed it with a big stiff-bristled brush. He splashed and scrubbed until he was satisfied it was clean. Then he sloshed a couple buckets of water across the floor.

"C'mon. I'll show you where Ike's boat is," Newsom said. They walked together past the main dock in front of the lodge and over to the long T-shaped docks farther along the shore near the boat launch ramp. Six open fishing boats were tied up along the length of the dock. Each boat was painted white with 'Glenwood Lodge' just below the gunwale on each side in pretty red letters and a large number painted at the bow - one through eight, one for each rental cabin. The two missing boats were being used by guests who were out fishing, explained Newsom.

Ike's boat was tied up there too. It was a dull green color, painted the same as his cabin, Pittella realized. Newsom called the Deputy over to one of the rental boats and pointed out a large smudge of green paint on the outside near the middle of the gunwale. Newsom said, "Just look at that mess. Ike didn't varnish his boat and the flat house paint he used rubbed off on my boat. I know it's going to ruin the lettering when I try to get the green off there."

"Well, the county will reimburse you, you know, because you were acting on behalf of the Sheriff's department. So just add it to the bill you're going to give us for the use of your boats and the refreshments you supplied," said Pittella. "You're the one who found Ike's boat, right?"

"Yup. Over in the bay on the north end of Ely Island. It was floating free, hadn't quite made it to shore yet. I pulled up next to it and held it up close to my boat in order to see if there was anything to see inside it. Didn't know the damned green paint rubbed off that like. Didn't even know it happened at the time. Didn't see nothing funny in the boat, so I grabbed the front rope and towed it back here."

"Too bad about that," agreed the Deputy.

"Funny thing though. I can't figure out how this other boat got the green paint on it too, 'cause I swear I didn't bump into anything when I tied it up just like it is now." Newsom showed the Deputy one of the other rental boats tied further out on the dock. It had the same large green smudge on its side. They stood next to each other silently for a minute, then Newsom said, "Well, I'll leave you to it. I've got to get those fillets wrapped and in the freezer. Stop back up at the lodge before you go, eh?"

"Okay, thanks. Will do," replied Pittella without looking up. He was still staring at the paint, letting his thoughts absorb this development without making any conclusions. There could be a logical explanation for the second boat's smudge, but he couldn't think of any way for the two smudges to look so much alike except from rubbing up against Ike's boat. The one rental boat couldn't have transferred the green paint to another rental boat because of their shape. The paint had to have come from a gunwale, not the side of another boat. Well, he thought, unless there's another fool out there painting his boat with the same green house paint, both of those rental boats rubbed up against Ike's.

He returned to Ike's boat and looked down into it for a minute before getting in. He leaned over and closely examined the gunwale along its entire perimeter and found, to his surprise, the paint had been scratched dull in certain spots on both sides of the boat.

Other than that, nothing seemed out of the ordinary. There was no fishing gear. The oars were on the seats. Most people didn't keep their oars in the oarlocks because they rattled and made too much noise when the motor was running. Pittella checked out the motor's gas tank and the two-gallon spare gas can. Plenty of gas. Not much of a motor - hardly big enough even for such a small boat, thought Pittella. It was the same old two-and-a-half horse Champion Ike had bought his first summer. He checked behind the seat, and yes, there was the requisite coffee can for bailing water but nothing else. 'For Pete's sake, Jake,' thought Pittella. 'You didn't even have a seat cushion or a life jacket.'

The Deputy stood in front of the back seat facing forward. The curved ribs of the fourteen-foot boat were exposed, no floor to make it easy to stand, he thought. He contemplated how he would have to fall in order to hit the back of his neck, where he would have to stand for that to happen. He moved his feet on the boat's ribs, rocking his ankles around to see if he'd lose balance. Hmm, it doesn't seem to make much difference because the ribs are so close together, thought Pittella.

He moved forward in the boat between the middle and the front seat and repeated the exercise. After a few more tries, he figured it was nearly impossible to hit the back of your neck in that little boat. He came to the conclusion you couldn't get far enough away from one side to fall backward and hit your head on it. He examined the gunwale again carefully one last time, but found no evidence that anything had hit it recently.

When he was done, he walked back up to the lodge and went in, screen door slamming behind him. Newsom looked across the big room from behind the counter and said, "Want a pop before your trip back to Tower?"

"Nope. But thanks. And you've been very helpful, Phil. I'd appreciate it if you could keep Ike's boat for a while just like it is. At some point we might need to take a closer look at it. Not sure there's anything more we need to do with it, but it would be good if no one took it out or anything," Pittella said. "I'll make sure to push your reimbursement through quick, so get your bill over to me as soon as you can. I know with only eight cabins, you're not bringing in the big bucks like the new place over there on Daisy Bay."

"Yeah, well. We like the quiet over here on this part of the lake," Newsom replied. "Don't be a stranger, eh, Harvey?"

Pittella knew he was referring to the fact that Daisy Bay now had two popular bars with bands playing several nights a week. The new one, The Idle Hour, just opened in June.

"Oh, one more thing. Do you know who has been using boat number six lately?"

"Sure. Number six goes with cabin number six. A guy up from Florida is renting it for several weeks. His name is Morgan. Just him, no family or anything. Seems like a stand-up guy. Dresses kinda prissy. You know, soft Italian loafers and fancy shirts. Keeps to himself. Oh, he's friends with that guy building the big cabin over on Pine Island. You know the place, don't ya?"

"Yeah, sure. Thanks a lot for the help, Phil. So long. Take it easy," said Pittella As he left to head home to Tower, his thoughts were as low as the sun hanging over Big Bay.

CHAPTER 31

The next day, Carl and Elsa sat down to eat lunch at the table – tomato soup, ham sandwiches, and two bottles of Schmidt beer. They had spent the morning doing odd chores around the cabin. Bruno, roused from his nap on the braided rug covering the middle of the floor, eyed his people sitting at the table, watchful for drops. Carl and Elsa talked about the past two days' events and then fell silent, thinking about the loss of their friend.

Taking the last bite of her sandwich, Elsa said, "I was really nervous when Harvey was here yesterday. I know he's a friend, but he's a Sheriff, for Pete's sake. He could have arrested us or something. I'm glad we told him, though. Not telling him would have bothered me."

"Oh, don't be ridiculous, honey. I know we shouldn't have gone to Ike's, but we didn't really do anything wrong."

Elsa went to the shelf where she had put the copy of the map and, after moving the dishes aside, laid it on the table. She ran her hands over the onion skin to smooth it out. "It sure seemed to be really old, that map," she said. "Remember there was a piece missing up at the corner? I wonder what was there."

Carl moved a finger along the printed outline of the lake, pointing out a few landmarks he recognized. "Here's our place," he said, "Hey, it shows the gold mine blasting sites on our backland. That's what those strange symbols are! They're blasting sites."

"You know, it shows a lot of those same symbols in different places all over the map," she said thoughtfully. "Look how many there are here on Pine Island," pointing to the area around Canfield Bay Portage, Elsa continued.

"So, do you think this is really a map from the 1860s, when people actually thought there was gold around here?" Carl asked her. "We know they never found any real gold. It was all iron pyrites. It's hard to believe a little bit of fool's gold made a lot of rich men poor back then."

"Yeah. That's what I read in that local history book I took out of the library a few weeks ago, too. There was a lot of hype, then no gold. So many people came at up here with gold fever, I think because the guy who explored up here and supposedly found the gold was a famous geologist who worked for the government. I forget his name. There was another town just to the east of Tower with, I can't remember how many hundreds of residents, several hundred anyway, even before Tower was built. There were shops, and saloons, a post office, and all kinds of stuff. The town was named Winton."

"Where is it?" asked Carl.

"It's totally gone now. Just think, a whole town built and abandoned in just a few short years. No gold was ever found because the geologist never wrote down exactly where the original samples had been taken and when he came back the second year, he couldn't find where he had been. Poor guy, he was disgraced by the whole thing and lost his reputation and job. It didn't stop all these other people from coming up here to try, though. It's strange to think that was only eighty years ago."

"Yeah, that is amazing. Maybe this map is from that time because Tower isn't on it, but Winton is."

"Maybe this is that geologist's map. Oh, I remembered his name. It was Eames, I think. The guy I read about. So, what do you think these pencil markings over here mean?" Elsa asked, pointing at a section of the map extending over most of the eastern end of Pine Island.

"I have no clue," said Carl

They both thought for a while, looking intently at the map in that area. They talked more about the searching for gold and what life would be like in this rugged country back then. How much work it would have been and how frustrating, too. They talked about how people would come to distrust one another and become paranoid about protecting their claims. Jealous of the other guy. Constantly fearful of being robbed or worse. How dangerous the blasting would have been. They wondered how many men had died, either murdered or by accident, during those rough times. They talked until it was very late. Finally, they had tea and a snack and went to bed.

As Carl turned out the bedside light, he said, "You know that small 'x' on the map? What do you think it means?"

"Well, if I were marking up a map, I'd only put an 'x' on it to show where the buried treasure is," replied Elsa.

"Well, that settles it then. It can't be gold. It must be buried treasure."

They laughed together about it. Then they laughed some more when Elsa suggested he look for her buried treasure.

CHAPTER 32

In the morning, Elsa was up first and, clanking the kitchen utensils around, seemed very determined to wake up her sleeping husband.

"What's up, honey?" asked Carl, finally acknowledging there was no more sleep to be had and getting out of bed. Breakfast was already on the table.

"I want to go to the 'x'," she said, opening the onion skin map and firmly pointing at the 'x' spot, "It must mean something. Something important!"

"Geez! You sure are hot on this," Carl answered. Coming around behind her to hug her and bury his face in her hair for a moment before looking at the map, he said, "But I have to admit, I'm kind of curious, too. So okay, let's go exploring." They ate breakfast and stacked the dishes in the sink for later.

They figured the 'x' on the map was inland on Pine Island, north of Big Bay and east of the entrance to Canfield Bay. It appeared to be close to the new cabin construction site, but they weren't sure if it was on Stark's land or not.

They debated about how to proceed. There were three options. The least desirable was to go to Stark, show him the map, and ask permission to tramp around in his woods. The second was to blatantly go ashore between Ike's and Stark's and head into the woods and, if they ran into anyone, give a cover story of checking out how the blueberry crop was coming. The third was to dock at Ike's and try to find a deer path back through the woods to where they thought the 'x' was. That option seemed to be the longest shot because the path would be deep in the woods, and the 'x' looked like it was closer to the shore.

Finally, they decided none of those was a good idea. Instead, being straightforward and truthful was the best tact. Well, almost truthful, they agreed, would be even better. They would go talk to their new friend, Mr. Stark. They wouldn't show him the map. They decided the quest for blueberries was a viable ruse for them. They would ask permission to walk around his land to look for blueberries. They didn't think he was the berry-picking type and probably wouldn't care if they got picked or who did the picking. Carl made a mental note to take a compass.

* * *

For the people who loved the Northwoods, berry picking, and blueberry picking in particular, was as much of a passion as fishing. During the few weeks of August when the blueberries were ripe, families would take buckets and pails and boxes - anything that was easy to carry and didn't tip over easily - and head to the woods for the day. It was common for people to check how they were coming along to see if it would be a bountiful season. Since the berry crop depended on the vagaries of the weather, how many berries there would be and when they would be ripe was different each year.

Some years, when other food sources were lacking, bears would tear up the blueberry bushes early in the season, looking for even the smallest unripe berry. Some years the weather was too dry, and the crop would be sparse. Then again, some years, there would be so many berries the ground looked blue.

Locals always wanted to know what to expect in August so they could plan when to pick and can the berries. Starting in early July, a car parked on the side of the road or a boat pulled up on shore in the middle of nowhere probably meant the owners were in the woods checking the blueberry patches to see how the berries were coming along. The locals knew the best rocky outcroppings near stands of big pines where the berry bushes and reindeer moss grew the best. Sometimes the patches would be an hour's walk back into the deep woods. Some even had names. There were no property boundaries when it came to berry picking. It was first come, first serve.

In the cafes and bars, people would talk about which patches would be most productive and when, just like they discussed where the fish were biting. They would share information about what they had scouted out, but they kept the details of where and when they planned to pick close to their chest. If it was a good season and everything fell into place, most families would only have to go picking for one day. Even in a year when there was a bumper crop, choosing the right day to go was crucial. Too early and the picking wouldn't be good – too many small or unripe berries made for inefficient picking and long hours cleaning out the duds. A day late and the patch would have been picked clean already, either by bears or people, sometimes both.

The one thing that really angered blueberry pickers was to come onto a patch that sloppy pickers had ruined. There was a right way and a wrong way to pick. The sloppy pickers, who were usually tourists, damaged the bushes by breaking the branches; or they grabbed berries willy-nilly, leaving bushes half full of ripe berries which made twice the work for the next guy to fill his bucket; or they picked everything on the bush, including the ones yet to ripen, which was equally harmful.

Carl owned a hand-held picker his brother had sent him from Sweden, where blueberry picking was equally important. It was shaped like a large flour scoop, with the back of it being a cloth pouch to hold the picked berries. The mouth of it had long, closely set tines which pulled through the bush like a comb, from the lower branches upward. The picker held at least a quart of berries, but it took almost everything off the bush, ripe and unripe, even some leaves, so Carl didn't use his picker. Besides, picking only the ripe berries was the truly honorable way to do it, leaving the small and unripe ones for the bears or for someone else to pick in a few days when they would be ready. Only if it was late in the season and all the berries were ripe, would Carl use his picker.

No one picked blueberries alone because it was easy to get disoriented and lost when you bent over for long periods, concentrating on berry picking. It was not uncommon for even groups of people to get lost, so the pickers usually chose a larger patch where they could pick for a long time. If they did have to spread out, one person would pick around the starting spot where the picnic baskets and larger berry containers were. That person would keep tabs on everyone as they returned to base to empty their full pails. They also kept watch for bears and sounded the alarm if anyone spotted one. Carl and Elsa picked together, but they each carried a shrill whistle in case they became separated. The whistles helped them find each other in the woods but also worked as bear deterrents because bears don't like loud or shrill noises.

* * *

Elsa packed some lunch staples – hardtack, a chunk of cheese, a length of summer sausage, and a couple of beers. The usual picnic necessities, like matches and a knife to cut the summer sausage, were already in the basket. Her lightweight jacket didn't have pockets large enough for the map, so she put it in the basket too. They were ready to go in no time.

As their boat approached the construction site, they could see that the workers had completed the concrete foundation, and the joists for the main floor had been laid. Carpenters were framing the walls. The whine of saws and the pounding of hammers sounded loud out over the water. Two guys were laying flagstones for a patio across the long front of the cabin. Off to the side, the backhoe was still working on the septic system.

"Ike wouldn't have liked all this noise, that's for sure," Carl said under his breath as they approached Stark's dock.

"Hello," Stark hollered out to them as he came out of his tent, "Come on up."

Elsa and Carl tied up the boat and made their way up to the large tent. Stark invited them in. Carl told Bruno to stay outside, and the big dog lay down with a thump right where he was standing. The solid canvas wall on the lakeside had been rolled up to reveal a full-length screened wall, a beautiful view, and a refreshing breeze. They were greeted warmly by Stark, who then turned to a man standing off to the side.

"Morgan, these are some folks from Chicago who have a cabin over on Daisy Bay. We met earlier this summer," said Stark. Everyone introduced themselves with handshakes and pleasantries, and they all sat down in the canvas camp chairs arranged in a circle on the Oriental rug.

Stark offered refreshments, but Elsa and Carl declined, saying it was too early for them and they had recently finished a late breakfast. "Morgan is the original developer of this place. My father's old partner back when they were going to create a vacation paradise up here in Canfield Bay," Stark said, "I invited him to come up and see what I'm building here after all these years." He smiled at Morgan and continued, "He's not much of an outdoorsman, though, and declined to rough it out here in one of my tents, so he's got a rental cabin over at Glenwood Lodge."

Morgan looked familiar to Elsa, but she hadn't been able to place where she'd seen him. With the mention of Glenwood Lodge, suddenly she knew. He was in the group of people eavesdropping when she made the call to the Deputy Sheriff. But she also realized something even more surprising, this was the man who had been staring at Ike during the parade in Tower.

Morgan, a gaunt man of about sixty, answered with a flat smile, "No, can't say I've ever cared that much for the Northwoods, but I couldn't say no to my godson's invitation. I've only been to Lake Vermilion once before and that was a long time ago and not under the best circumstances."

"Morgan was here when my dad disappeared. He was the last one to give up on the search, too. The authorities wanted to quit after a few days, but he convinced them to keep looking, at least for a few more days," said Stark, "and for that I'll always be thankful. As least I know everyone tried their hardest."

Turning to Morgan, Stark said, "I told them all about what a lousy son-of-a-bitch my dad was. You know how I feel about him."

After giving Stark a patronizing look, he turned to Carl and Elsa to explain. "As much as I've tried to encourage my godson to forgive and forget, to move on, you know. He can't seem to get past being abandoned. He was so very young when it all happened. At the time, I couldn't believe Nathan would have embezzled money and fled to Canada. I thought he was a good man. He was my partner for over ten years, but we lived next door to each other most of our lives, so I knew him for many, many years."

"That must have been terrible for you both. I don't mean to be indiscreet but isn't it possible he died or drowned in the storm," said Elsa.

"Well, it's doubtful in my mind, because Nathan was such an avid outdoorsman. He would have been prepared for any circumstance in the wilderness, no doubt. And to tell the truth, even if he did die in the storm, it doesn't change the fact he embezzled the money and ruined so many lives."

"That's right. He's dead to me either way. He left me and my mother either way. Actually, I'd like to think he did die in the storm," said Stark with a pout.

"The lake certainly has its share of tragedies. Did you hear Ike Iverson drowned just the other day? He had the little cabin just east of here," said Carl.

"No, I didn't hear. I've been too busy with my project to pay attention to the locals," said Stark.

"Yes, I did hear about it. That must have been traumatic for you to find him like that," said Morgan, "Did you know the man?"

Carl looked puzzled, "How did you know we found him?"

"Mr. Morgan was there when I made the call to the Deputy Sheriff from Glenwood Lodge, weren't you, Mr. Morgan?" Elsa said.

"Yes, and I helped with the search for his boat later that day, although it wasn't me who found it. I think it was the lodge owner who did," Morgan said.

"That was kind of you. Yes, we knew him pretty well. We'll miss him. He was such an interesting person," said Carl. "How long will you be staying here at the Lake?"

"I'm not sure. Stark is trying to convince me to buy a piece of land and build here too, but I'm not inclined to do so. The mosquitoes, the lack of amenities, just aren't for me. I've become quite accustomed to Florida. I like the warm weather and my game of golf too much, and I don't fish."

"Well," said Elsa shifting in her seat to change the subject, "we actually came to ask you something." She smiled at Stark and continued. "We wondered if you would mind if we left our boat at your dock and explore your backland a little. We'd like to look for blueberries."

"Huh. That's a new one on me," Stark said, looking puzzled. "I guess that would be all right. I own about sixty acres back in there, but I couldn't begin to tell you where it starts and ends. I'm not really too keen on people tramping all over my property, but..." He looked like he wanted to say no but could not think of a logical reason to.

Elsa and Carl looked at each other and laughed.

"Sorry for laughing," Carl said, "but I think you'll find when it comes to blueberry picking time, your property ownership won't matter a hoot. People have been berry picking on Pine Island for years and years. But take heart, it only lasts a short while and most people are very respectful of the land where they pick and certainly wouldn't pull up to your dock, so you won't be bothered by them. I guess we were being just a little forward thinking we could leave our boat here since you were so friendly the other day."

Stark chuckled, too. "Oh, I see. So, you're telling me I shouldn't shoot any trespassers right now? Glad you clued me in. I guess I wasn't aware of the local traditions about berry picking. Well, I don't mind if you tie up at my dock, you seem like decent people, but I wouldn't want anyone else to. We've had so much trouble with vandals creating problems with the construction, I'd shoot anybody who I thought was behind it," Stark said.

"Well, I can understand you'd be upset. Still, your cabin looks like it's coming along. Are the problems still happening?" said Carl.

"Up until late last week, every few days there would be something. We're at least three weeks behind and I've lost thousands of dollars in materials. At one point, I considered giving up for this year. It will be a stretch to get the roof finished before I have to leave for home. The latest prank was drilling holes in the roofing shingles. Can you believe it? Someone drilled one-inch holes right in the middle of each bundle. The guy was so devious we didn't even hear him. It was done during the night, and he never made any noise so it couldn't have been done with a power tool. It must have taken an hour at least to ruin so many bundles. I hope his arm fell off from fatigue. Fortunately, he didn't get to them all, but it still is a huge loss of money and a time setback because we have to reorder from Duluth. I am so angry about it."

"Wow, this guy is serious about not wanting this cabin to be built!" said Elsa, "And you really don't have any idea why someone wouldn't want you building here?"

"Like I said before, no, not really. A lot of people lost money when my dad disappeared, but that was twenty years ago," Stark replied, "I think it must be mischievous young punks, probably Indians. I've talked to the Deputy Sheriff about it, but I don't think he's done much or even cares."

Elsa and Carl stood to go. "Well, we'll go berry hunting, if you don't mind. Thanks for letting us use your dock. We'll be sure to give you some berries if we find any to pick later in the summer," said Elsa.

They all went outside together. Carl, Elsa, and Bruno started walking up the hill to head into the woods behind the new cabin when Elsa stopped suddenly. "I forgot something in the boat," she said and trotted back down to the dock. Grey went back inside with a wave, but Morgan had already begun walking toward his rental boat from Glenwood Lodge tied up at the dock opposite the Swanson's.

Elsa and Morgan arrived on the dock at the same time and made cordial gestures at one another. Elsa was a little flustered from running down the hill. As she got into the boat, she realized Morgan would see her take the map out of the picnic basket. She awkwardly turned her body so it was between Morgan and the basket and quickly took out the map and put it in the armpit of her jacket. She hoped he didn't see what she had done but she had no way of knowing for sure. She grabbed the kitchen paring knife from the basket at the last minute when she realized that otherwise it would look like she hadn't retrieved anything.

Morgan looked directly at her with no expression when he offered her a hand to get from the boat onto the dock. She couldn't give him the hand with knife, so she tried to ignore him. But he leaned down and took her elbow to help her up. There was nothing she could do when the folded onion skin map dropped onto the dock from under her jacket. She quickly bent to pick it up, folding it smaller to hide what it really was. "Got to try to find the same patch as last year. It was great picking," she said, waving the folded map back and forth, hoping to make it hard to see. She hurried past him off the dock and up the path. She could feel his stare on her back.

CHAPTER 33

Carl and Bruno were waiting at the back side of the construction where the woods loomed dark. Elsa joined them, and they walked along the edge until they saw a narrow break in the trees – a deer path. Deer don't like to get poked in the eye any more than people do, so they use the same paths as much as possible to go between places, like favorite grassy areas, stands of cedar trees that they love to eat, and easy access to the water's edge for drinking. While deer paths are not easy passage for people and they often meander in the random directions, they are better than just striking out into the woods.

Pine Island, along with almost all the land surrounding Lake Vermilion, had been deforested fifty years before. The trees Carl and Elsa walked through were new growth, aspen, birch, different kinds of conifers, ash, and lots of underbrush. They pushed their way up the hill, which didn't even appear to be a hill yet. Yes, the ground slanted upward, but with trees all around, it was hard to tell. Rocks were everywhere, and sometimes the path became steep, so Carl and Elsa had to use their hands to climb. Bruno ran ahead, unfazed by the incline. Then finally, the sloping eased, and room-size spaces opened. That trees grew up on top of the hill was amazing considering most of the ground wasn't earthen at all but was a single mass of rock. It was like walking on the bellies of reclining dinosaurs, a massive mound of motley grey granite. The small crevasses in the rock, like wrinkles, were filled with dirt made over time from decomposed leaves and pine needles. Enough rain was caught in them to grow small scraggly bushes, some wild roses, some gooseberries, some just scraggly grasses, but most importantly, lots of blueberry bushes. Reindeer moss and lichen spread across the barren rock like blemishes on the giant abdomen.

"Whew," said Carl, "That was a climb." They sat for a minute on a couple of small boulders next to each other on the surface of the enormous rock mass. Elsa had given Carl the map to put in his pocket when they started up the hill. Now he opened the map and refolded it to show the part of Pine Island where they were. They pondered how far they had come and where exactly on the map they were sitting. Where exactly was the 'x,' they wondered. They made a plan, taking a hint from whoever had made the pencil lines on the map, to walk in a straight line for a set distance, then turn left for a certain number of steps, then turn left again to walk back parallel to the first line. This made an elongated zigzag pattern, which would cover all the ground if they could just stay parallel. Elsa would concentrate on counting their steps, and Carl would closely pay attention to the compass.

They regretted not bringing the picnic basket and decided they should get moving. First, they made a pile of small rocks pointing the way back down the hill to Stark's. Next, they looked around for a particular size rock, long, narrow, flat ones. There were a few odd rocks here and there, cracked off larger ones by many cycles of freezing and thawing. They filled all their pants and jacket pockets with the small stones to use as markers at the corners of their search area. Carl got his bearings with the compass and started walking. Elsa followed, counting steps out loud. It was slow going over the rough terrain, not following a deer path. Bruno constantly ran ahead, then back to his people. He was interested in so many wonderful smells but knew he had to be on alert, so he stayed close. They had to take their time, too, to look around for whatever it was they were looking for, considering they didn't have a clue what that was. After half an hour, they had made two loops of the pattern and stopped to reconsider their plan.

"I don't know," said Carl, "this is pretty hard work. Are you sure you want to continue this fool's errand?"

"We can't give up yet. It should be a little easier once we get past this area here on the steep part of the hill."

"Okay, then. How about this?" said Carl after a minute of thought, "Let's keep at it for another hour and a half. By then we'll really be hungry and thirsty anyway. We'll end this zigzag on the western end of a loop and cut back to our starting point. Sound like a plan?"

"Yep. Sounds like a plan," Elsa said. And they took off again, counting, stopping to look around, and so forth.

After another half hour or so, they had, as Elsa thought they would, come away from the hill so they no longer had to go up and down it with each loop. This was easier going, flat land with typical trees and bushes. They came to a marshy section and had to walk around the end of it, veering from their straight line. They argued when they couldn't agree on where to go from there. Finally, Elsa gave in, so they skipped the whole section past the end of the marsh and kept going, skirting the mushy ground altogether. Bruno checked it out and came back to them with muddy paws and a bunch of burrs.

They rested for a few minutes, sitting on some downed trees in their path. "Sure, wish we had a beer," said Carl.

"We're almost done. Sorry I didn't grab the whole picnic basket when I had the chance, instead of just that stupid knife," said Elsa. Carl always carried a pocketknife, so the kitchen knife was not only unnecessary but awkward to carry. They had taken a thick piece of birch bark and folded it around the knife after first sliding the blade into two slits in the bark. At least it wasn't cutting into his back pocket. Farther on, she noticed an odd piece of wood sticking upright out of the ground. It almost seemed like a grave marker, Elsa thought. She walked over to it and said aloud, "It is a headstone! But not a stone!"

Carl looked up, confused. He had been concentrating on the map and hadn't heard what she said. "What is it, honey?" He joined her as she knelt to get a closer look.

The cross was made of one piece of wood and stuck out of the ground about two and a half feet. A pile of rocks held it steadfast. The horizontal arms were very short, only about ten inches wide. It was hardwood, as evidenced by the fine grain in it. "There's something carved on it," said Elsa, rubbing her finger across the surface. "It's an R, then an I, and another R. Then there are some numbers, which are…" she leaned even closer and scratched away some moss. "7,1,2,1,9,2,8". She stood and brushed off her knees. "Oh, I get it. It's 'R.I.P. July 12, 1928'."

Carl looked at his wife with his jaw dropped. "What are you, some kind of clairvoyant? How did you know we should be looking here?" He shook his head. "I just can't believe this. One day you spot a floating body. And now you find a hidden grave." He came close and hugged her to him.

Elsa pulled back. Her face was somber. "Let's look at the map again. Do you think this spot is the 'x'? This is really creepy," she said.

They sat back down on the log and opened the map. They talked it over and decided that if their counting and calculations were a bit off, this could indeed be the spot marked by the 'x.'

"What should we do now?" she asked Carl.

"Let's just sit here and think for a minute," Carl answered. And they did. Bruno joined them, stretching out on his side near them.

Finally, Elsa said, "I'm going to make a copy of the carving." She walked around in the trees until she found what she was looking for. During their first camping trip to Lake Vermilion, she had noticed the surface of the inner layers of birch bark bruise easily, leaving marks wherever it was scratched. She had written little love notes to Carl using a pencil-sized stick and thin birch bark.

Now she looked for a fallen birch with a large piece of loose bark. There are many, many pale pink layers between the outer paper-white layers and the thick tan inner layer. With all layers intact, birch bark is exceptionally strong and stiff, as the Native Americans were well aware. But Elsa wanted a thin inner layer. She tore off the entire piece from the fallen tree and had Carl help her carefully tear away the heavy outer layers. She peeled off layers of the soft pink inner bark, thinning it from each side until it was very thin, like a sheet of paper. Then she asked Carl for the kitchen knife from his pocket. She went over to the cross and held the thin bark against it.

"Help me here, please, Carl," she said.

He held the bark firmly as she rubbed the spine of the knife back and forth around the entire area that was carved. She had done this before when she and her parents had visited Westminster Abbey in London when she was a girl. Vendors in the plaza sold pieces of charcoal and sheets of paper to the tourists to make 'rubbings' of bas reliefs inside the church. With her parents' help holding the paper in place, she had carefully rubbed the image of a ghostly skeleton in long robes holding a sword engraved on a sarcophagus in the Abbey's huge crypt. They had the rubbing framed when they got home from their trip. It was one of their favorite souvenirs and hung in their front hall.

The birch bark rubbing worked just fine, and after a few minutes, they had a clear imprint of the carving, along with the general outline of the cross. Folding the bark would ruin it, she knew, so she rolled it tightly with one of the thicker layers of bark she had peeled off before and put it down the front of her blouse, which was tucked into her corduroy cargo pants.

Before they left the grave in the woods, they foraged around the nearby trees and found a few dried Y-shaped branches they could break easily. Carl took each one and broke off the stem of the Y and left the two other legs as long as possible, making a large wishbone shape. They made five of them and set them on horizontal branches of trees in a circle around the grave. A few had to be adjusted to even out the weight of the two legs. These out-of-place branches would jump out at someone looking for them but would most likely not be noticed by anyone else. They would rock in the wind, perhaps, but not fall off. They placed one of the long narrow rocks at the base of the trees, pointing toward the grave.

They made their way back to the pile of rocks they had built as a marker at the start of their quest. Then they headed down the hill toward the lake and Stark's cabin site. They grabbed some sample blueberry twigs as they left the rocky ledge as evidence of their venture.

Morgan was nowhere to be seen, but Stark came out of the tent when he saw them through the screen wall and shouted a greeting at them. They wanted to avoid him and headed to the dock. They waved a 'thank you,' waved the twigs, and hopped in their boat. Bruno took his place on the pile of life jackets, and they headed home.

Elsa cut a few slices of cheese and sausage and handed them to Carl as he steered the motor. She ate a few, too, then opened a beer, took a few gulps, and passed it to Carl. She turned around and moved to the front seat and let the wind blow in her face the rest of the way home. She felt she needed to clear her mind, and the wind was refreshing.

When they got home, they had a real lunch of leftover meatballs and spaghetti Elsa heated up in a saucepan. Bruno didn't even look twice at the food but just plopped down on his bed, exhausted. As they ate, they looked at the rubbing held down at the end of the table with a book on each corner to uncurl it.

"Do you think it is really a grave? I mean, not a pet grave but a real grave?" Elsa asked.

"Well, the size of the marker is pretty over the top for a dead cat," said Carl, "And why 'R.I.P.' and not 'Spot' or whatever its name was, if it was a pet?"

"Then again, why not a real name if it was a person?" she said.

They talked about the interaction with Stark and the new person, Morgan. Elsa told Carl about him helping her out of the boat and that he had seen the map.

"The way he looked at me when he saw it gave me the creeps."

"You know," Carl said, "there was something about that guy I just didn't like. I have no idea what it was, but I sure wouldn't have him as my lawyer."

"I think we need to tell Pittella what we found. If it's a person buried up there, someone needs to know about it. If it's a pet, well, we'll have egg on our faces. What do you think?"

Carl was staring at the date and finally replied absentmindedly, "Sure. We should tell him."

Elsa looked at him. "What're you thinking?"

"That date. It's twenty years ago. Isn't that when Stark said his father disappeared?"

"You're right. It is. But Stark disappeared. No one ever said he died. Maybe he left but didn't get a chance to come back for the money he had buried there."

"That doesn't make any sense. Why would you put R.I.P. and a date, especially a current date, on a marker for buried money?" Carl said.

"Yes, I suppose I'd mark buried money in a different, less obvious way," said Elsa, "But I would mark the map with an 'x'."

"What if it's Stark himself who is buried there. What if

someone killed him for the money he embezzled and buried him there?"

"And the big question is, why did Ike have the map?"

"Hmm. I really think we should tell the Deputy. We have too many questions. This may be more than we want to chew, even if we could bite it off, to paraphrase an old saying," Carl said, "Why don't we drive into town and talk to Pittella?"

CHAPTER 34

It was late afternoon by the time they got to Tower. Bruno enjoyed the ride with his head out the back windows. The Frazer had lots of room for him with the back seat folded down. He went from one side to the other, taking in all the passing scents. A beautiful day for a dog and humans, too.

They drove straight to the City Hall building, parked in a visitor's spot, and walked through the lobby and down the hall to the Deputy Sheriff's office. It was empty. Bruno sniffed around the back of the desk, then came and sat by Carl's feet as he and Elsa discussed what they should do next. They decided to go down the street to the Tower Café to see if Pittella happened to be there having a cup of coffee.

They didn't see his car out front, but they went in anyway to get a cup of coffee and maybe a piece of pie for themselves, leaving Bruno in the car with the windows down. Edna was working the counter, and they passed a knowing look between them as they took their seats on the fixed swivel stools. Edna had worked there for years and acted like she owned the place. She greeted them with two mugs and a pot of coffee. They nodded when she asked if they wanted some.

"Hey, Edna," said Carl. "What kind of pie do you have?"

"I got apple, lemon meringue, pecan, and cherry."

"I'll have lemon meringue," said Elsa.

Carl said, "Pecan for me, please. Hold the ice cream."

When she came with their pie, they asked if she had seen Deputy Pittella recently. In her usual tone, which implied her superior knowledge of all things, she told them he was down at the boat slip since that's where he had told her he was going. They finished their pie and coffee and left a generous tip for Edna, the all-knowing.

While the East Two River was the closest water to the Deputy Sheriff's office, it was not where he kept his boat. That was down at Hoodoo Point in a newer, larger boat house shared by the Fire Department and the Sheriff's Department. It was a mile and a half to drive but gave direct access to the waters of Lake Vermilion.

With Bruno still loaded in the back of the Frazer, Carl and Elsa took off for Hoodoo Point. A small airport on the flat point of land separated Pike Bay from the rest of the lake. Both seaplanes and airplanes could land, fuel up and take off there. There were hangers near the runway as well as over the water to accommodate both. The public safety boat house was just past the airport. They pulled in directly behind the building and saw Pittella coming out of the door. He turned and locked it, then walked over to their car and leaned in to talk to them through their open car window.

"Hello again. What brings you out here?" Pittella asked.

"We'd like to talk to you for a few minutes, if you have time," said Carl.

"Sure, I was just heading back to the office, but how about we talk out here. Leave your car where it is, and we'll go sit at the picnic table over there by the shore."

Bruno trotted ahead as they walked to the shady area in a stand of birch. Carl and Elsa sat down across the table from the Deputy and proceeded to tell him about their exploration of the section of Pine Island inland behind Stark's and Ike's. They mentioned talking to Stark and meeting Morgan but didn't go into details of their conversation, thinking it wasn't important. They took out the map and spread it on the table. They described how they searched in the zigzag pattern for the 'x' and what they had found. Elsa unrolled the rubbing they had made on the birch bark and held it flat for Pittella to see.

The Deputy didn't say a word. He just looked back and forth between Carl and Elsa. "I'd say you two are a regular Nick and Nora. Although, I must say Asta isn't my kind of mascot. I much prefer a big black lab like Bruno," he said, referencing the Thin Man detective series popular on 1930s radio. After hearing his name, Bruno went over to the Deputy for a couple of hearty pats. "And how industrious of you, making a copy of the map in the first place."

Pittella then turned his attention to the rubbing and the map. After a few minutes, he said, "Well, I know one thing. There shouldn't be a body buried out there from 1928. Maybe some Indian or trapper bones from the 1700's but not with a grave marker like this. It probably is just a pet, but I can't leave it to chance, so I guess we'll have to go out there with a shovel or two and see what's there. Do you think you can find the place again?" he asked.

"I think so," said Carl, "We left markers and it shouldn't take long if we're not doing that crazy zigzag cover-every-inch pattern. Just tell us what you'd like us to do."

"I'll pull up to your dock tomorrow morning about 9:30. If you'll come prepared to spend some time to help us find the spot, I'd appreciate it."

"No problem. We'll be ready. Do you mind if Bruno comes along in your boat or should we plan to leave him at home?" Carl asked.

Bruno sat up when he heard his name. "Don't mind at all if he comes along," the Deputy extricated himself from the picnic bench. He patted the dog and walked them back to their car. "See you in the morning, then, eh?" he said.

Carl and Elsa waved goodbye as they drove away.

CHAPTER 35

The Sheriff's Department boat was a 24-foot Chris Craft, a 1947 front cabin launch, with a powerful inboard engine, which rumbled as it shifted into neutral to coast up to the Swanson's dock. The Deputy had Korchenko with him. They were both holding on to the dock when Carl, Elsa, and Bruno came down the path. Carl got in first, carrying a small padded canvas cooler. He clicked his tongue to tell Bruno to jump in. The Deputy extended a hand to Elsa. Still holding on to the dock, he asked Elsa if they had brought their copy of the map. When she said yes, he shoved off, put the big boat in gear, and slowly pulled away from the dock. In a matter of a few minutes, they were in Big Bay. The Chris Craft hummed as it cut through the water, providing a smooth ride for the five passengers.

The dock at Stark's cabin was barely long enough for the Chris Craft, but Pittella could see the drop-off was steep, the prop would be safe. He crept forward nose in, the stern of the boat extending past the end of the dock. The four carpenters working on the cabin didn't even look up. Two other guys were busy laying the patio stones in a complex pattern, the work almost complete halfway across the front of the cabin.

Stark was waiting for them outside his tent, hands on his hips, an angry look on his face. "What can I do for you, Deputy? Or have you come with news for me? Like who has been destroying my property." he said.

"No, Mr. Stark. I'm sorry to say I have no information for you about the vandalism you've been experiencing. Right now, I'd like your permission to walk through your property," said Pittella.

"May I ask why?" Stark said, then turned to Carl and Elsa and added angrily, "What's going on? Why are you two here again? What did you do yesterday on my land?"

"We have reason to believe there might be a burial site on your property," answered Pittella.

"Aha! I thought it was Indians all along! It makes sense. That's who's been doing the vandalizing. Protecting some stupid Indian mound or burial whatever and now you're going to tell me I can't move another rock on my own property because of it. Or, even better, some obnoxious archeologists are going to harass me in court to stop my cabin from being built and then come here and tramp all over my land. This is really the last straw. I can't believe this!"

"We won't know any of that until I see what these people found yesterday. So, do you mind if we go and take a look? Perhaps you'd like to come along," Pittella said, his voice reasonable.

"Of course, I'm coming," he said. He turned and went into

his tent, complaining about harassment and his troubled construction woes from inside. He came out, putting on a long sleeve shirt, and said, "Let's get this over with."

The five of them hiked up the hill single file, Carl leading them to the pile of rocks they had left the day before at the top. When they all got there and stood together in a small circle, Pittella took the map out of his jacket pocket and handed it to Elsa. She pointed at the 'x' and how they came to find it. She explained how they had used Y-shaped branches as markers and what they should be looking for. Carl estimated where the base of the hill was on the other side, and instead of walking the complex back and forth pattern, he led the group directly down to the flat woodsy area. Stark complained the entire time. When they didn't see any Y-shaped markers, they all spread out, walking slowly, looking at the lower limbs of every tree. Korchenko called out first, saying he found one. Then Elsa found one and could see another from where she stood. From those three points, it was easy to find the grave.

"What is this place? This is no Indian mound!" exclaimed Stark. He stepped up to the marker and read it out loud, "R.I.P. July 12th, 1928." He froze, his hand in midair. He turned to the Deputy, color drained from his face, and said, "That's the day my father disappeared."

"What do you mean, disappeared?" asked Pittella. He had been on the job as Deputy Sheriff for eight years that summer and remembered the case well, but he asked Stark to explain anyway. Pittella listened carefully as Stark gave him a shortened version of what he had told Carl and Elsa about his father. No one said a word but just stood for a few minutes thinking. Then Carl opened his camera case and took a few photos, adjusting the shutter for the dappled sunlight coming through the treetops. Pittella, Stark, and then Korchenko took turns taking a closer look at the cross and the carved inscription.

"Well, I guess we should get at it," Pittella said.

Visibly shaken, Stark sat on the log that had beckoned Elsa and Carl to sit the day before when they had first discovered the grave. Carl and Elsa stood off to the side, Bruno lay down at their feet. The four of them watched as the work began.

Korchenko had carried two shovels they had brought in the boat. He gave one to Pittella, and they set to work gently removing thin layers of leaves and dirt in a band several feet out from the marker, trying to avoid the area where logically, if it were a grave, the head and chest would be. They shoveled lots of small rocks out and to the side as they dug. They concentrated on disturbing the earth as little as possible. After a half hour or so, the trench was three feet deep, two feet wide, and about six feet long. Pittella had stopped digging when there wasn't room for both of them to work in it. He stood at ground level, watching Korchenko in the trench, still working carefully, taking only a few inches of dirt away at a time. The soft soil crumbled in whenever it was touched, spilling into the hole. Over and over again, Korchenko had to clear where he was standing. Roots and small rocks hindered his progress. Suddenly, the shovel made a soft thunk sound. He stopped and kneeled down to feel in the dirt for what he had hit.

He stood and presented the Deputy with a human long bone. "I'd guess this to be a thigh bone," he said flatly, climbing out of the trench with a grunt and a helping hand from the Deputy.

* * *

Pittella instructed Korchenko to stay at the grave site, and the rest of the group retraced their steps back to Stark's cabin site. Turning to Stark, the Deputy said, "I probably don't have to tell you not to leave until I get a chance to talk to you, but to make it official: Do not leave the property until then."

Pittella looked over at the workers who were taking a break, sitting on the odd pile of lumber or slate stones, drinking from their thermoses. He walked over to them and explained the situation. He took out his notebook and asked each of them for their names and addresses. He told them to stay on-site until he could ask them a few more questions. They nodded and shrugged their agreement and started to talk among themselves again.

Elsa and Carl walked Stark to his tent. He looked pale and shaky. As he opened the flap to go in, he turned to them and said, "I suppose you think I should thank you, but you can forget that. If that's my father in that grave, I don't know what I'm going to do. I've spent my whole life hating him. Now what? I'm supposed to feel sorry he's dead? Well, I don't. I hated him when he left us, and I'll hate him until I die." His voice was quiet, but it quaked with anger as he spoke. "You two need to get the hell off my property. Now."

The Deputy patted Bruno, who had accompanied him over to the workers, and they went down to the dock together where Elsa and Carl were waiting. He told them all to get in and asked Carl to shove off.

Pittella looked grim on the ride to Glenwood Lodge. Two bodies. On his watch. Were they connected? He felt somehow they were, but he didn't know how…yet. He would find out, though. That much he was sure of.

When they pulled up to the dock, Newsom was at the lodge door, holding the screen open. He motioned the group into the lodge and on into his office.

"I need to use your telephone, Phil. We've got another situation on our hands," said Pittella. "While I'm doing that, I wonder if you could find a way to get Carl and Elsa home. Loan them a boat or find someone to take them by car, maybe. You can add it to the bill we're racking up here."

He turned to Carl and Elsa, "You two should go on home. I'll stop over to talk with you tomorrow."

"C'mon," said Newsom, "I'll have my daughter take you home in our boat."

Carl and Elsa sat together on the back seat while Carrie drove the run-about across Big Bay, taking them home. As they passed the construction site, Elsa leaned close to Carl so he could hear her over the noise of the motor. "I don't know why, but I have a feeling Ike had something to do with that grave."

CHAPTER 36

The Tower News had run the advertisement for the dance the week before. Carl and Elsa planned to go as soon as they saw it. The Idle Hour Tavern usually had a local three-piece polka band on Saturday nights, but this Saturday, the live music was Tony D'Amato and the Three D's, touring around Minnesota from the Twin Cities. The group was billed as "The four-piece band with the big band sound." Tony D'Amato was a crooner and sang Sinatra's favorites.

Carl and Elsa had heard the band on the radio and liked their music. Now, in the aftermath of finding two bodies, they decided they needed to have some fun. They would make an evening of it, have a nice dinner at Bay View Lodge, then head over to Idle Hour for the music and dancing.

Carl was a great dancer and loved to work up the momentum to twirl Elsa off her feet. She would laugh that throaty laugh as he swung her around, and when he set her back down, he felt twenty again. He was glad he had brought the brown leather-soled shoes. They were a few years old but none the worse for wear because he only wore them dancing. He called them his Fred Astaire shoes. They were made of the softest Italian leather, and the inside was fawn-colored calfskin. He felt good in his pleated, dark green gabardine slacks and beige short sleeve shirt. And he had remembered to splash on a little of the Aqua Velva Elsa had given him.

Elsa was getting her clothes out of the small closet when he came up behind her and wrapped his arms around her, his face in her hair. "Mmm, you smell good," he said.

"You smell better," she turned and replied with a kiss.

He sat and casually played an old Swedish tune on the harmonica as he waited for her to finish getting ready. Elsa put on a full skirt, a rich dark brown with a contrasting stripe near the bottom. The cap-sleeved linen blouse was the same color as the stripe, a pale yellow, making the outfit look like a dress. Always the practical dresser, she had on a pair of plain brown flats, primarily because they were comfortable and had smooth soles to dance in. She took along a beige shrug, all she would need to keep warm later in the evening.

The Idle Hour was located at the end of Daisy Bay and sometimes they would go by boat. It was a pleasant boat ride, not far at all by water. But it was much farther to Bay View Lodge, on the other side of Birch Point, the two-and-one-half mile-long spit of land separating Daisy Bay from the western end of Big Bay. So, they decided they would drive the Frazer. Bruno would get to stay at home.

Bay View Resort was the classiest resort on the lake. It was where old money came to vacation on Lake Vermilion, staying in the well-appointed log cabins with maid service. In the beautiful lodge, they would drink and dine on first-class fare, whiling away the evenings schmoozing, playing cards and genteel games with other well-dressed city folks who were also roughing it in the Northwoods. The lodge, constructed of enormous pine timbers, had vaulted beamed ceilings and massive stone fireplaces. It was decorated with Indian hand-woven rugs, a giant bear skin on the floor in front of the lobby fireplace, taxidermized game and fish hung high on the walls, and soft welcoming cushions strewn on rough-hewn pine furniture.

The Maître d' seated them at a table by the window overlooking the manicured lawn, the many docks, and the smooth waters of the bay reflecting the colors of the setting sun. They chatted and watched the activities below where other diners, showing up in city finery in their luxurious cruisers for a gourmet meal and a visit with friends, were met by valet dock boys who tended to the boats. They ordered manhattans.

"You know a while back I came here with Werner and Gertrude, before we met. They took me out to celebrate me getting my citizenship," Carl recalled as they waited for their drinks. "I had driven up by myself to fish for a week after I had passed the citizenship test."

"That was certainly nice of them."

"It was quite a night, I remember," Carl said. "You'd never in a million years guess who was having dinner right over there." He nodded his head toward a table in the back.

"No, I wouldn't," she laughed. "Tell me."

"Al Capone and a bunch of guys."

"When we got here, the Maître d' told us the dining room

was closed. But when Gertrude told him that we were from Chicago and what we were celebrating, he went over to Mr. Capone and asked if we could stay for dinner seeing as how we were from Chicago and all. He laughed and said sure we could stay. He even bought us a round of drinks."

"That's something! I mean, Al Capone!"

The waiter brought the menus and their drinks.

Carl and Elsa sipped the sweet, mahogany liquid from Marie Antoinette coupes while they discussed the menu options. The chef had studied at a famous culinary school in New York, and the menu promised incomparable flavors. Eventually, Elsa decided on filet mignon with béarnaise sauce, asparagus, baked potato, and a chilled avocado mousse. Carl chose a top sirloin with mushrooms in red wine sauce with mashed potatoes, green beans, and a Waldorf salad. They started the meal with shrimp cocktails served in footed, etched glass two-piece chillers. They ate leisurely and drank a bottle of cabernet between them. When coffee and dessert was offered, they opted out, knowing their evening was far from over. The meal was delightful, and they were in mellow spirits when they left for Idle Hour and a change of pace.

* * *

They could hear the jukebox playing when they pulled into the gravel parking lot. As they entered the foyer of the clapboard, one-story building, Carl and Elsa ran into some men trying to leave. The tiny room, added to the outside of the building to keep the heat in and the cold out when the door was opened, might have succeeded in doing so if it had been just a little bigger. But as it was, both doors were being held open as the five people awkwardly negotiated the small space. The three men who smelled of smoke, fish guts, and whiskey were oblivious of their own smells, but couldn't help leaning in toward the attractive woman and breathe in hers - Chanel No. 5. "Pardon me," they each mumbled as they brushed past her. Finally, Carl was able to let the outer door close after them and Elsa had hurried through the inner door.

A small corkboard hung on the wall between the two doors. Carl paused to glance at the ads and notices pinned on it, noting a few boats, motors, and other odds and ends for sale. Across the top was a permanent legal notice in large letters which said women were not allowed to enter unless accompanied by a man. Carl shook his head in disbelief at the archaic state law and went in to join his wife.

It was a simple joint, built more for drinking and dancing than eating. The exits to the outside were directly across from each other bisecting the room, with an aisle from front to back. One door led out front through the tiny foyer to the gravel parking lot, the other led to the back where the outhouses and the path down to the dock were. The fireplace took up the short wall at far end, and booths lining the two long walls surrounded the dance floor which took up half the building. The U-shaped bar with the kitchen behind it took up the other half. The wood floor had no finish, and there were no carpets or rugs. The walls were knotty pine, and the built-in booths were made from the same wood. Not a padded seat in the place. This was an everyman's bar. No valet boat service here either. Food was served on melamine plates with thin metal silverware and brown paper napkins. Besides burgers, the menu offered pasties made spicy the way Finnish miners liked them, porketta with mashed potatoes, patty melts with red coleslaw, and all-you-can-eat fried fish on Fridays. Tap beer was the drink of choice, with highballs a close second.

Inside, the pervasive smells were different kinds of smoke - cherry tobacco a few men were smoking in their pipes, cigarettes, a faint smell of burnt food, and of course, the fire in the fireplace. The fire was just a small one and probably would be allowed to burn out. The room would get too warm later when the crowd got larger, and people were dancing.

Carl and Elsa made their way along the row of booths on the far wall and found that the one nearest the fireplace was unoccupied. They sat next to each other on one side so they could watch the band and still be able to talk to each other as it promised to be loud being so close to the music. When the waitress came, all perky with pigtails on either side of her head perched high above her ears, she asked, "What can I getcha?"

When Carl replied they'd like beer, she offered up with a smile, "Schlitz, Blatz, Schmidt, Shaefer, or tap."

"What's on tap?" Carl asked.

"Hamm's, the beer refreshing," she singsonged. So, they ordered Hamm's. Finally, the jukebox was silent, and the band fired up.

The first song was a familiar standard. Carl slid out of the booth and offered his hand to Elsa, "Honey, would you like to dance?"

"Been waiting all day for this!" she replied with a smile.

They passed the next hour sipping beer, listening to Tony D sing in his smooth, polished voice and dancing the fox trot, the two-step, and a few waltzes, obliterating for a short while all the strange and morbid events of the summer.

When the band took a break, Elsa headed for the ladies' room. She gave Carl a kiss as she slid past him to leave. She put on her shrug, gathered her purse, and walked the length of the dance floor toward the bar and the back door leading out to the facilities. Directly in front of her, sitting at the bar with their backs to the dance floor, were Stark and Morgan. They were talking heatedly, but she couldn't hear what they were saying because the jukebox was playing again now the band had stopped. They didn't notice her, and she passed by quickly, hoping they wouldn't.

Once out the door, she aimed for the second outhouse, designated as being for ladies by the doe carved in the door. A young woman in her twenties and dressed to the nines was waiting her turn, moving in place to the jukebox music playing inside. Elsa smiled at her as she came up and stood behind her. The young woman smiled back. Almost immediately, the outhouse door opened and was held by her friend who was exiting. The two tittered at each other and traded places. It wasn't long before the second girl came out, this time holding the door for Elsa as she left.

When she went back into the Idle Hour, she took a sharp right into the small powder room just inside the back door. A folding chair and a small table sat in the corner. A round mirror hung above a sink and a long loop of towel hung on a bar to the right. The bare light bulb on the ceiling wasn't the best for applying lipstick or rouge, but at least there was a place to wash your hands and powder your nose. The two women she had seen outside finished up at the sink and left as she entered. Elsa washed her hands and felt the towel for a dry spot to use. She primped her hair a little, and applied some Revlon "Sweet Talk" lipstick she carried in her purse. Giving her shoulders a lift as she shored up her good spirits, casting away unwanted thoughts, she went back into the dancehall.

She slipped by the bar without being seen by the two men who were still arguing. The band had started up again by the time she got back to the booth where Carl was waiting.

"You won't believe who's sitting at the bar," Elsa said close to Carl's ear. "Our new friends Stark and Morgan."

"Well, it is a good place for a beer and some food," Carl said noncommittedly.

"They were arguing pretty seriously. I mean really angry at one another."

"That guy Stark is not a happy man, that's for sure. But we came here to have fun. Forget about them. Come on. Let's dance."

"OK, I guess I'm just being overly dramatic. You're right. Let's do this polka!"

When the band announced they were taking a final break and would play only one more set, Elsa again made her way to the outhouse. This time Stark and Morgan were gone.

The two small outhouse buildings, surrounded by scrub trees and bush, stood next to each other, perpendicular to the main building. This afforded a little privacy but not much. She knew the dock was straight down the long hill from the back door, but poor planning had put the outhouses directly in the way. The path to the dock had to veer around them in a semi-circle, then head back to the straight line down the incline to the water's edge. As she reached to open the door with the doe cut-out, she heard loud voices coming from further down the path. One of them sounded like Stark. She didn't open the creaky door.

Instead, she quietly followed the path around the small buildings toward the lake.

She came to the bend in the path where it turned to go down the slope and stopped to listen. There was a half-moon that would have been bright enough to see by if fast-moving clouds didn't cover it frequently. She couldn't see Stark and Morgan, and she was certain they couldn't see her, but she could hear them arguing. She could tell they were trying to keep their voices low now, whispering their agitated words at one another. She couldn't tell which man was speaking.

"So, it was you!" one voice said, getting louder.

The men had stopped walking, their shoes shuffling on the path, as they turned to face each other.

"Keep your voice down!" the other voice said in a harsh whisper.

"So, YOU killed him!" the voice said, now sounding hysterical.

"After what he did, I had to!" the other voice said.

"But he hadn't done anything to you. He didn't deserve that, I'm sure of it."

"You have to keep your mouth shut about this. There's no proof of anything, so just keep your damned mouth shut."

Elsa had been creeping forward but stepped to the side when the two men had stopped to face each other. A twig snapped underfoot as she moved off the path. Her breath caught in her throat, too loudly she feared.

"Shhh. I think someone is there," one of the voices whispered.

Their footsteps hurried away. She couldn't bring herself to step out from her cover where she would be in clear sight if they turned around. Their feet clomped on the dock, and she could hear them untying their boat. I've got to hurry, she thought. She had to see who had been talking. She got up her nerve, turned the corner, and hurried down the path as quietly as she could. The clouds covered the moon for a few crucial minutes as she scurried closer to the dock.

Just as the clouds moved past the moon, she stepped to the side between two trees near the end of the path. She got a good look at the boat as the two men started up the motor and pulled away. It was, as she suspected, the boat she had seen tied up at Stark's dock - the "Grand Plan." She ran back up the hill to the Idle Hour and made her way through the crowd dancing the fox trot to the booth where Carl was waiting. She didn't sit down but leaned over and said urgently in his ear, "We have to go! Now!" Carl could see she was upset and immediately got up, then, taking her by the hand, led her through the crowded dance floor and out the two foyer doors.

"The tab!" Elsa exclaimed.

"It's all right. I had just finished paying before you came back," he said as he held the car door for her.

He went around to the driver's side and got in. Without turning the ignition key, he turned to face her. "What's going on? Are you all right?"

She took a deep breath and told him what had happened, trying to recount every word she had heard. She felt a fool for not having had the nerve to step out and confront the men. Carl assured her she had done the right thing. They were, after all, talking about murder. It wouldn't have been smart to let them know she had overheard them.

"You're right, I know. But what do we do?" she asked him,

her heart still racing.

"Let's see. It's about one in the morning and we have important information regarding a murder. I'd say we had better go wake up Harvey," said Carl. "Don't you agree?"

She nodded, looking out the windshield, her lips pressed tightly together.

CHAPTER 37

It only took four sharp raps on the front door before Pittella opened it. He was wearing flannel pajamas and sheepskin slippers. His right hand was hidden behind the door, resting on the gun belt that hung on the wall of the small entryway.

"What on earth are you two doing here at this hour?" he asked, motioning for them to come in. They followed him into the living room just off the hallway to the right. Pittella switched on a lamp and told them to sit down. Minnie came in behind them and asked if they needed anything, water, coffee, a drink. Her long black hair fell straight almost to her waist, but even in the low light, Elsa could see how much her hair had turned gray. The chenille robe she was wearing was large on her and made her seem smaller, frail somehow.

"Oh, Minnie," Elsa said, "I'm so sorry we woke you." The two women exchanged a brief hug.

"There is no problem, Elsa. We're used to late night visitors and phone calls. It's so nice to see you again. Are you sure you don't want a cup of coffee?"

They declined Minnie's offer, and she left the visitors with her husband. Elsa began to tell him what had happened at the Idle Hour.

"Whoa, just a minute," the Deputy interrupted. "Are you sure? Okay. Slow down and start from the beginning. Let's hear this all again."

Elsa stood and walked back and forth across the carpet as she retold the events of the evening, more slowly this time, concentrating on getting every word correct. When she was done, she sat back down and said, "That's what I know. I couldn't tell you who said what, but that is definitely what was said."

Pittella sat forward in his chair, elbows on his knees, hands clasped, and said, "Well, much as I hate sitting here in my PJs at one in the morning, you did the right thing coming straight here. I'd bet on it that those two aren't going anywhere tonight. But just to make sure, I'm going to rouse Korchenko. He lives just a couple doors down from here. I'll have him stake out Glenwood Lodge to make sure Mr. Morgan doesn't leave. And I'll give Gruben's a call to let me know if Stark shows up to get his car. I'm pretty sure I heard that's where he launches his boat from. So, unless they went there directly from Idle Hour and left already, we'll be able to keep track of them."

The three of them talked for a while longer. "Now I want you two to go on home and get some sleep. I'll stop by later tomorrow or the next day and let you know how things turn out," Pittella said. He walked them to the door and stopped before opening it. He stood for a long moment staring at the door handle.

"You know. I'm having second thoughts. I'm thinking it might speed things along if you went with me tomorrow to talk to Stark and Morgan. Primarily, I'd want you to just be witnesses to the conversation. But I might call on you to state what you heard tonight if I think the conversation isn't going the way it should. Do you think you're up for that, Elsa?"

Elsa and Carl exchanged a meaningful look, and Carl answered for them both, "Of course, Deputy. We'll do whatever you need us to do."

Pittella described his plan to them and finally opened the door. "Drive carefully," he said. "Watch for deer."

CHAPTER 38

The next morning, the weather continued fair and calm, with large high clouds moving quickly in front of the sun, causing alternating shadow and bright light just as they had done the night before with the moon. Pittella pulled up to the Swansons' dock right on time, where Elsa and Carl were already waiting. They had left Bruno in the house.

"Thanks for coming along. Last night I was thinking we'd provoke a little conversation by having you repeat what you heard at the Idle Hour," Pittella said, looking at Elsa. "I'm thinking that will produce some kind of look or tell as to which one said what, which I can then build on. We don't have much in the way of evidence here, but based on the high emotions you overheard, I think we can lay us a little trap. And I need you two as witnesses. You've proved yourselves good observers and pretty darned unflappable. So, please, just stay quiet until I ask you something. That okay with you both?"

Carl and Elsa both nodded. "We're up for whatever it takes, Harvey," Carl said.

Elsa tied a scarf under her chin to keep her hair from flying in the wind. The big boat sped across Daisy Bay, then across Big Bay to Glenwood Lodge. Earlier, Pittella had called Phil Newsom from his office in Tower with instructions for Korchenko. The Patrolman was waiting for them at the main dock. He looked tired, having spent the early morning hours in his car watching the resort's parking lot from a vantage point up the road. Stoic as usual, Korchenko nodded a good morning to Elsa and Carl as he secured the boat. Pittella got out and went up the path to the lodge and disappeared inside. He returned a few minutes later with Morgan walking casually at his side. The three of them got in the boat with Carl and Elsa, and Korchenko pushed away from the dock. Pittella put the engine in reverse, turned, then headed back the way they came and over to Canfield Bay.

At Stark's dock, Korchenko secured the boat as the rest of them disembarked and headed up to Stark's tent. Holding the flap open for them as they approached, Stark invited them in and half-heartedly offered them coffee. They all declined. He looked contrite and hung over. He had been sitting at the table inside his big tent having a breakfast of bacon and eggs. A stainless-steel coffee pot was on a tray at one end. Stark threw the napkin he had been using onto his plate.

At Pittella's suggestion, they all sat down on the camp chairs randomly set around the Oriental rug. The canvas walls were lowered, so the space felt cramped. Pittella remained standing where everyone could see him. He then turned to Stark and thanked him for allowing the Swansons to join them.

"I have some pertinent information about the grave on your property and I believe they will have an interest in it as well," he said.

He took a small notebook from his jacket pocket, flipped a few pages, and continued, "Based on the evidence the medical examiner discovered on the remains of the body on your back land, we can now say for sure it was your father, Nathan Stark. The ME determined the cause of death was a blow to the back of the head with a sharp, irregular shaped blunt instrument, such as a rock. Based on this, he has declared the death to be a murder." Pittella paused to look at each person in the room. Elsa was composed but a little pale, Carl passively interested. Stark was leaning forward, intently listening. Morgan was sitting back, one leg crossed over the other.

"Let me remind you, I was the law enforcement officer who investigated Nathan Stark's disappearance in 1928. So, this news is extraordinarily interesting to me as the missing persons case had remained unsolved to this point. The additional information which the ME found, I think, is the crucial thing, however, because it gives a motive.

With a somber pause, Pittella folded his notebook and put it in his pocket, immediately extracting from the same pocket a small manila envelope. He opened it and pulled out several sheets of paper, all of the same odd size. They were folded, but he did not unfold them.

"In Stark's pocket, there were a few pieces of paper, hastily folded and, fortunately, well preserved inside the canvas-type material of his pants. These were torn from the 1928 calendar Aronson's used to keep track of their deliveries that year. Fact is, they cover the period of July and August. The calendar was a bound book with each page showing a week."

Stark interrupted, "What does a calendar have to do with my father's death?"

"Perhaps I should explain. In the 1920's and 30's, Aronson's Boat Livery was the only company on the lake which had barges. Any building materials that were going to be used on an island or, for that matter, anything big at all like a stove or icebox, regardless of which lumberyard or store it was bought from, had to be brought out to any property that didn't have road access on one of Aronson's barges or delivery boats."

Pittella again paused to see if everyone was following, but he didn't notice any changes on their faces yet. He knew the next part was crucial, so he took his time in telling it.

"Now, what's so interesting about these particular pages of the delivery schedule, seeing as there was nothing much on them? That's what I asked myself. Let's assume Stark was murdered on the day he disappeared, July 12th. Why did he have these particular pieces of paper in his pocket? The pages only showed a few deliveries."

He unfolded the sheets, paused while he looked at them carefully, and looked up at his audience, still uncomprehending, except for one person who had shifted backward in his seat.

"There were several deliveries in early July, before the 4th. Then on the 7th, Aronson's delivered the tents and supplies to your grand opening site. A delivery of gardening supplies, soil and some plants was scheduled for the end of July to Preston Bradley's place out on Black Duck Island. And a new icebox and some furniture were to be delivered to Ravenswood Lodge on August 6th. As well as a few others scheduled for later in the summer." Pittella paused again and looked around the room, stopping at Morgan. "You, Mr. Morgan, understand the implications of this, don't you?"

Morgan pressed his back further into the canvas chair. His face tightened, but he said nothing.

"There were no deliveries scheduled for Canfield Bay because you hadn't ordered anything, had you, Mr. Morgan?"

Pittella continued to stare at him. "There should have been several deliveries by the time your campground's grand opening occurred in July and lots more scheduled for the rest of the summer. I remember interviewing the guests at your grand opening. The main complaint they had, other than the storm, of course, was that no work had been started on the community buildings and docks which they had been promised would be part of their real estate purchase. Without supplies and materials, how could you build that glorious lodge and all the other amenities you and your partner, Mr. Stark, had planned? But there were no plans to actually build anything, isn't that true, Mr. Morgan?"

Morgan was now sitting forward, ready to respond. He had ordered his thoughts and calmly began to explain it was all Nathan's doing. That Nathan had been the man in place, in charge of ordering, and he, Morgan, just took care of the legal paperwork, not the building or financial part of the project. Nathan, he said, had told him not to worry about anything, so he hadn't. Nathan had told him he would order everything that was needed because he was on site to take charge of that. Nathan took the money. Nathan was a full partner and had access to the accounts. Nathan had emptied all the money from the accounts before coming up for the Grand Opening. He knew he'd be close to Canada and could just canoe over the border. From there, he would be scot-free. Nathan left for Canada with the money. That's what happened.

Morgan expertly recited the story he had concocted twenty years ago and had repeated to himself innumerable times. The story which made him out as the victim. As he talked, he began to realize how many holes the story actually had and that the more he spoke, the more it sounded like he was complicit in the scam. He realized, too, that Pittella must have found out that while Nathan had access to the accounts, Morgan had been the one to receive the money from the buyers. That he had actually been responsible for the books and would notice missing funds. His voice and face began to change. His eyes began to dart realizing he had painted himself into a corner with his pat story full of lies - the story which had been so easy to defend when it was assumed Stark had absconded with the money. He could see now that if Stark were dead and the money missing, it was only logical that people would think that he, not Stark, must have taken the money. Whether Stark had stolen it on his own or Stark and Morgan were partners in the scam, he was left holding the bag. He turned pale and started to sweat.

Stark, across the Oriental rug from him, had become increasingly agitated as Morgan talked. His face had darkened, and finally, he burst out shouting. "You son of a bitch! You took that money! You ruined my life! You ruined my entire life!" Pittella quickly stepped in front of Stark and told him to calm himself and sit back down.

Stark gave the deputy a withering look and sat down with a grumble. Pittella again took his place where he could see everyone. He allowed the tension in the room to continue to build as he put the pages away and took out his notebook, slowly flipping pages before he calmly turned to Morgan.

"Let's take a minute here, Mr. Morgan, to think about what you have just told us," Pittella said. "It's clear from everything we know now, Stark didn't take the money, or if he did, someone else took it from him along with his life. It is also pretty clear from what I've read and heard about Stark, he wasn't the one in your partnership who would have taken care of the details like dealing with a builder or ordering lumber and supplies. He was a nice guy, a great salesman, but not one who would have been able to figure out how to embezzle that money. You were the paperwork guy, Mr. Morgan, and you would have been the one to get bids, hire a builder, pay for materials and supplies, and so forth. You would have done those tasks, Mr. Morgan. Not Mr. Stark. Isn't that right, Mr. Morgan?"

"I think what really happened, Mr. Morgan, is that when your partner, Nathan Stark, arrived for the grand opening, he was astounded to find that no work had been done on the project. He asked you about it, but you blamed scheduling difficulties with Aronson's or the builder. You had some clever and plausible excuses, I'm sure. He didn't believe you, however, so he went to Tower to find out the truth. Which he did. He found out what you already knew. There was never going to be any vacation paradise on Canfield Bay. That you had embezzled the money. You two fought about it and you killed him. You picked up a rock and hit him in the back of the head. Your best friend. Your partner. You murdered him. Didn't you, Mr. Morgan?" Pittella's voice had escalated as he stepped nearer to Morgan, imposing and intimidating as he looked down at the seated man.

Morgan sprang to his feet and cried desperately, "No! No! It wasn't like that." He looked back and forth between Stark and

Pittella. "I needed the money to get away. I couldn't take another year, another minute, in that God-forsaken Duluth. I was dying there. I couldn't breathe. I had to have money to set myself up in Miami. Those rich people wouldn't even miss such a little bit of their money. They were all wealthy asses, looking down their noses at us as if we were some back-country hicks." He stopped and panted, his fear showing, eyes wide now, darting back and forth.

"He fell. He fell and hit his head. I didn't kill him," his voice dropped to a whisper as he sat back down. Even as he said the words, he realized how hollow they sounded. He knew they were true, but who would believe it. And, in the end, he knew in actuality he had killed him, just not the way they thought.

Pittella let it sink in for a moment, then he spoke in a subdued voice, "And you thought no one would ever know. But all those years ago, Ike saw you kill your friend and partner, back there in the woods, didn't he, Mr. Morgan? And, then the first time you come up here since then, you bump into Ike. After all these years. What luck! And Ike recognizes you, doesn't he, Mr. Morgan? Perhaps you two see each other in town at Zup's or at the 4th of July parade. He recognizes you and tells you what he remembers - that he saw you hit your friend - but you tell him he is mistaken. That he has you mixed up with someone else. You ask around to find out who he is and where he lives. When you realize his cabin is right over there, you're sure he knows your dark secret. You go to his cabin and confront him. He turns his back for a moment. You grabbed the paddle he'd been working on and hit him in the back of the head. You put him in his boat, towed it out into Big Bay and dumped him overboard. Then you let the boat drift away. We know it was you, Mr.

Morgan, because the green paint from Ike's boat rubbed onto your boat while the two boats were tied together when you dumped the body. You killed him, too, didn't you, Mr. Morgan?"

Morgan leaped to his feet and cried out, "I didn't kill that old man. He did!" and pointed to Stark.

Up to this point, Stark had been leaning forward, still, as if frozen in place. He stood up and shouted, "He deserved it, the crazy old bastard. Did he really think he was going to get away with it? That I would stop building my dream house because he dumped some damned nails in the lake, or drilled holes in the shingles, or ruined the cement? Did he? Well, he found out, didn't he?"

"When I went over there to tell him he couldn't stop me with his stupid pranks, you know what he told me? That I couldn't build on my property because there was gold there, and it was his gold. Hah! There's no gold! Everybody knows that. Then he started saying there was a graveyard there, not gold. He said soldiers were buried there. He'd watched them die and then he buried the soldiers. On Pine Island. Hah! He was totally off his rocker."

"I could see he'd never quit. He was nuts! A total nutball! So, when the old man told me he was going to get his shotgun, I took the paddle and hit the bastard. He deserved it," Stark said again.

Morgan started to laugh, a huge rumbling laugh that shook his chest. His laughter filled the tent.

"What's so damned funny?" asked Stark.

"It was me who sabotaged your damned building project, you fool. When you first told me about your plans to build right here, I was worried you'd find a pile of bones. I couldn't have that, so I made a few inquiries among old acquaintances in Duluth. Thompson seemed to fit the bill, and I arranged for him to be recommended to you. And you hired him. Of course, I pay him twice what you're paying him to find ways to discourage you from building this place. He's been very clever, don't you think?

"I swore I'd never come back here, but I had to keep you from knowing the truth. So, when you invited me to come see it for myself, I accepted your invitation. I thought I'd be able to find what remains there might be from your repugnant, stupid father and could get rid of it. When I got here, I immediately went to where I thought Nathan's remains should have been, but it wasn't as easy as I anticipated, what with twenty years of growth and all. I figured some animals, foxes or wolves maybe, would have made short order of the body, but there might be a bunch of bones lying around. But I couldn't be sure, and I knew if the body was found, I'd be suspected of taking the money. I had hoped Thompson's pranks might even be enough to get you to give up. After all, it's just a stinking cabin you'd probably never visit very much anyway. Hell, if all else failed, I was going to pay him to burn it down. But you, you're such an idiot. You went and killed an old man over some stupid dream. A dream that wasn't even yours. You're building this place just to spite your father. What a worthless piece of shit you are – just like your father was!" Morgan sputtered the last words.

Stark's eyes were wild. "You were my godfather. My father's best friend. All these years you acted like you cared about me, but you were just pretending. You lying bastard! You ruined my family! You took my money! I had to grow up in a crowded tenement apartment in backwater Wausau, sharing a bedroom with my fat cousins who hated me. And all the while you were lounging in Miami in luxury. With my money! You bastard! Now you tell me you're the reason I killed that old man! It's all your fault! You killed my father! You made me kill the old man. Now, I'm gonna kill you!"

Stark leaped across the room onto Morgan, knocking him down. Morgan and Stark were swearing and rolling around on the floor, swinging ineffectively at each other. Korchenko, who had been standing guard outside the tent, came rushing in. He and Pittella pulled the two men apart. Korchenko grabbed Morgan, crawling on all fours, trying to sneak out of the tent. He yanked him to his feet, put handcuffs on him, and stood holding him by the upper arm. Pittella wrestled Stark to a prone position on the floor and put the cuffs on him right there on his Oriental rug.

When everyone was standing and ready to leave the tent, the two men in handcuffs, Pittella said, "Just one more thing, Stark. Why were you in Morgan's boat the day you killed Ike?"

It was Morgan who answered, "Hah. That was a fluke, now, wasn't it?"

"Care to explain?"

"I needed to talk to Thompson alone. I wanted to give him some new instructions since Stephen wasn't showing any signs of giving up on the building. So, when I went over to visit Stephen that day, I pretended to be admiring that ridiculous project and slipped Thompson a note which said to tell Stephen he needed to go to town. When he came into Stephen's tent later and asked to use his boat, that he needed the big boat to get some supplies in Tower, I said I'd like to go along. And you in your rage against that old man couldn't wait for your beautiful boat to get back so you took that measly little bilge bucket you arranged for me." Morgan turned to sneer at Stark and said, "Hah! You should see my yacht I keep on Biscayne Bay. You and your paltry Northwoods ambitions make me sick. And best of all you never even suspected Thompson had been doing my bidding all that time. You really are just as stupid as your father was."

Without anything further being said, the two law enforcement officers took the cuffed men down to the boat. Elsa and Carl followed behind and stopped on the dock while the others got in the boat.

"Hop in. We've got to go to Glenwood Lodge where the vehicle is. You can get a ride home from someone there," said Pittella offering Elsa a hand. "Things didn't go exactly as I thought they would but I'm glad you came along. Amazing how guilt just has a way of coming out under the right circumstances, no matter how long it's been buried. I'll be busy for a day or two, but I need to get an official statement from you. Would you mind driving into town tomorrow morning to do that?"

"No problem, and don't worry about us getting home. We'll be fine," said Carl as they climbed into the boat.

CHAPTER 39

The four of them were sitting in Pittella's office having coffee the next morning. Bruno was on the floor by Carl's feet. Pittella set his mug on the desk and leaned back in his chair.

"It all fell into place when I saw the grave marker. I knew then the two murders were connected. For as long as I can remember, Ike has made at least one paddle each summer. He liked to whittle and sand the wood outside on his porch where he didn't have to clean up the mess. He had a stockpile of clear ten-by-two cedar boards which he special ordered every couple of years. He made me one a few years ago." Harvey paused to wipe at his eye and sat forward, elbows on the desk.

"Anyway, when I saw the grave marker, I recognized his work even though it wasn't very much like a paddle, having square corners and all. I think Ike must have used the one he was working on at the time to carve the inscription on and he hadn't gotten to shaping the end yet. When we dug it up, the buried end was definitely the start of paddle. Cedar never rots, so it made a good headstone."

"I actually thought the letters on it looked like the notes we saw on the map. We know now Ike didn't kill Stark, so why would Ike have buried Stark's body? Why would he put up a grave marker?" asked Elsa.

"Well, I really don't know. I immediately thought, early on, it was Ike who buried the body, but I doubted he had killed anybody. Nope, I really didn't think that could be it," Pittella said, shaking his head. "We might never know why he did what he did. He was a tortured soul, more than any person I've ever met. I do know he had a wife at one point, but it was WWI that changed him, and he moved up here to get away from his nightmares. He was as close to a real hermit as you can get. But you just could tell that inside all that silence was a good heart."

"Stark said Ike had rambled on about dead soldiers and having to bury dead soldiers. Maybe he was reliving some terrible memories when he saw Morgan kill Stark. Maybe he did what he had done after a battle or something like that. He did the best he could by making the grave marker with what he had. Maybe they had made wood crosses on the graves of the dead soldiers back then," said Elsa.

"Could be. I guess we can't be sure, but it's possible that's what happened," Pittella said. "Morgan, now, that guy is a real snake. His story about Stark hitting his head might be true, but there isn't a jury who wouldn't convict him anyway because of what he did afterward. A good prosecutor would make sure of that.

"It was a big surprise to me when Morgan said Stark murdered Ike. I had my money on Morgan all along. Perhaps my predisposition to suspect Morgan had to do with my first impression of him back in 1928 when Nathan Stark disappeared. I had been Deputy in Tower since 1919 and had seen some truly slimy characters what with Prohibition and all. Morgan gave me a real bad feeling even back then. He hadn't done anything wrong we could prove but he came across as if he was guilty of something. Back then, without a body, there was nothing we could do. And the embezzlement case was out of my territory. But all that's resolved now thanks to you two. Some people just don't have whatever it is that keeps the rest of us from doing away with the people we don't like. I guess we found out both of those guys are cut from the same bad cloth."

Pittella opened a folder on his desk and took out some photos. He slid them across the desk toward Carl.

"By the way, the photos you took the day Ike was murdered were very helpful. When we examined the ones you took from high up on Indian Point, we could see two boats pointed away from Pine Island. The two boats were somehow really close together but there's only one person visible. I think that's Stark disposing of the body over the side," Pittella said, leaning to point at one of the photos.

"Wasn't he trying to make it look like Ike hit his head and fell into the water?" asked Carl, "Why not just leave him in the water by his dock? Why did he take the body and the boat out further into the lake?"

"I don't think he was very clearheaded about what he did. I believe he pitched Ike's body overboard thinking it would sink and it probably did for a bit, but bodies do strange things in water. He probably felt the boat wouldn't be found for a while and that would give him time to get back to wherever he needed to be," replied Pittella.

"Those photos you took of the body out there on Gull Island made a difference too," Pittella continued. "The details of the neck injury faded over time and the ME used those photos to verify what he thought was cause of death. Again, thanks for the quick thinking. You're quite the photographer, by the way."

"I saw a lot of death when I was stationed in Italy, but the injuries we saw were even worse. The pain some of those guys had to endure was hard to comprehend. The best way for me to handle it was to depersonalize it, to think of how a camera would see it. I had had a camera with me for a short time at the beginning of the war. Don't get me wrong, I never took pictures like that but, for a short time, looking through the lens let me pretend what I was seeing wasn't real. Even after I lost the camera, I would focus on just a small area or a certain section of the scene in front of me, as if I was looking through the camera lens. Anything to keep from thinking about what was really happening. It might sound strange, but it got me through. Ike was a friend, but I couldn't stand to look at his body like that. I couldn't let myself think that was really him. That's why I took the photos. I'm glad, though, that they helped," Carl looked down, a bit overwhelmed with the emotions he was feeling. Elsa reached across and took his hand.

Pittella paused a moment before continuing, "And thank you, Elsa, for your wild theories. Oh, I mean, keen observations."

They all laughed at that, and the mood lightened.

"The fact you noticed the sweep pattern on the path was really important. The ME found traces of blood and hair on the edge of the paddle, dirt and grass on the end, and Stark's fingerprints on the shaft. Without the paddle we might not have had much physical evidence.

"And once we realized Ike's death wasn't an accident, the only reason I could think of that Ike had been killed was that he knew something or had something someone wanted. When you came up with the map, Elsa, I thought you might have found what it was. The fact it had been sitting out in the open like that, though, made me reconsider. If that's what the killer had wanted, why leave it there? And you were crazy enough to follow your gut, which told you the map did play an important part in all this. Traipsing through the woods, now that was way beyond anything I could have imagined.

"We've still got a lot of details to get out of both Morgan and Stark. All in due time. They're not going anywhere. You might have to testify at their trials, but hopefully it won't be necessary. In any case, I'd appreciate it if you both would write up your statements while you are here. It might take a while and that's okay with me. Take as long as you need. We can bring you some food if you want."

"We came prepared for that, so no problem," said Carl.

Pittella walked them into the next office and introduced them to the City Clerk. She provided them with pads of paper and pencils and a place to write. The next couple of hours went by quickly as they each wrote it all down. Bruno snored most of the time from under the table. When they were done, they called the city clerk over. She thanked them and told them she would type up their statements over the next day or two, and they should come back any time after that to sign the official versions, which she would notarize.

They walked back to Pittella's office and peeked in. Harvey

was behind his desk. Korchenko was still gone.

"Come on in," he said.

Bruno wagged his way around the desk for another treat, but Carl and Elsa stood in the doorway.

"We think we'll head home now, if that's okay," said Elsa.

"Sure, sure," Pittella said, digging another dog treat out of the drawer. "Did Charlotte mention you have to come back to sign your statements?"

"Yes, she did. We'll stop in to read and sign them at the end of the week, if that's okay," said Carl.

"Sure, sure. Thanks again. I hope the rest of your summer is uneventful. Stop in and see us before you leave for Chicago, if I don't see you when you come in to sign your affidavits."

"We will. But I hope we'll see you and Minnie at the Old Settlers' Picnic. Take care," replied Carl. Elsa waved. Bruno woofed.

CHAPTER 40

The rest of their summer was uneventful, just as Pittella had wished. They went into Tower several more times after signing the affidavits. They fished almost every day and caught their limit most of the time. They ate more walleye than they thought was humanly possible. The weather held, and they completed many of the small projects around the cabin they had wanted to get done. In short, life went on.

They were invited to dinner and a sauna with some acquaintances on Birch Point the first week in August. It was a delightful evening, and after an enjoyable meal, the group separated in two and took turns in the sauna. The ladies went first, then the men. Afterward, feeling exhilarated and squeaky clean, they had dessert and a nightcap.

When they got home and were getting ready for bed, Elsa said, "Say, Carl, I think we should consider doing a little building project next summer."

"So, you loved the sauna that much? You really want to build one? Well, it's not a bad idea at all. I really enjoyed it, too. We could build it to the right of the boathouse close to the water," said Carl, as he crawled under the covers.

Elsa laughed and said, "Well, that would be terrific. I do think we'd use a sauna. But I was referring to a different building project." She crawled in beside him and rested her head on his extended arm.

"What building project? What are you talking about?" he said.

"Well, I'm pretty sure we're going to need another bedroom. There just isn't room enough in here for a crib."

Carl surprised the both of them by sitting straight up in bed and making happy whooping noises he didn't know he could make. When he calmed down, he held his wife close, pecking kisses all over her face.

"I am the happiest man alive," he declared. The night got even better for the two of them, and then they finally fell asleep.

* * *

In mid-August, they attended the Old Settlers' Picnic at McKinley Park. They met up with the Peylas and had a great time listening to old-time music, playing horseshoes, eating bouya stew, and drinking beer. The program included a tribute to an honorary Tower citizen, the Reverend Doctor Preston Bradley. He graciously accepted the award and pledged to continue contributing to the library fund saying Lake Vermilion was one of his favorite places in the world to read. They visited with Harvey and Minnie at a picnic table where they sat with their daughter, son-in-law, and new grandbaby. Carl and Elsa grinned at each other as they cooed over the chubby little girl. They basked in the small-town ambiance and the beauty of the Northwoods and Lake Vermilion and stayed until sundown.

A few days before they were to close up the cabin for the season, the Swansons went into town. Carl and Bruno waited on the sidewalk while Elsa stopped at the Post Office and told Midge to forward their mail to the Chicago address she gave her. Then she went next door to the Tower News and arranged to have the weekly newspaper sent to their home by mail.

They dropped in to say goodbye to Pittella. He was sitting at his desk writing something. He looked tired.

"Hello, Harvey. We just stopped in to say goodbye. We're leaving in a couple of days," said Carl.

"We won't keep you. You look busy," said Elsa.

"I guess you could say that. Someone stole a car from the marina's parking lot yesterday. Just filling out some paperwork about it," said Pittella. "Thanks again for your help with Ike's murder case. Say, I've got something I want to give you."

He pulled open a desk drawer, and Bruno was immediately there. He gave Bruno a treat and said with a laugh, "Besides a treat for Bruno, that is."

He took out a manila envelope and handed it to Elsa.

"These are some letters I found at Ike's place and the map, too. I figured you might as well have them since we were informed by his sister the family didn't want any of his belongings once I told her there was nothing of much value. They had written him off long ago. I gave the little bit of furniture he had to a needy family on the reservation. I kept the last painting he was working on. It's not finished, of course, but I still like it. There are a few other items in the box over there that we saved from his place. If there's anything in there you'd like, please take it."

Elsa went over and looked in the box. Leaning up against it was Ike's palette. It was a thin, flat, odd-shaped piece of wood with a thumb hole near one rounded edge. With dried paint smudges of all colors, well-worn from years of use, it appealed to Elsa.

"I'd like to keep this, if that's ok," said Elsa.

"Sure. Take it."

She gathered everything up. "Thanks," she said.

"See you next summer. Take it easy, Harvey, and give our best to Minnie," said Carl, as the two men shook hands.

"You, too. Have a good trip back home," said Pittella.

This time Carl went upstairs with Elsa to return her library books. He watched with a smile while she took the time to put them back where they belonged on the shelves before they headed home.

CHAPTER 41

Two days later, Carl suggested they take a last boat ride before they put up the boat. They wouldn't fish because they already had more than they could take with them home to Chicago in their cooler anyway, and their hearts just weren't in it. Carl knew what Elsa needed - a fast boat ride with the wind in her face. He decided they would ride around Pine Island clockwise. Elsa packed a few things to nibble on and a couple of bottles of Hamm's.

The lake was very calm, the air crisp with the promise of a new season. They took off at full speed and headed to Gruben's. "Let's get a last ice cream and settle up our tab. It will save them sending us a bill," Carl said as he tied up. Bud was heading down the slope to the dock when Carl shouted, "It's ok. We're coming up."

They went inside the old school building-turned store and greeted Mrs. Gruben, telling her they wanted to pay their tab.

She reached back to the box sitting on the shelf which held fifty or so small receipt books. She pulled out the one with Swanson written on the spine.

"Add two ice creams to that please, Mrs. Gruben," said Elsa.

They each picked an ice cream out of the small chest freezer sitting just inside the door. It was new that summer and sported two small removable fold-back lids to access the boxes of frozen treats inside. Elsa chose a Dreamsicle, and Carl an ice cream sandwich. They tore off the paper wrappers and threw them in the old bucket at the end of the counter before going back out the door. They sat side by side on the green swinging bench hung from the ceiling of the screened-in porch where Bruno had been waiting. From inside, they could hear the hand-pull adding machine ka-chunking loudly as Mrs. Gruben totaled up the individual items listed in the little receipt book with their name on the cover, summing up their purchases of the summer.

Carl reached over and took Elsa's hand as they looked out on the picturesque wooden bridge to Isle of Pines, the large, corrugated metal boathouses, the long docks, and the single huge rock everything was perched on. Finally, it was quiet except for the creak of the swing and the occasional tap of Carl's shoe to keep it going. When they finished their ice cream, they went inside the store and paid Mrs. Gruben, who thanked them, "Okay, then. Have a nice winter, eh?"

"You, too," said Elsa.

Bud came out of the shed where the minnow tanks were kept and waved at them as they got in their boat.

"Take care now. See ya next year," he said. He called Bruno over for a last treat and patted him for a long minute before the dog ran to the dock and jumped into the boat. He gave a woof as they pulled away.

Carl drove slowly through the no-wake zone under the bridge and between the reef and mainland. Once clear of the hazard markers, he cranked up the motor and took off full speed with Pine Island on his right. Directly behind the boat the water was smooth on the surface but roiling underneath, melting into the white foam of the wake which spread into the v-shaped waves disappearing into the distance.

Facing forward on the front seat, Elsa tilted her head up to absorb it all. She could feel the lake patter on the boat's bottom through the soles of her shoes on the ribbed floor. The continuous splash of water against the sides sent shiny droplets flying out from the hull, transparent and transient like good wishes disappearing into the blue water.

The rich greens of the forest were already flecked with gold and red. Fall was imminent. It was the light greens that changed. The evergreens would retain their rich dark colors. The few maples always turned first in August. Next came the bright yellow of the poplar leaves. Even some of that was already evident to Carl and Elsa as they watched the shore fly by.

They cruised past Moccasin Point, through the markers and small islands there. They passed by Shadowland with its trellised archway which seemed to stand guard at the end of the dock, the name painted in script letters on the curve of the arch. Elsa wondered what lay at the end of the shrouded path, perhaps a cabin with secrets, unseen, deep in the woods.

Then on around to the right, skirting St. Paul's Island and the reefs near it, and on past St. Mary's Island into the long east-west stretch of lake on the north side of Pine Island. To their left, just a few miles away was Canada and the Quetico

Provincial Park. The water slid by under the hull of their boat, smooth as glass. It was a glorious day without a cloud in the sky and not a breath of wind. They passed Trout Lake portage, Morcom Inn visible a little further to the east. They slowed as they turned south, passing tiny Sunset Island.

They came around the eastern end of the big island and slowed even more going through the narrows by Glenwood Lodge. Phil Newsom was standing on one of the smaller docks in front of a rental cabin. He waved as they passed by. They waved back. They cruised slowly through the small archipelago of islands in the bay before it yawned open into the expanse of Big Bay. They looked over at Indian Point and their favorite picnic spot, exchanging a look that said without words, 'let's do this again next year.'

Following the south shore of Pine Island, Carl slowed the motor to trolling speed long before they got to Ike's. He drove close to the shore, looking at the interesting rocks at the water's edge, the overhanging cedar trees trimmed evenly from the deer eating them in the winter, and the stands of birches and balsam along the way. A deer path led down to the water.

As they came up to Ike's dock, Elsa said in a whisper, "Look. There. It's Ike's fox." Carl put the motor in neutral and turned to look where she was pointing. The fox was sitting on the path by the corner of the cabin. It looked directly at them for a long moment as they drifted slowly by the end of the dock. Bruno wagged his tail and let out a solitary woof.

Finally, the fox broke its stare, turned, and disappeared behind the cabin.

ABOUT THE AUTHOR

Karen Engstrom writes short stories and historical fiction. *The Fox* is the first of a trilogy set in 1950's northern Minnesota. Her short stories have been published in *Minnesota Stories, A Collection of 20 Fiction Stories about the State We Love*; *Minnesota Not So Nice, Eighteen Tales of Bad Behavior*; *WINK Magazine*; and *The Star Tribune*.

When she's not writing, Karen spends time making handcrafted fountain pen inks for a family company, Anderillium Inks. She is a native of Illinois and currently lives in Independence, MN, with her longtime partner and their ever-napping dog and cat.

Stay tuned for *Shadowland* coming soon!

9 781964 354026